PASCAL'S WAGER

PASCAL'S WAGER

A Novel By

NANCY RUE

Multnomah®Publishers *Sisters, Oregon*

PASCAL'S WAGER
published by Multnomah Publishers, Inc.

Published in association with the literary agency of Alive Communications, Inc.
7680 Goddard Street, Suite 200, Colorado Springs, CO 80920

© 2001 by Nancy Rue
International Standard Book Number: 1-57673-826-4

Cover image by Tony Stone Imagess

Multnomah is a trademark of Multnomah Publishers, Inc.,
and is registered in the U.S. Patent and Trademark Office.
The colophon is a trademark of Multnomah Publishers, Inc.

Printed in the United States of America

The quotation by Blaise Pascal that appears on page 6 is
taken from: *Mind on Fire*, James M. Houston, ed.
(Minneapolis, Minn.: Bethany House Publishers, 1997), 130–131.

For information:
MULTNOMAH PUBLISHERS, INC.•POST OFFICE BOX 1720•SISTERS, OREGON 97759

Library of Congress Cataloging-in-Publication Data:
Rue, Nancy N.
  Pascal's wager / by Nancy Rue.   p.cm.   ISBN 1-57673-826-4
  1. Mothers and daughters–Fiction. 2. Philosophy teachers–Fiction.
  3. Aging parents–Fiction. 4. Atheists–Fiction. I. Title.
PS3568.U3595 P3 2001   813'.54–dc21   2001003167

01 02 03 04 05 06—10 9 8 7 6 5 4 3 2 1 0

Either God exists, or He does not. But which of the alternatives shall we choose? Reason cannot decide anything. Infinite chaos separates us. At the far end of this infinite distance a coin is being spun, which will come down heads or tails. How will you bet? Reason cannot determine how you will choose, nor can reason defend your position of choice. Let us weigh the consequences involved in calling heads that God exists. If you win, you win everything; but if you lose, you lose nothing. Don't hesitate, then, but take a bet that He exists.

BLAISE PASCAL

ONE

I was late getting to the Faculty Club that night, the closest I could come to not showing up at all. I hated to admit that at thirty years old, I still found it intimidating to say no to my mother. But, then, who wasn't cowed by Dr. Liz McGavock—hematologist extraordinaire, administrator de la créme, power in an Evan Picon suit.

I'm not exaggerating. I wish I were.

The air that October evening was chilly and damp as I hurried across the Stanford campus, past the mission-style buildings that breathed academia. All *I* could breathe was my mantra: *Don't let her get to you, Jill. You're thirty—she's fifty-five. You haven't had time to accomplish as much as she has. She can't knock you down for that. She can't knock you down for anything.*

But I could feel my face twisting into a smirk as I cut across the grass and took the last few steps to the club at a virtual canter. Who was I kidding? One appraising look from my mother, one switchblade remark, and I'd be down for the proverbial count.

I hurried up the walkway feeling like a truant sixth-grader. Unlike most such facilities that are housed in old, traditional, ivy-covered buildings, the Stanford Faculty Club was a modern affair that looked like someone's upscale, rambling rancher. Who knows—maybe it was designed that way to give it a homey touch. My mother certainly felt at home there after twenty-five years on campus, although tonight she was the guest of honor.

The front door opened, and an undergrad, attired in the traditional garb of the campus banquet crew, chanted "Good-evening-are-you-here-for-the-anniversary-banquet?" as if he were reading it off a teleprompter.

I'm not here for the cuisine, kid, I wanted to say to him. But I just nodded, and he pointed toward the door to the main dining room. So, Mom had made the big time. They'd opened up the Taj Mahal of banquet rooms. Not surprising.

I forced a smile at the kid and made a beeline for the ladies' room.

Fortunately, nobody was in there, though if every stall had been full it wouldn't have stopped me from doing what I did, which was to survey myself coolly in the mirror. Good paternal genes had given me fair skin of a decent texture, dark eyes, and dark hair. My mother had been pontificating since I hit puberty about the need to wear makeup in order to look polished. I never wore any. She'd also held forth on more than one occasion about how much more professional I looked with my hair up. I pulled out the clip that held it in place and let it fall down to my shoulders in its straight, dark panels.

I could almost hear her saying, "If you insist on wearing it down like a Russian wolfhound, at least don't drag your hand through it. You might as well bite your nails or pick your nose while you're at it."

I neither picked nor bit, but I did rake my fingers through my hair and shake it out so that it had its usual tousled, I-do-not-have-time-to-think-about-my-hair look. Then I slung my purse over my shoulder and, with one more rake through the hair, I headed back toward the dining room, my black jacket flapping behind me. I was so unpolished that my mother would probably come down from the podium with a can of Pledge.

Forks were already clinking when I walked in. Big, teddy-bear Max stood up at a table near the front and waved to me with his usual effervescent enthusiasm, his signature shock of dark, wavy hair tumbling onto his forehead. Everyone within a two-table radius brought his or her respective head up from the smothered chicken and cold broccoli to stare. It was always hard to tell whether Max was directing Beethoven's Fifth or just saying hello.

He was in Jewish-mother mode when I got to him. Make that New *York* Jewish mother.

"I was worried sick," he said, gesturing toward his plate. "Look at this. I could barely eat."

"Only because it isn't veal scaloppini," I said. And then I submitted to the customary kiss on each cheek, which I always tolerated because there was no sense doing otherwise. Max never asked me if I *wanted* to be fawned over like fifth-century sculpture—he just did it.

"Sit down, sit down," he said. "I had them cover your plate. It's probably stone cold anyway. You want me to order you another one?"

"No," I said. "I don't think it'll make much difference."

"I've given up on banquet food improving." Max's words were always more *gushed* than spoken. "I've tried to tell them—heaven knows, I've tried. A university of this caliber—all the guests we have...Jill, honey, eat, eat. God forbid you should still be on the dessert when your mother gets up to give her speech. You know everyone here? What am I—I'm a miserable host. Jill McGavock, Liz's daughter—"

There was probably no need for an introduction. From the expressions on the four faces that looked back at me, they had been hearing about nothing but me and my whereabouts since they sat down. And they were undoubtedly relieved that I had finally arrived so Max would move on to another topic. Not that he wasn't charming—but enough already.

"Dr. Wang from pathology," Max was saying. "And his wife, Stephanie. Look at her. Is she a picture? Beautiful lady."

"Definitely," I said to the mousy woman with the bad perm. "We've met."

"Ellen Van Dyke," Max continued, gesticulation in high gear.

"New in hospital administration. Fascinating. You'll hear her stories about China—she's an expert." And with a raised hand, "No, Ellen, you are. Don't argue with me."

"I can't wait," I said.

"And this is…what am I, slipping? What is your name again? Please forgive me?"

The man whose arm Max was by now wringing like a dishrag grinned. "Sam Bakalis," he said. "I tagged along with Ellen. Free food."

"You'd have done better standing in line at the soup kitchen," I said. "That's a little higher on the chain."

Sam grinned again and nodded toward my plate. "So does that mean your share is up for grabs?" Then he squeezed Ellen's hand and said, "No, seriously, I came for the delightful company."

"Save it, Sam," she said. "You've heard all my China stories. And so has just about everybody else here, so you're going to be spared tonight, Jill."

"Stop by her office and see her slides, though," Sam said.

"So, do you work at the hospital, too?" Max said, nodding at Sam.

"No, no, I'm in the philosophy department."

What are you, the file clerk? I thought.

He obviously wasn't. Stanford Hospital administrators didn't date the office staff. But this Sam person didn't look like your standard academic. Not that there was a *look*. When you were riding across campus in the middle of a flock of bicyclists, you saw staff members wearing everything from berets to dreadlocks. But few of them did the I-look-like-a-student thing, and Sam had it down to an art form. He had dark curly hair that was on the shaggy side, which sneaked out over his ears as if he'd spent the money his mother had given him for a haircut on baseball cards. His eyebrows were thick—no professorial trim at the barber. And he smiled—no, *grinned*—more than most people in academic pursuit. Besides all that, his shirt and blazer both had an almost-rumpled look, as if he'd pulled them out from the bottom of the stack on the chair.

He must be looking for a wife, I thought. *Don't look at Ellen. She falls more into my mother's class. Women in Gotchy shoes don't marry guys who look like unmade beds.*

I looked up then to find the unmade bed in question staring back at me.

"Max tells us you're a graduate student," Sam said.

"I am," I said. "Fifth year." *And I don't go for unmade beds either. Or any beds, for that matter.*

"Math, right?" Dr. Wang said.

I nodded and pushed my plate aside to see if the salad was any better than the rice pilaf.

"Math. You're a sick woman, Jill," Ellen said. "But I'm sure your mother is extremely proud of you."

"Proud?" Max said. "She's a peacock when she talks about Jill!"

Even though that was definitely not accurate, Max could never be convinced otherwise. He was completely biased when it came to my mother. I'd discovered years ago that the Liz McGavock he saw and the one the rest of us had to live with were not the same person.

"So, fifth year," Sam said. "You're pretty far into your dissertation then."

"I am," I said. "I'm close to proving my thesis, actually."

"Good thing," Dr. Wang said. "Don't you have to finish in five years?"

"You don't have to finish, but you don't get funding after five. And, yeah, they wonder about you if you can't pull it off by the end of that time."

"And your thesis is—?"

I looked at Sam, who was surveying me through his thin-rimmed glasses. What I hadn't picked up on before, when I was putting him into the secretarial pool, was the intensity in his eyes. They were hazel, kind of a neutral color, but focused, as if there were something behind them fine-tuning their lenses.

"Do you actually want to know what my thesis is?" I said. "Or are you just being polite?"

"*Polite* isn't a word I'd use to describe Sam," Ellen said with a laugh.

"Besides, differential calculus doesn't usually constitute small talk," Dr. Wang said.

"I guess I have no choice but to say I really want to know." Sam was still grinning.

"If they had just put a little basil in this sauce," Max said, "it would have made all the difference."

"Nice try, Dr. Ironto," Sam said to him. "But let me just get my question answered before we go off into the culinary world."

Max looked like the host whose tea party has just been crashed by the Hell's Angels. He knew me.

"So how much algebraic topology have you had?" I said.

"None," Sam said. "I didn't even know it existed."

"I'd have to give you a crash course, then. You sure you have that kind of time?"

Sam grinned again. "Sure. I should be able to get that down before they bring the dessert."

I set my fork on the edge of the plate and folded my hands. My eyes locked onto Sam's. "I'm specifically in the area of K-theory, working with vector bundles. We can take any shape and assign a vector space, so that for every point on the shape we end up with a vector bundle. K-theory studies those vector bundles."

Sam's full lips were twitching. "Ah, that certainly clarifies it for me. How about the rest of you?" He grinned while surveying everyone around the table.

"I'm good to go," Ellen said.

"Okay, but here's my real question," Sam said. He leaned over his broccoli. "Why? Why do you want to fool around with *shapes* in the first place?"

"Because I can," I said.

"She has a terrible image problem," Max said, straight-faced. "We've tried therapy, but still, always with the inferiority complex."

"All right," I said. "I do it because it's beautiful."

"*Math* is beautiful?" Mrs. Wang said.

Ellen was shaking her head. "No, Jill. A sunset at Half Moon Bay is beautiful. A German chocolate cake is beautiful. Geometry is not beautiful. What were you saying about basil, Max?"

"No, really, indulge me here," Sam said. "I'm intrigued."

He had yet to take his eyes off me. I, in turn, was holding my own in the who's-going-to-look-away-first contest, even amid the banquet chatter and dish clatter that was going on around us. No man won that competition with me.

"So it's all about the beauty of it for you," he said.

I leaned forward. "That's pretty simplistic."

"So work with me. I'm a layman."

"For me, yes, it is about the elegance of it. What I'm working on is going to help us understand the mathematical big picture."

"So, you're learning math so you can…learn math."

"Again that's a little simplistic. If you have to have a *practical* reason, K-theory has some applications to quantum physics." I shrugged. "But there isn't much applied math here at Stanford."

"That would be too mundane, wouldn't it?" he said. "I try to make a practical application in the philosophy department and they're ready to give me the hemlock."

"What is it exactly that you do there?" I said, eyes still fixed.

"I teach."

"You're a TA."

"No, I'm a professor. But not tenured. Don't be too impressed."

I wasn't. But I *was* surprised. The Midwest twang and the

shaggy do had me fooled. And I don't fool easily.

"Ah, the *pièce de résistance!*" Max said, with more fervor than was warranted by the slices of carrot cake that were being served.

I knew he was ready for a subject change, and I reluctantly let him make it. If I ever cut anybody slack, it was Max. He hated any dissonance that didn't come from a Rachmaninoff piece. At that moment, he was bowing his silver-streaked head to each of us as the cake was being distributed, as if he'd baked it himself. As he handed me my piece, his soft brown eyes practically begged me not to mar my mother's special night. I gave in and looked around for the mother in question.

She was at the head table, of course, next to Dr. Grant, chief of all the Stanford labs. Her face was turned away from me as she talked to him, more than likely treating him to her opinion about something. Anything. There was nothing she couldn't hold forth on with complete eloquence at the drop of a toupee. I didn't have to hear her to know her voice was deep and rich in Grant's ear— that her articulation was impeccable, that every word was slicing into him like a scalpel. As always, she was almost perfectly still as she talked. My mother never seemed to feel a need for gestures or anything else that didn't contribute to the collected image she projected.

Right about now, I thought, *Grant is probably saying to himself, "Is this woman human?" Don't give yourself credit for an original thought, pal. I've wondered that all my life. The real question is—*

But the real question faded right there in my frontal lobe as my mother turned her head to address the tuxedo-clad gentleman on her other side. I could see her face, and it stopped me cold.

Did I miss the cyclone she survived to get here? I thought.

That was only a slight exaggeration considering the package my mother always—*always*—presented to the world. I'd expected the thick mane of dark hair peppered with gray to be in its perpetual cut-fashionably-short, not-a-hair-out-of-place condition. The square, handsome face to be flawlessly made up. The 22-karat understated gold necklace to hang in tasteful elegance against something in pure silk.

What I saw was a woman who had thrown herself together en route to the banquet and hadn't bothered to look in a mirror since then.

She was at least two months past the last due date for a haircut. The Riot Red lipstick she saved for evenings at the opera with Max looked like it had been applied with a crayon. And although she was indeed wearing a silk blouse, the points of its collar were at right angles to each other, fouling the two—make that three—chains she was wearing. Two of them silver. One of them gold. As hard as it was to believe, I looked like I'd just had a Merle Norman makeover compared to her.

Max was leaning toward Ellen, hanging on her every word, but I nudged him anyway.

"Why does Mother look like she's running from the glamour police?" I hissed in his ear.

Max shifted his gaze to the head table, and his smile melted into I'm-looking-at-Liz mode. "Isn't she a beauty? Your mother's a beauty."

"Not when she's playing fashion fugitive. Look at her, Max!"

He did and then nodded. "She should have worn the diamond earrings. I told her, 'Wear the diamonds—this is the night to drip with them.'"

I gave up. Max himself was donned in his customary ascot and velvet jacket, and as always his hair was even more tousled than mine. Someone who always looked as if he'd just finished conducting the 1812 Overture could not be counted on to reliably assess grooming.

I considered asking Stephanie Wang. She wasn't exactly cover girl material herself, but she'd probably been around my mother more than I had in the last six months.

Which is not my *fault,* I reminded myself. *What am I supposed to do when she doesn't return my calls?*

What I had done, of course, was tell myself I was better off *not* having to listen to my mother's latest evaluation of my life. But at the moment, that wasn't the point. The point was, Dr. Elizabeth McGavock did not show up to functions given in her honor looking the way she did right now.

I looked across the table at Stephanie, but both she and Dr. Wang were obviously engrossed in what Sam Bakalis was expostulating about to Ellen. Stephanie looked like she was mesmerized by his eyebrows.

"So let me ask you this," Sam was saying. "I know for a long time you've been able to determine that a baby, before it's even born, has genes for certain diseases. But is it standard procedure now to run those tests?"

"It isn't standard," Ellen said, "but we *can* do it if there's reason to suspect the fetus might be at risk. You know, family history, that kind of thing."

"You used the word *fetus,*" Sam said. "Does that reflect your views on life before birth?"

Stephanie Wang giggled nervously. "Maybe we'd better get back to that basil, Max."

I have to admit, the current state of my mother's style sense slid out of focus. This was too good to pass up.

"And does your picking up on her use of the word *fetus* reflect *your* views?" I said.

Sam met my gaze head-on. "It does, actually. Why do you ask?"

"Are we talking religion here?" I said. "I'm only asking because if we're about to be spiritually mugged, I need to find another table."

Sam raised both hands. "I'm unarmed. But I do reserve the right to present a viewpoint."

"Just be forewarned: I don't think science and religion are going to mix at this table." I looked at the Wangs. "Am I right?"

Stephanie looked like she'd rather be having a root canal.

Dr. Wang folded his hands neatly on the table. "I'm open to a lively discussion."

Max groaned. "How lively do you want it?"

"What, are we going to see verbal WWF?" Ellen said. "Should I clear the table?"

Sam's eyes were still on me. "I can stay above the belt if you can."

I hated that. The minute you started to debate with a man, he had to pull out a sexual innuendo. But I forced myself not to narrow my eyes at him.

"You're on," I said. "Now?"

"No, I think it was my turn to counter," Sam said, his eyes focused in even more. He obviously relished an argument as much as I did. I doubted that he hated losing one as much, though. "You're saying there is no blend of science and religion."

"Not if you're going to be completely rational, no."

"You're a mathematician."

"She's brilliant," Max put in.

"Then you've heard of Pascal. Blaise Pascal? Father of geometry?"

"I think you would have to build a case for his paternity, but yeah, I'm familiar with Pascal."

"I'm a little rusty," Ellen said. "Refresh my memory."

"Seventeenth-century mathematician," I said. "He did some work on vacuum theory. He's credited with developing the first calculator?"

"They named the computer language after him," Dr. Wang said. "The same fella, yes?"

"Yes," Sam said. He was all but licking his chops. "Physics, math—he was pure science. All about rationality. The whole ball of wax. But after his conversion to Christianity—"

"Conversion from what?" I said.

"From what I'd guess you'd call perfunctory piety," Sam said. "He went through the motions, but he didn't internalize any of it. Anyway, after his conversion, he continued to invest all of his energy in science. Matter of fact, his most productive scientific work was ahead of him. But my point is, he was also about to deepen his understanding of human nature, and *that* is what he's best known for."

"So he studied psychology," I said. "That's considered a science."

"Mmmm, that's debatable," Dr. Wang said.

"And it's a moot point, anyway," Sam said. "He didn't study psychology. He studied faith."

"In what?"

"In God."

I pulled my eyes away from his long enough to roll them. His eyebrows shot up.

"You don't believe in God," he said.

"Uh, let me think about it—no." I knew my voice sounded spiky, but that's because I was vaguely disappointed. I'd hoped for an interesting debate. "You will never convince me that there is some spiritual force that controls everything."

"Why?"

"Because it can't be proven."

"So you only believe in things for which there is hard evidence."

"Right." I gave a dismissive shrug. "I'm a mathematician."

"You deal with infinity in mathematics?"

"Ugh, this is bringing back memories of college math," Ellen said. "Dr. Rosenberg, 8:00 A.M., Tuesdays and Thursdays." She shuddered. "I'm going to need another piece of that carrot cake."

Max looked relieved to oblige and raised his hand to hail a server. I turned back to Sam's intense eyes.

"Yeah," I said. "Mathematics has an infinity of infinities of propositions to expound. *And* they are infinite also in the multiplicity and subtlety of their principles. Those that are supposed to be ultimate don't stand by themselves—they depend on others, which depend on still others, and thus never allow for any finality." I slipped in a smile. "How do you think every math grad student finds a thesis to prove? Anyway, that's infinity."

"I have a headache," Max said. "More wine!"

"Infinity," Sam said, "sounds an awful lot like God to me."

"To you maybe. To me it sounds like a concept."

"Which you can't prove unless you someday find the end of it. Never finding the 'finality,' as you called it, doesn't prove there is no finality—it just means you haven't found it yet."

"And your point is?"

"My point is that just because you haven't found God yet doesn't mean God doesn't exist."

Dr. Wang tapped his spoon against his wine glass. "I think round one goes to Sam."

"No," I said. "The round isn't over yet." I homed in on Sam again. "What visible difference does believing in a 'God' make? I *don't* believe, you *do* believe, but both of us are going to die. Show me the difference."

"Now we're getting into the *nature* of God. If you're looking for a God who is going to allow you to live on earth forever, you're not going to find that God because that God doesn't exist."

"Besides," Ellen said, "I think there's more to life than just hanging out until you die."

"I'll drink to that!" Max said, lifting his glass. "To all that is in between. Good music, good friends—"

"Good conversation," Sam said. He tilted his water glass toward me.

Now I know, I thought, *why I always wish born-again Christians had never been born the first time.*

Sam had gotten preachy, as far as I was concerned, and I was again disappointed. There was something attractive about him. His intensity—no, his casual command over his intensity…no, maybe it was his chin.

Would you stop! I scolded myself. *He's a pompous jerk you don't have time for.*

"Coffee, anyone?" Stephanie Wang was saying. "Last call before the speakers."

I nodded at the kid with the coffee pot who stood at her elbow. I was going to need some caffeine for the rest of *this* evening. I was about to reach for the cup when Sam put his hand on top of mine. I glared at it, but that didn't seem to have the freeze-drying effect my glare usually had on guys reckless enough to try to play touchy-feely with me.

"What?" I said.

"Just consider this one argument, and then I'll drop it."

"Could I have a signature on that?" I said.

He reached inside his jacket and took out a pen.

"I was speaking figuratively," I said.

But he was already scrawling his name across a cocktail napkin. I noticed the skin on his hands was smooth and olive-colored. Not that it mattered.

He pushed the signed napkin toward me, and I gave it a bored glance. His eyebrows were expectant.

"Go for it," I said. "What's your argument?"

"It's not an argument exactly—it's more of a wager. And it isn't mine. It's Pascal's."

Dr. Wang snapped his fingers in recognition. "Pascal's Wager."

"You've heard of it," Sam said.

"Yeah, but give me a refresher course," Dr. Wang said, smiling at me.

Sam leaned back in his chair and folded his hands behind his head. My mother, if she'd been at our table, would have been appalled. *He learned his social skills in a pool hall,* she would have said.

"It goes like this," Sam said. He focused on the chandelier as if to get his cues from it, and yet his eyes went beyond it. He was being a little dramatic as far as I was concerned. But I listened, as did everybody else at the table. Even Max looked entranced.

"At the far end of what we're calling infinity," Sam said, "a coin is being spun. It will come down heads or tails. How it lands will reveal to you whether there is a God—heads—or whether there isn't—tails. You have to wager. We all do. A choice has to be made."

"I've made mine," I said. "Tails."

"Based on what?"

"Based on reason."

Sam dug hungrily into his pants pocket and produced a nickel, which he placed on his thumbnail. "Can you reasonably tell me how this coin is going to land if I flip it?"

I shook my head.

"Reason can't make the choice for the figurative coin either. We've already established that reason—hard evidence—can't prove either way. So the wager posits this: If you wager that there *is* a God and you live your life as if there is one—if the coin comes up tails—you've lost absolutely nothing. But if it comes up heads and there *is* a God, you've won everything."

The eyes I'd been watching all through dinner took on a fiery quality, as if they were in the throes of some deep passion. I went for the cream and stirred my coffee.

"I remember that now," Stephanie Wang said. "I read it—it's the wager that every man makes."

"But I'm not so sure about every woman," Ellen said. She was half smiling at me.

"Heads is a safer bet," Sam said.

"I'll pass," I said. I nodded toward the podium where some campus muckety-muck was adjusting the microphone. "Looks like it's show time."

Everyone else started scraping chairs and rearranging themselves in their seats. Sam just looked at me. I waited for, "Can we finish this discussion over coffee sometime?" But it didn't come. I had to concede the eye-holding contest and shift my focus to the front. The introduction of Dr. Elizabeth McGavock was just winding down.

"Tonight, as we hear her speak, I'm certain it will become clear to you why we are honoring not only Dr. McGavock's twenty-five years at Stanford Hospital, but also the quality of work she has done in that time. Ladies and gentlemen, Dr. Elizabeth McGavock."

The room erupted into applause, and my mother rose from her seat. In the instant it took her to get from there to the podium, I placed a wager I had absolutely no doubt about. I would have staked my last four years on it: Dr. Elizabeth McGavock was drunk.

TWO

I sat there staring like an idiot.

The administrator who had just introduced her held out his hand to shake hers. She stared at it for a good three seconds before she took it and let him pump her arm while she gazed into his face—as if she were having trouble putting a finger on just who he was.

He took her by the elbow and ushered her to the microphone amid the waning applause. As she gripped the sides of the podium, a vague smile crossed her face.

"Hi," she said.

Hi? I wanted to shout at her. *Hi? You* are *drunk!*

Except that my mother never consumed a drop of alcohol. Ever.

I put my lips close to Max's ear. "Since when did she start drinking?" I said through clenched teeth.

He looked at me as if I'd just fallen in through the ceiling. "What are you talking about?"

I jerked my head toward the podium. Mother had relaxed her death grip on the lectern, and her eyes were now focused on the audience.

"It's hard for me to believe I'm being honored for twenty-five years of service," she was saying. "The difficulty is not in accepting that it's been twenty-five years. Has it only been that long?"

There was a ripple of laughter through the dining room. Max looked at me smugly.

"No, it's the *honoring* part that surprises me," she said. "After what I've put these people through during that time, I'm amazed they aren't asking for early retilement—*retirement.*" She paused, fixed a smile on, and turned to the head table. "Or are you?"

They laughed appreciatively. Max started a round of applause. I stayed locked in on my mother. *Retilement?* No, there was definitely booze in her immediate past. I craned to get a glimpse of her now-vacated place at the table, in search of a wine glass.

"It has been a journey for all of us," she went on. "I can't speak of anybody else's. I'm only here to shlare—to *share*—my own experience at Stanford Hospital."

I bored my eyes into the side of Max's face, but he didn't look at me. He was hearing it too, though, I knew. His proud expression looked as if it had suddenly met with a stun gun.

Across the table, Ellen Van Dyke cleared her throat, and I realized there was a long pause going on up at the podium—an interminable pause in the public speaking world. My mother was gazing at the audience with an empty grin on her face. If it had been anyone else, I'd have assumed she was waiting for the next car in the train of thought. Max reached over and grabbed my hand.

"So," Mother said finally, "my journey. Yes, it escaped me for the moment!"

And then she threw her head back and laughed, a juicy, snorting sound that came straight out of her nose. One hand left the podium with a jerk and made contact with the glass of water in front of her. She watched as it dropped to its side, the same look of dismay on her face that Max and the Wangs were now wearing on theirs. In the drop-dead silence that followed, I could hear the water dripping over the edge of the lectern and onto the floor.

My mother gaped at it for a moment, and then her persona suddenly snapped back into place—as if it had just been off in the ladies' room powdering its nose while Liz's body kept the audience entertained.

"This is why I became a well-educated woman," she said. "I could never make it waiting tables!"

While the audience roared—more out of relief than glee, I was convinced—I gave Max a sharp jab.

"I'm telling you, she's half schnockered," I hissed through clenched teeth.

"She's stressed," Max said. "That's all it is. She's fine now. It's just the stress."

I folded my arms and tried to focus on the "journey" my mother had been promising to recount for the last five bungled minutes. Max was patently wrong. The only theory more ridiculous than her being *drunk* was her being *stressed.* It didn't happen. The woman oversaw dozens of medical technologists while they juggled ten different machines that ran thirty blood tests at a time—and she seldom even smudged her makeup in the process. The word *stress* never crossed her lips.

She got through the speech without any further overturning of the stemware or obvious lapses of memory. But the slurring of her words was so noticeable to me that I kept sneaking glances around to see if anybody else was picking up on it. If restless repositioning of chairs and faces squinted in concentration were any indication, it wasn't escaping anybody.

The final "thank you" was no more out of her mouth than the audience came to its feet *en masse,* clapping. I suspected as I joined them that they were determined not to give her a chance to say anything else. I hoped that from a standing position I could get a better view of my mother's wine glass, but Sam Bakalis was blocking my view. I noticed only in passing that he was a lot taller than he looked sitting down.

When the formalities were finally exhausted and my mother was in possession of an engraved plaque, I skipped the good-byes to the Wangs and the rest and told Max to meet me in the hall.

It took him a good ten minutes to get out there, during which I raked my hand through my hair enough times to *drive* my mother to drink. I knew I was obsessing, but I got that way when I was thrown completely off balance. Most disturbing of all: My mother had been the one to do the throwing. She might have been critical, judgmental, domineering, and cold, but at least I always knew what to expect. That woman who had practically slobbered her way through a speech to her colleagues was nobody I had ever seen before.

In mid-rake number forty-two, I spied Max's bearlike form emerging from the dining room and waved him over. It took him another two minutes to get to me with people stopping him for hugs and handshakes and brief dialogues on Paderewski. I was ready to chew glass by the time I was able to get my fingernails into his velvet jacket and drag him into a smaller hallway off the main one.

"Okay, Max, *what* is going on?" I nearly shouted.

"What are you talking about?"

"You know exactly what I'm talking about," I said. "Mother looked like Robert Downey Jr. up there."

"I don't know—"

"She slurred every other word. She forgot what she was going to say. She *snorted*, for Pete's sake! You can't tell me you didn't notice. You were practically cutting off the circulation in my hand."

"All right, calm down." Max took my arm and tucked it through his, trying to stroke my fingers.

I wrenched myself away. "You saw it."

He shrugged. "So she was a little off."

I drilled my eyes into him and put my hands on my hips. He drooped like a scolded spaniel.

"Something was wrong. She was distracted," he said. "I told you it was the stress."

"Since when does she let something as benign as a job where people's lives are in her hands get her down?" I said. "She thrives on that."

"Maybe not so much anymore."

I could tell Max wanted to grab my hands again. I kept them firmly planted on my hips.

"When was the last time you saw her?" he asked. "I mean really saw her—sat down and talked to her?"

I could feel my jaw stiffening. "It's probably been six months. But that's been her choice, not mine. She doesn't return my calls. She barely answers my e-mails. When I do happen to get her on the phone, she always has some reason to dash off somewhere."

"You see?" Max said, bringing out the soothing voice. "She's too busy. Anybody is going to crack sooner or later under the kind of schedule she keeps."

"Are you saying she's about to have a breakdown?"

"I'm saying you're jumping to conclusions. Your mama is under a lot of pressure, and that's all. But I will tell you this, though God forbid I should try to give you advice—"

"Let's have it," I said tonelessly.

He reached for my hands again, prying them right off my hips to squeeze them in his. "Try again to spend some time with her. Make her meet you for lunch. You two share some nice antipasto."

"Now I think *you're* the one who's on the verge of a break-down," I said. "Who do you know that can *make* my mother do anything?"

"Just promise me you'll try."

It was clear he wasn't going to let go of me until I agreed, so I nodded. Then, as soon as he went off in search of my mother, I hightailed it out of there.

I called Mother the next morning from my office in the math department, and I did get her on the phone—by disguising my voice and telling Alma, her secretary, that I was from the bank. Liz kept a tight watch on her finances. I knew that would get her scurrying to the phone.

"It's Jill," I said when she picked up.

There was a brief pause. After last night's performance, it

crossed my mind that she might be trying to recall who the heck Jill was.

"Alma told me you were someone from the bank," she said. ‹

"I think Alma's getting a little ditzy," I said. "Isn't it about time for her to retire?"

"I'm sure you didn't call to check on Alma's work status. Was there something else?"

I didn't answer right away. Her words were as pointed as ever, each one carefully selected to go into me as cleanly as a needle. But the thickness I'd heard in her voice during her speech was still there. Good grief, had she already downed a couple of Bloody Marys to take the edge off of her hangover? Max was even more clueless than I'd realized. How could he have missed this?

"Jill, I don't have time for this. Why don'tcha crawl me back when you have something to shay?"

It took a moment to interpret. "No, no, I just wanted to set up a lunch date with you."

"I have lunch plans today."

"So how about tomorrow?"

"I'm leaving for a conference. I'll be gone until Monday."

"So Monday then," I said. "Noon?"

"It takes me a day to get out from under the work that pliles—piles—up while I'm away—"

"Okay, Tuesday. Next Tuesday."

There was another pause. I thought she was considering hanging up on me.

"What is this about, Jill?" she said finally. "You're not usually this ang-shush to spend time with me. "

Ordinarily by that point in such a conversation with my mother, I would have said, "And I'm not now either. Call me when you've got a minute, okay?" But "crawl" instead of "call"? "Ang-shush" instead of "anxious"? I had to get her to lunch—and I'd probably need a delegation from Alcoholics Anonymous with me.

"I just need to talk to you," I said.

"Are you out of money?" she said.

"No," I said. The hair on the back of my neck was starting to bristle. She wasn't too drunk to get my hackles up.

"You're not going to finish your dishertation in time, and you want me to intercede for you for more funding."

"No," I said. "It isn't about me, Mother. It's about you."

"What about me?"

"I'll tell you when I see you. Next Tuesday, noon. I'll meet you at Marie Callendar's."

Then I was the one who hung up on her. "You owe me, Max," I said.

"Oh, I'm sorry," a husky voice muttered from the doorway.

I looked up to see a tall, skinny girl peering in with apologetic gray eyes. It was Tabitha Lane, a freshman in my Math 19 class, the one who always reminded me of an adolescent giraffe. I'd totally forgotten she was coming by this morning.

"Sorry about what?" I said. "Come in."

"I thought I heard you talking to somebody," she said. "I can come back later if this isn't a good time."

"It's fine," I said. I turned around and cleared off a seat on the straight-backed wooden chair next to my desk. Then I had to find the matchbook I always put under one leg so it wouldn't rock and drive me nuts. Most of the furniture in graduate student offices, at least in the Alfred P. Sloan Mathematics Center, looked like it had been salvaged from the Stanford attic. I kept talking as I hunted under the desk for the matchbook. "You've got an appointment. I was just on the phone."

"I thought maybe you were talking to that guy you share your office with."

"Alan Jacoboni?" I said. "He never comes in until at least noon, the slacker. You know, you'd think with the amount of tuition people pay to go to this school, they could afford a chair that doesn't require—"

I stopped in mid-sentence at the sound of wheels rolling

across the office floor. Tabitha was entering on roller blades.

"What the heck?" I said, looking up at her.

"Oh, I'm sorry!" Her face went pale under the spattering of freckles that covered her nose and cheeks like carelessly thrown confetti. "Do you want me to take them off? Are they too noisy? I can take them off—"

"No," I said, still staring. "You can wear them in here. The question is, why?"

"It's so much easier to get around campus with these," Tabitha said. "I was ending up late to, like, every one of my classes, and they frown on that around here and so then I saw this girl in my dorm putting them on and I go, what are you doing, and she goes, they're totally the best, so I asked my mother to send me mine and of course it took, oh, maybe three weeks for me to get them because the mail is so slow—"

"Well, good. Whatever works for you," I said. It was no wonder she talked like she was hoarse, I thought. Overuse of the vocal chords. "I have to ask, though, how do you deal with steps?"

Tabitha cocked her head, her short, blunt-cut, reddish hair spilling against her cheek. It would have fallen straight into her eyes if she didn't have it pulled back with the clips that made her look even more like Rebecca of Sunnybrook Farm. There was a small outbreak of tiny pimples on her forehead, but she was obviously making no effort to conceal them.

"I can't skate down them," she said, "so I just walk down backward. I don't know why, but I just tried it and I haven't fallen yet, but I do wear these kneepads so—"

"Great," I said. "Have a seat."

I pointed to the chair, and she skidded crazily toward it, sank into it, backpack and all, and let her feet roll out halfway across the room. She really did have the longest legs I'd ever seen on a girl, accentuated by the shorts she was wearing. Only the pink top that was fluttering at her waistline assured me that those legs didn't come straight out of her neck.

I sat down in my desk chair and looked at her, waiting for her to state her business. She just looked back at me, eyebrows furrowed over her big gray eyes in an expression of deep consternation. Her face wasn't bewildered and confused like the rest of her; it was just concerned.

"So," I said. "What can I do for you?"

"I need help." Then her arms came up for no apparent reason and flopped back down on her lap.

"With Math 19?" I said.

"Yes," she said.

"Okay," I said. I flipped open my grade book and ran a finger down to Lane, Tabitha. Yeah, she needed help, all right. She'd failed the first quiz, and although she turned in every homework assignment, it was clear that calculus was still a mystery to her.

"What exactly is it that you're not getting?" I asked.

"All of it."

"Okay," I said. "Let's start with my explanations in class. Are they confusing you?"

Her eyes got bigger, if that was possible. "Oh, no!" she said. "No, you're a great teacher! I totally understand everything you say! It's just when I get back to my room to do the problems, it's, like, gone. Plus, I can't even study in the dorm. It's so noisy all the time—people are talking and going in and out all hours of the night. It's like, yikes, you know? So I go to the library and I look around and see all these people who are so smart and they obviously understand everything they're doing and I don't and I just start thinking I'm going to flunk out and be so humiliated and then—I just can't do the problems."

Fortunately, she had to stop to take a breath. I took the opportunity to offer the only really compassionate thing I could ever think of to say to kids who were in over their heads.

"Look, math isn't for everybody," I said. "I'm sure you do a lot better in courses for your major."

She blinked. "Math *is* my major."

I had to bite my tongue to keep from saying, "What are you, a masochist?" Instead I flipped open my date book and picked up a pen.

"You're going to need tutoring at least twice a week," I said. "When can you come in?"

She disentangled herself from the backpack and pawed through it. I stifled a groan. Spending two hours a week with an eighteen-year-old who was short on confidence and long on non-stop monologues punctuated with the words *like* and *totally* wasn't what I'd had in mind when I applied for the coveted fellowship at Stanford.

I told Alan Jacoboni about her that afternoon while he was waking up over a cup of Starbucks coffee. Why I ever discussed anything with the man was beyond me. I'd have been content to sit in the office in total silence, actually getting work done, since I was teaching a course on my own that quarter *and* getting pressure from the department to organize a teaching seminar for the other graduate students *and* being available to see students three hours a week *and* trying to finish my dissertation *and* getting it together to apply for post-doc positions. But Jaboni never seemed to have much to do except talk in that educated Southern accent that sounded phony to me—although who would *want* to put that on was a question I couldn't answer.

"How does a child like that get into Stanford in the first place?" he said.

"High school grades. Test scores," I said.

"And she's flunking out?"

"Not yet."

"Good luck, darlin'."

He smiled for no apparent reason, the way he did at the end of almost every sentence, and then propped up his feet, legs clad in cargo shorts, on his desk. As usual, he was wearing sandals, in spite of the fact that his feet were gargoyle-bony. It was his macho pose, one he had adopted early on when he'd discovered that he was the best-looking graduate student among the males in the math department. Math guys tended to be on the geeky side, so the fact that Alan was somewhat hip and played up his basic attractiveness made him look like Leonardo DiCaprio in a room full of Woody Allens.

I personally didn't think he was all that handsome. He kept his generically brown, curly hair cut close to his head so it didn't go wild on him, and he was going to be fighting the proverbial battle of the bulge someday if he didn't stop living on beer and Cheetos. At twenty-eight, it was about time. Okay, so when he was dressed in nice slacks and a sport shirt and loafers he looked relatively attractive, but he usually schlepped around in shorts and T-shirts when he wasn't teaching, and he didn't do "sloppy-casual" well. He tended to just look sloppy.

He was still leaning back in his chair, hands behind his head, checking me out with his eyes, as if he hadn't been looking at me every day for the last four years.

"What?" I said coolly.

"Darlin', I bet it's days like this you wish you were already out there knocking down the big bucks instead of in here tutoring pathetic little airheads."

"I'm not crazy about the 'pathetic little airheads,'" I said. "But I'm not here to learn how to make big bucks."

"Oh, bilge! We all are. What really burns my biscuits is when I get an e-mail from one of my fraternity brothers telling me he's going to Cancun for a week. He's got a bachelor's in business and he's already making six figures a year. I've got twice the education and I'm still living like a pauper." He lifted a foot so I could see the large hole in the sole of his sandal.

"Nice," I said.

"You can't tell me that doesn't bother you," Jacoboni said.

"It doesn't bother me." I made a huge deal out of opening a

file folder and studying it intently, pencil behind my ear. He didn't pick up the clue that, for me, the conversation was over.

"It bothers *me*. But not for long. Once I'm out of here, I'm heading straight for industry. Then I'll be flying to Cancun for the week*end*—in my private jet. Oh, yeah, baby."

Since he was obviously not going to shut up, I turned and surveyed him with one of my I-see-through-you-pal stares.

"If you want to work in industry," I said, "why did you come here? We have less applied math than almost any other school."

"Because it's *Stanford,* honey. All I have to do is say the name and CEOs drop their dentures."

"Oh," I said. The stare wasn't working. I went back to the file.

"I like being one of the two oddballs around here," he went on. "You and me, darlin'."

"Excuse me?" I said.

"The two of us are the oddities. We keep our moods cool and our eyes on the prize."

I was grateful that Peter and Rashad showed up just then asking Jacaboni to come "see something"—undoubtedly the latest grad student scribbles on their office chalkboard.

"Sure," Jacoboni told them. "I don't have anything else to do."

He winked at me as he left. When he was gone, I feigned throwing up in the trash can, just for my own benefit.

I had Tuesday's lunch date marked in red on my calendar, and I'd circled it three times so I wouldn't forget. Mother, on the other hand, was still in her lab coat as she sailed into Marie Callendar's at 12:15. She didn't look much different than she did the night of her dinner, except that now she was wearing no lipstick at all. It made her look a little like a disheveled corpse.

"What?" she said to me as she slid into the booth. "You're looking at me like you've been waiting for two hours. I'm not that late."

I shook myself out of my stupor. "No, you're fine."

"I don't see why you wanted to meet all the way over here when there are places to eat on campus," she said.

She propped her menu in front of her, which gave me a chance to shift my face out of stunned mode. Not only did she look even more unkempt than the last time I'd seen her, but her voice was more slurred in person than it had been over the phone. It did nothing but confirm my drinking theory, and at this point even Max couldn't have persuaded me otherwise.

The problem was, if *I* was noticing it, it probably wasn't escaping the people she was seeing every day—her colleagues, her employees, her superiors. I stared at my own menu without really seeing the words. If it was up to me as her dutiful daughter to say something to her about it, both of us were out of luck. Suddenly, I could conjure up the scene that would occur if I calmly said, "Mother, it's time for you to admit you have a drinking problem." I would be filleted with her icicle of a tongue and left for dead right there in the Marie Callendar's booth. What had I been *thinking*, asking her here for a dressing down?

I hadn't thought at all, actually, and I was totally unprepared. It was throwing me—again.

"What can I get you ladies?" said a perky little waitress.

"Chicken potpie, order of corn bread, salad bar," Mother said and then slapped her menu closed.

Perky and I exchanged momentary blinking stares, and then I hurriedly ordered the French onion soup. By the time the waitress was bustling away, Mother had already polished off her own glass of water and was reaching for mine.

"I'm sure she'll come back with a pitcher," I said.

My mother drained my glass and set it down. "So what is this all ablout, Jill?" she said.

I leaned forward, as much to get a whiff of her breath as to speak. I couldn't detect any alcohol, though she seemed to have bathed in Clinique.

"Don't you want to go get your salad first?" I asked.

"What salad?"

"You ordered the salad bar."

"I did not."

"Oh," I said. "I thought you did."

"You thought wrong. Now what did you want to talk to me about? As soon as I eat, I have to get back to the lab."

My stomach tightened. This was such a role reversal. It had always been my mother summoning *me* to an interrogation lunch or commanding *my* presence at a cross-examination dinner. I raked my hand through my hair and then winced, waiting for the inevitable "Stop that, Jill." She didn't say a word.

"I just wanted to spend some time with you," I lied. "Find out what's happening in your life."

"Why?"

"Why? Because you're my mother, and I haven't had a whole conversation with you in six months."

"I've been busy. And as you can shee—*see*—I'm fine."

I got nowhere from then until the food arrived. From the way Mother had ordered, I expected her to devour it like a half-starved dog, but she picked at the crust of her potpie with her fork and then set it down. It occurred to me vaguely that I had never seen her eat a potpie anyway.

"Do you want to order something else?" I said.

"Since when did you start prashtishing—prashticing—your maternal instincts on me?"

And since when did you start talking like you have a mouth full of couscous? I wanted to say. I did muster up the courage to get out, "Is there anything wrong? I mean, are you feeling all right?"

Big mistake. She slid her plate aside so she could get her elbows on the table and fold her hands close to my face. Her small, blue eyes were intense as they locked right onto mine. My upbringing snapped into place—the thousands of times I'd been told to *look* at my mother when she was speaking to me.

"There is nothing 'wrong' with me," Mother said. "I am perfectly intact, functioning quite normally, thank you very much. Now rather than *insinuating* for the rest of the afternoon, I suggest you get to the point."

I was actually relieved that my mother had suddenly returned— collected, eloquent, and razor sharp. Until she abruptly snatched up her handbag and lurched out of the booth.

"I have to get back," she said.

Then she gave that vacant grin I'd seen on the night of her award banquet and literally bolted from Marie Callendar's, nearly mowing down Perky en route to the door. I stared after her until long after my French onion soup had gone cold.

THREE

Three nights later I realized how much of my think time was being consumed by the mental video of my mother. On my nightly run on the Stanford Loop, it occurred to me that for the last three nights I hadn't clocked myself, checked my heart rate, or monitored the effectiveness of my pre-run hydration. The minute I hit the first hill, I was completely preoccupied with the memory of her flipping back and forth from sloppy drunk to coherent doctor to schizophrenic bag lady.

My life at that point was neatly compartmentalized, and the Loop was where I went to concentrate on the fitness compartment. I'd turned into a runner in high school, when my mother had informed me that I had to take up a sport so as not to become lazy. The fact that I was already in advanced placement classes, National Honor Society, two academic fraternities, and private piano lessons three times a week made cross-country track the only option. Six weeks in the fall and it was a done deal, and it was enough to assure my mother that I was not going to lapse into a vegetative state.

Secretly, I fell in love with running—not the competition, but the idea of being out there alone on the road with no one in my face. Everywhere I'd been since high school—at Princeton for undergrad work, at Mercer County Community College in Trenton when I was teaching—I'd always found a place to end the day with a run. Here the place was the Stanford Loop.

Situated in the Stanford hills west of the main campus, toward

the ocean side of the peninsula, it consisted of a long, hilly, winding trail that challenged me physically—or, to use the vernacular,
kicked my butt. At its highest point, you could see the San
Francisco Bay, the Dunbarton Bridge, the San Mateo Bridge, and
Hoover Tower—the main landmark of the Stanford campus. On
clear days you could make out the Bay Bridge and sometimes
even the city itself, though most of the time the fog curled around
San Francisco like a pair of protective hands.

Personally, I appreciated the solitude of the Loop more than
the view. Unlike a lot of the people who went up there, I was
unconcerned about the recent Stanford edict prohibiting anyone
from leaving the main path to follow the myriad of bunny trails
that wound among the widely scattered trees. To do so, we were
told, would irreparably damage the ecology of the area. All I
wanted was a path where I could run literally for hours and not
have to speak a word. Where I could pass other joggers who were
in search of aloneness and not even feel the need to nod for the
sake of politeness. Where I could focus fully on the fitness compartment.

At least I *had* been able to do that, until my mother wouldn't
get out of my head. Working, teaching, dealing with Tabitha,
putting up with Jacoboni, all of those compartments kept me too
busy to wrestle with my mother issues the rest of the time. But
once I hit the hills in my Nikes, my concentration went down the
toilet.

Look, I told myself the evening I finally put it together, *you
can't let this mess with your head. Mother is a big girl. If she can't see
she has a problem, you're not going to be able to do a thing to change
that. Now get your tail on up this hill and stop obsessing.*

The first hill was a killer, shooting up for three hundred yards
at a thirty-degree incline, and I prided myself on taking it on as a
formidable opponent without batting so much as an eyelash. I
normally latched my eyes onto the top and didn't waver until I
was standing there, and then congratulated myself on the fact

that my thighs were still crying out for more. That night I took about two strides—pictured my mother lurching out of the booth at Marie Callendar's—and was ready to bag the whole run. Only sheer stubbornness kept me going.

By the time I got to the summit, I was breathing like a locomotive—no concentration whatsoever on controlling my inhale-exhale pattern. I actually started to get a stitch in my side, which hadn't happened since about freshman year in college, and I slowed to a walk, hands planted on my hips in self-disgust. Thus, I was completely at my best when a figure just ahead of me leaped over the fence that caged us on the path and practically scared me out of my Spandex.

He didn't see me. In fact, he continued on at a long-legged, lazy lope as if he *hadn't* just emerged from forbidden territory. That was fortunate, as far as I was concerned, because even from yards behind I could tell it was Socrates himself—Sam Whatever-His-Name-Was from the night of my mother's dinner. I'd rather have run into Alan Jacoboni at that point.

As I waited to let him get beyond catching-up distance ahead of me, I had a brief lapse and considered the fact that he had great legs. Nice muscle definition. Confident stride. Smooth, golden-olive skin—

I turned abruptly and headed back the way I'd come. If beating myself up about my mother and fantasizing about some religious fanatic's legs were my only two thought choices, I *did* need to bag the whole run.

The next day, I was wishing those *were* my only choices. When I got to my office, there was a Post-It note stuck to the door. *Jill,* it said, *See me ASAP.* It was signed *NF.*

NF. Nigel Frost. *Dr.* Nigel Frost. My advisor. The man who held my future in his hands at that juncture.

As I was going up the stairs to his office, Deb Kent was on her way down, her eyes blinking furiously in her contact lenses as usual. Deb seemed to be in a constant state of high-level stress. You'd have thought she was running IBM.

"I was going to come looking for you," she said. "Do you realize you and I have to do a tea in a couple of weeks?"

"If it's not today, I'm not worried about it," I said.

"That's because you're organized. Some of us don't have minds that function like Day-Timers, okay?"

She tossed her naturally frizzy mop of chocolate brown hair and flipped open her calendar. I attempted to edge past her, but she actually put out a hand to stop me.

"It's the one before the seminar on wavelets or something. Doesn't matter, I don't know 90 percent of what they're talking about at those things anyway."

Deb had a point there. Guest speakers came in to give seminars on a fairly frequent basis. Hence, the "tea"—a tray of bank cookies, a loaf of sourdough bread or two, a little fruit and a hunk of cheese—which grad students took turns setting up beforehand. The speakers were so specialized that you practically had to be a specialist yourself in the topic field or most of it was likely to blow by you. But everybody knew that was the case. I could never see why Deb claimed it made her feel like an illiterate moron.

"I'll pick up some cookies," I said. "This is not the inaugural banquet, Deb. Relax."

"Okay, okay, you're such a calming influence. Nothing bothers you. How do you do that?"

I shrugged and started up the steps again.

"Where are you going?" she said. "I thought you had a class this morning."

"I have to see Nigel."

"What a way to start the day. I hope you've had at least three cups of coffee."

Actually, I didn't usually drink coffee. Jacoboni called me an "oddity" there, too, because I didn't kick off every day on a caffeine high. I definitely didn't need it for a chat with Nigel. We had a great relationship: I did the work, he approved it, we both looked good. I didn't see how cappuccino could improve on that.

His office door was open, and he was standing up at the dry-erase board on the wall, tapping his chin with a marker. Most of the time I saw him behind his desk, so when I did come upon him standing up, it always struck me how big he actually was, which was probably part of the reason most undergraduates in his classes found him intimidating. He was definitely rotund, but in a distinguished way. At least he had the good taste to go to a bigger size than he'd worn in his forties, rather than let his shirts gape open at the buttons or his belly hang over his belt.

I tapped lightly on the door. "Dr. Frost?"

He turned and looked quizzically over his half-glasses, then gave me a brisk nod. I'd noticed my first year there that the gray fringe that was left on his balding head matched his moustache exactly, in content as well as color.

"Come in," he said, slipping the half-glasses into his shirt pocket. He headed in his typical unhurried fashion toward his desk. We were going into advisor-student mode. It was a safe bet he was going to bug me again about doing a teaching seminar.

"I got your note," I said. "Did you want to talk about—"

"Sit down," he said. "There's something you need to read."

The half-glasses went back on, and he scanned his neatly organized desktop with his eyes. Jacoboni could have taken a few lessons from him in office decorum. Heck, maybe Nigel was going to assign me a new officemate.

"Take a look at this." He produced a copy of *K-Theory*, which I recognized as one of about three hundred journals published monthly for math fanatics. "Page twelve," he said. "It's marked."

"More background reading?" I asked. "I thought I'd covered all that already." Covered it—ha. I'd read my eyes into an almost permanent bloodshot state my third year before I'd started my own research.

"Just read it," he said.

His face was, as usual, impassive as he rocked back in his chair and crossed his legs. You could never read him, which was probably another thing that intimidated his undergrads. Tabitha would have complete cardiac arrest if she ever got into one of Nigel's classes.

I flipped open the journal to the page marked with one of Nigel's ubiquitous Post-It notes and glanced at the title. Tabitha and everyone else disappeared when I saw the title of the article: "Topological K-Theory of Algebraic K-Theory Spectra."

No way. My eyes darted far enough down the page to confirm what the title suggested.

I looked up at Nigel. He was watching me, glasses in hand, face without expression.

"He proved my thesis," I said. "This is my dissertation."

"More or less."

"How much less?"

"Not enough, I'm afraid."

I stared at the offensive page and tried to keep my lip from curling. I'd been scooped. Some math geek from the University of Washington had done the same research I was doing, and he'd reached his conclusion before I had.

My mother had never allowed me to swear; she'd always said it was a cop-out from expressing yourself with eloquence. Too bad. I wanted to blue the air. As it was, I flung the journal back onto Nigel's desk, where it landed on the neat piles like an inkblot.

"So what does this mean?" I said. "Do I start all over? Find a new thesis?"

"Not exactly," Dr. Frost said.

"Not *exactly*? If I have to backtrack at all, it's at least a week added on—and I don't have that kind of time. What does 'not exactly' mean?"

He continued to look at me, until I realized I was standing up, driving my index finger into the desktop. I dropped back into the chair.

"It means you can keep what you have," he said. "You'll just have to take it further than he did."

"Go further, go backward—it still means the same thing in terms of time. I'm so close. How many people on my committee will have read that article?"

"I didn't hear that," Nigel said sternly, looking at me over the tops of his glasses, which had by then found their way back to his nose.

"No, you didn't because I didn't say it. I just…thought it out loud."

"Well, don't think it. We don't breach integrity here."

"I know. I don't want to duplicate somebody else's research. I wouldn't sleep at night. Not that I'm going to be doing any sleeping anyway. All right, what do I need to do? Come up with an amended proposal?"

"Give yourself a day or two to fume," he said.

"I don't have a day or two—" I caught myself and consciously put on a calm face. "And I don't need to fume. There's no reason to. Every graduate student knows this is a possibility. I'll have a new proposal on your desk by, say, Friday, and then I'll double up on my time on the weekends and get caught up. I'll blow Mr. University of Washington right out of the water. Anything else?"

Nigel took off the glasses again and slipped them back into his pocket. He placed *K-Theory* back on its pile on the corner of the desk. Finally, he leaned back in the chair again and crossed his legs.

Come on, Nigel, I thought. *If I don't get out of here so I can drag my hand through my hair, I'm going to drag it through what's left of yours.*

"I don't want to see a proposal until Monday. You need to take the time to determine how you're going to proceed. You may want to discuss it with me a bit, should you get into a bind with it—"

"I'll be fine," I said. "I don't anticipate any problems. I'm well enough acquainted with K-theory to anticipate the challenges."

Yeah, even my mother would have been proud of that exit line.

What I knew she wouldn't be proud of, I thought as I finally escaped Nigel's over-the-glasses scrutiny, was the fact that there was now a good chance I wasn't going to finish my dissertation before my funding ran out. The thought of asking her for money was about the most bone-chilling thing I could imagine.

By that afternoon, I had gone after my hair with my hands so many times that Jacoboni took one look at me when he came in and said, "Did you get the license number of that semi?"

Fortunately my cell phone rang just then, or I probably would have said something like, "Are you referring to the one that dragged *you* in here?"

"Jill!" Max said when I answered. "It's your Uncle Max."

"Hi," I said. "What's up?"

If he noticed my clipped tone, he didn't let on.

"Have you seen your mother since we talked? I'm not nagging you. Heaven forbid I should nag."

"Yes, I saw her."

I moved out into the hall with the phone. Jacoboni had taken a sudden intense interest in his computer screen, a sure sign he was homing in on every word I said. The hallway itself was resembling Highway 101: Every freshman on campus was following Tabitha's lead and skating through Alfred P. Sloan on roller blades, and that was compounded by the group of five male second-year grad students who seemed to be forever in the halls. I took the phone out the end door to the courtyard and sat on the edge of the circular planter that was overgrown with wandering Jew.

"You still there?" Max said. "Jill?"

"Yeah. Look, Max, I had lunch with Mother, and I know you think she's the queen of Sheba, but I *know* she's got a problem." I gave him the *Reader's Digest* version of our lunch date. He groaned with increasing drama at every plot twist.

"Nobody acts like that unless she's seriously hitting the bottle," I said.

"You actually smelled liquor on her breath?" Max said. "I'm just asking?"

"No, but who could tell with the amount of perfume she was wearing? Since when did she start bathing in fragrance and forgetting the smaller niceties—like combing her hair?"

"The stress is getting to her. I knew it—I saw it coming—but does she listen to me?" Max sniffed. Any minute now he was going to start blowing his nose. I could feel myself stiffening. I was already squeezing perspiration out of the cell phone.

"What do you want me to do about it, Max?" I said. "I told you—when I even hinted that she might have, oh, a headache, she practically cleared the table. Do *you* want to be on the receiving end of one of her tirades?"

"I don't want to ruin a beautiful friendship. You, she'll forgive. Me, she'll put out with the garbage."

"Oh, come on, Max, you two have been friends for twenty-five years. And if she comes after you with her saber tongue, you'll stand there and take it until she's worn herself out. If she comes after me, I'll say things I'll regret and put even *more* distance between us. That's why I don't get into it with her, ever."

"What are you talking about—what distance? Her whole world revolves around you!"

"Then you and I aren't orbiting in the same solar system. She has been avoiding me for six months. There was a time when I cringed every time she called me. Now if my phone rang and it was her, I'd probably lose consciousness. Look, I tried, Max, and it didn't work. After our little incident at Marie Callendar's, she's not going to make another lunch date with me for a long time."

"She said you were having lunch next week."

"What?"

"She told me she was meeting you again for lunch next week. She said you discussed it."

"Where was I? I'm telling you, the booze is getting to her."

"It's not booze."

"Then how do you account for—"

"Last night, I finally talked her into letting me come over and cook dinner for her. I fixed everything she likes. Polenta with gorgonzola, my stracotto al barolo—that's the beef braised in red wine sauce—"

"Enough with the menu, Max. What happened?"

"I told her, 'Go upstairs and take a hot bubble bath and when you come down, it will be a feast to die for.' While she was up there—God forgive me—I went through every cabinet, every closet, the pantry. Not a drop of alcohol, just like always. Nothing. Nada. Not even a cork in the trash can."

"You went through the garbage?" I said. "Tell me you weren't wearing your velvet jacket."

"Silk shirt. I hope the coffee grounds come out at the cleaners."

"Coffee grounds? Since when did she start drinking coffee?"

"She didn't. It was left in the pot from the last time I was over. I had just dumped it into the trash, then I stuck my arm in there. Maybe I'm the one with the problem?"

"When was the last time you'd been over there?" I said.

He paused. "Two weeks ago."

I switched the phone to the other ear. "What are you thinking?"

"Nothing. I'm not thinking. I don't want to think. But you go over there, Jill. You check on her."

"What do you want me to do, dismantle the garbage disposal? You went through everything. She's obviously not drinking at home."

"It's not that."

"What then?"

The usual rich tenor of his voice was thinning out until it was almost shrill.

"I got her talking about her work," Max said. "And she says to me—you won't believe this, Jill—I couldn't believe it myself—"

"Try me."

"She says 'I was looking through the…the…oh, that thing, that instrument we use to see things magnified.'"

"The microscope."

"Yeah. Exactly. That's what I had to say. She talked all around the word, and that wasn't the only time."

"But she wasn't drunk." I said. "You're sure?"

"You know what I think? I will *tell* you what I think. I think she's depressed."

"That's everybody's answer to every malady they can't figure out," I said.

"No, depression affects the mind, the powers of concentration. I know musicians who suffer—oh, it's terrible—they can't even tune an instrument."

"She's not some melodramatic artist—no offense—but she would never let herself fall into something like that. You've never heard her lecture about antidepressants and support groups? She could've pulled Sylvia Path right out of the oven with that one."

"Then show me I'm wrong," Max said. "Go over there and find out I've built another mountain out of a mole hill. I will kiss your feet. I'll cook you whatever you want. You want lo schinco? You always loved my schinco."

"You don't have to ply me with food," I said. "I'll go over there. When did she say we were having lunch?"

"She was vague. Next week was what she said."

"Okay, so maybe I'll just drop in Saturday. You think she'll be home?"

"That I know. She's always home on the weekends. She won't put her nose out unless I carry her."

"I have a life-sized picture of that," I said, sarcasm dripping.

"You'll call me when you've seen her?"

"Yes."

"Day or night. You have my number?"

"Yeah, Max."

"Don't make me wait. I won't sleep until I know."

C'mon, Max, I thought as we hung up. *I thought I was obsessing. A little Valium wouldn't hurt you any.*

I got through the rest of the week by keeping things in their proper cubbyholes. I prepped for and taught classes and held office hours and tutored Tabitha during the day, and then after my Loop run—during which I didn't run into Socrates again, thank heaven—I stayed up most of the night figuring out how to expand my research to reach a new conclusion. When I did sleep it was sprawled out on the couch in my apartment, my laptop blinking at me from the coffee table so I wouldn't actually go into REM and lose my train of thought.

I was bleary-eyed by Saturday morning, but I had the new proposal done and safely tucked into my desk drawer at the office, ready to be delivered to Nigel on Monday. It was so invitingly quiet in the building that I was tempted to prop myself up at my desk with a cup of Earl Grey and get work done. No Tabitha. No Jacoboni or Peter or Rashad or Deb or bevy of second-year grads. If there were a heaven, that would be it.

But Max would never let *me* sleep again if I didn't go over to my mother's. My only hope of avoiding verbal bombardment came from knowing that she'd actually told Max she was going to see me again. That is, if Max was telling me the truth. I was beginning to think he'd do just about anything to make sure my mother didn't drop out of his life—short of selling his pasta maker and his conducting baton.

I knew Max hadn't been lying to me or even exaggerating a little when I pulled my Miata—bought secondhand from Max—up to the house on Mayfield. He had, in fact, left out the most important information. The oleanders had grown past the lower windows and were on their way up to the second floor. The grass hadn't been cut since probably July—and it was October. There was a soggy Sunday paper lying in the middle of the lawn.

Okay, so the yardman quit. Big deal, I told myself firmly as I retrieved the paper and plopped it into the large garbage can that was still parked at the curb. If memory served me correctly, trash pickup was on Wednesday. Yardman or no yardman, Liz McGavock always had the trash can back behind the garage before the truck got to the other end of the street.

I knocked on the front door, a "courtesy" I had been paying my mother since the first time I'd gone there when I moved back to Palo Alto four years ago. I had opened the door and called out, "Mother, I'm home!" Her initial greeting had included, "From now on, wait for me to answer the door."

That had been my first clue that her encouragement to quit my teaching job in Trenton and at least apply for a fellowship at Stanford had been purely in the interest of my career, not because she missed me and wanted me close to her. There had been no argument when I said I wanted to live in graduate housing at Escondido Village rather than move back in with her, but she'd definitely kept close tabs on me the first two and a half years— only because she wanted to supervise my studies and oversee my friendships and keep surveillance over my activities, just as she'd always done. She said she wanted to guide me in becoming, as she put it, a strong, independent, intelligent, well-educated, and culturally astute woman. Nothing more. When she'd stopped calling six months ago, I'd told myself I was better off beyond her scrutiny.

Now, as the front door swung open, Mother greeted me in a half-open bathrobe. Black bikinis and a white bra did more than peek out from under it. The sight of me didn't seem to surprise her or prompt her to cinch up the robe. She just smiled vaguely at me and said, "Oh. Come on in."

"Did I wake you up?" I said.

"Don't be ridiculous. I'm up at dawn—you know that."

I also know you stood over the yardman with a pair of tweezers and a magnifying glass, but look what happened to that.

"I was at the office early, so I thought I'd come by," I said. "I figured you'd have the tea made."

"No, as a matter of fact, I don't," she said.

"Oh," I said. "Do you mind if I make a cup?"

"Help yourself."

"You want any?"

"Any what?"

"Tea."

As I trailed behind her to the kitchen, I tried not to wonder whether she'd be any more alert if I offered her a gin and tonic. I glanced back at the foyer and craned to see into the living room. So far everything looked, as usual, compulsively neat and orderly. The Hans Hofmann and Willem de Kooning prints were still on the walls. I caught a peek of the baby grand piano—my mother's only frivolous possession. Everything else in her house was rigid and decidedly unfeminine. She preferred clean lines, she'd always said. Everything uncluttered, unfussy.

So it still seemed—until I got to the kitchen and saw a mound of dirty dishes the size of Mt. Shasta in the sink. I pretended not to see it as I opened a cabinet to get a mug, but it was empty and I was forced to paw through the pile to locate one to recycle.

"Did you have a dinner party last night?" I said.

"No. Why?"

"Oh, I don't know. It was Friday night—you like to entertain—" *And you have enough dirty dishes in here to have served the entire Santa Clara Valley.*

I found the English breakfast tea and pretended to be choosy about which bag I picked from the box as I mentally groped for another approach. I was so bad at being subtle.

"So...Max said he was over for dinner this week," I said finally.

"Yes, and he talked insheshantly."

"Incessantly," I corrected automatically.

"That's what I said."

"Just confirming. What was he going on about?"

"Music-school politics—about which I could care less and he knows it. Why he felt it nesheshary to tell me that the chairman—no, don't use that!"

I stopped with my hand on the door to the microwave, tea mug ready to go in.

"Why not?" I said. "Is it broken?"

"I can't tolerate the noise it makes," Liz said.

"What noise? Is there something wrong with it?"

"It beeps. I said I can't—can't—"

"Tolerate it," I said.

"Do not finish my sentences for me. I am perfectly capable of expressing my own—"

She was cut off by the ringing of the phone, which caused her to jump as if the thing had exploded. Then she snatched up the receiver and said into it, "What is it?"

I set the mug of still-cold water with its floating tea bag on the counter and worked at keeping my teeth from falling out of my mouth. My mother had never been known for her phone cordiality, but it was beneath her to be outright rude. What the *heck* was going on? She couldn't stand the microwave beeping? She was jumping at the telephone ringing?

I paused and listened. Except for Mother snapping into the receiver, there wasn't a sound in the house. Normally on a Saturday morning, she had NPR on, but a glance at the radio revealed the plug dangling from the shelf. If she didn't like what was on, she would at least put some classical music on the CD player. In fact, the only thing close to bizarre I ever saw the woman do was stand in the living room and conduct a concerto that was coming through the speakers. But the place was completely silent. I didn't even hear the clock ticking in the foyer.

I'm blowing this whole thing out of proportion, I thought. *Max has got me freaked out.*

I made myself go into the entrance hall to look at the black-oak grandfather clock that kept stern tabs on the comings and goings of the McGavock house. The pendulum hung motionless behind the glass door. It wasn't like Mother to let it run down. By now, I strongly suspected she'd stopped it on purpose.

I got back to the kitchen just in time to hear Liz say, "I do *not* have time for this. Under no shircumshtances are you to call here again!" She then yanked the phone set off the wall and dumped it into the trash can.

"I need a cup of tea," she said to me. "Fix me a cup while you're doing yours, would you?"

"Sure," I said. "I'll put a kettle on the stove."

When I turned on the faucet, I saw my hand shaking.

I spent the rest of the day over there. Mother went back to bed after she took two sips of the tea. I didn't comment that it was only 10:00 A.M. I just did the dishes, made some sandwiches for lunch out of what wasn't moldy or shriveled in the refrigerator, and did my own search for telltale signs of alcoholism—or even drug abuse. It never seemed to occur to my mother that it was unusual for me to hang around her house like that. In fact, half the time, I wasn't sure she was even aware I was there.

But I was aware of her. How could I not be?

Saturday afternoon, she kept asking me what time it was, even though she was wearing a watch and there were three clocks in the kitchen alone.

Saturday night, she rambled on about campus politics—something she'd claimed that morning to care nothing about. She went nonstop for forty-five minutes without once looking at me.

The next morning, I called to tell her I'd be there at noon so we could go to lunch. When I got there, she'd already eaten and was napping on the living room couch. I put on a CD of Bach fugues and she came up off the sofa shrieking, "Turn that off! I can't stand that noise!"

Yet there were stretches of time when she seemed normal. She talked about a new resident at the lab who didn't seem entirely committed to his work, something she abhorred. I was relieved to see her straighten the CD cases because she was always a control freak about tidiness. In the midst of one rambling monologue she said, "I am quite happy with my current state of affairs, and if anyone has a problem with who I am that is unfortunate, because I have no intention of changing." I was sure then that the whole idea of her somehow losing it had been a figment of my imagination, if not a total hallucination.

But then she would abruptly get up and go to the refrigerator and stare into it, or wander off to take her fourth nap of the day. I was left wondering, *Who is this erratic woman, and what has she done with my mother?*

The most telling thing of all was that not once during the entire weekend did she ever say a word about me. There wasn't a single attempt to exert control or even question my most recent moves, decisions, or choice of lip gloss.

I knew it was time to find out what was going on.

FOUR

I stayed up half the night Sunday, surfing the Net. No, actually, I was ransacking it. If I didn't find some kind of answer by morning, I was going to be bald.

I bit the bullet and started with Alzheimer's. The minute it crossed my mind I went into major denial, but it was the only thing I could think of that might even remotely explain the changes in my mother's behavior. After scanning one Web site, I was sure I was on the wrong track.

Alzheimer's involves a loss of memory. Mother was losing words and being somewhat absentminded, but she didn't seem completely forgetful. The things she was doing were deliberate—like not using the microwave because she couldn't stand the noise and being outright rude to people on the phone instead of just coldly brusque. And there was nothing under Alzheimer's disease about slurring words—or showing up at the front door in your underwear and casually exposing yourself to the neighborhood. This whole thing with Mother was about language and behavior—and just plain judgment.

I hate to admit it, I thought, *but maybe Max is right. Maybe it is a bad case of depression.*

There was a vague sense of relief, but even as I tried to get a few hours' sleep and then attempted to move into my dissertation compartment for a possible meeting with Nigel, I couldn't shake the nagging thought that there was something more fundamentally wrong with my mother than the blues.

My biggest clue was the abyss that had formed itself between us. I'd always complained about the distance she kept from me emotionally. We'd never been affectionate with each other—I couldn't imagine anything more phony. And we'd certainly never "bonded"—a word I disdained anyway. But in the past when we'd been together, she had always focused her attention on me. Sure, she was usually critical, but at least she *saw* me. There had been a connection, even if it made me want to scream.

Right now there was no connection at all. Throughout my hike from Escondido Village to Sloan Monday morning, I couldn't fix Nigel and the new thesis proposal in my head. All I could picture was the look on my mother's face when I left the night before. She was sitting in her study reading when I finished the supper dishes and went in to say good-bye. She looked up at me from the book in her lap, and I fought not to gasp. For a moment, the vibrant intelligence that had always given her eyes life was gone. Her face looked absolutely flat.

The moment had passed then, but it wouldn't leave me alone now. And it had to. I had Nigel's face to worry about.

He wasn't in his office yet when I got there, so I put my new proposal in his box and tried to jam myself into the teaching-class compartment. Nothing doing. Tabitha showed up about five minutes after I got back to my desk. There was evidence in the puffed-up slits that she'd been bawling her eyes out. However, crying hadn't slowed down her speech patterns any.

"Hi, Ms. McGavock," she said. "I know I don't have an appointment, so if you have other stuff you have to do right now I can come back later, but I thought I'd try to catch you before you got too busy because I really need to talk to you."

"Sure," I said, giving the stack of yet-to-be-looked-at homework papers only one pointed glance. "What's up?"

"I'm just—" The gangly arms flapped as if the poor kid were trying to take flight. I motioned toward the chair.

"The tutoring's not helping?" I said as she skated her way over.

"Oh, no, I think it is. You've been so supportive and everything and I think I'm getting the problems better—but I thought if I could just, like, talk to you about this other thing, it might help me concentrate better because I'm just *really* freaked out."

"I can see that," I said dryly.

I opened a drawer and pulled out a purse-size package of Kleenex, which she accepted gratefully. She managed to get a tissue out and blew her nose.

What am I now, a guidance counselor? I thought. *Don't they have people with master's degrees to handle this kind of stuff?*

"Did you try what I suggested?" I said. "Did you find a study carrel in the library?"

She nodded, fingers still pinching the Kleenex over her nostrils.

"Didn't help, huh?"

"Oh, yeah, it did! Like I said, you're so good at all this. That's not the problem. The problem is, I'm *so* homesick!"

I groaned inwardly. Maybe if I looked at my watch about twenty times she'd get the hint that I did not want to play Mommy this morning. I restrained myself and nodded. Active listening, my mother had always called it.

"I knew I'd be a little bit homesick. You know, miss my parents and my brother and my dog and all my friends and some of my teachers—"

"Uh-huh."

"But I thought I'd make friends here and be over it by now. I mean, it's, like, October."

"It *is* October," I said.

"But there's nobody here like me. I'm not expecting people to be my clones or anything, but everybody here is so into dating and partying and competing for grades, and I'm not—so—"

In my experience those had been the usual reasons for going to college, but I kept nodding. If I said anything else, the girl was likely to get hysterical.

"So, like, this whole weekend, I studied in my room and I ate all my meals by myself and everybody else was out doing—well, I don't know what they were doing—and then yesterday in church I was praying about it and suddenly I just started crying and I couldn't stop. I haven't stopped since. I slept in the lounge last night so my roommate wouldn't hear me."

"Don't you have an R.A.?" I said.

"It's a guy. I don't think I can talk to him."

I could see her point. No guy would have sat through this much without telling the kid to get a life. That, of course, wasn't an option for me. We were supposed to "be there" for our students.

"I just thought maybe if I got it all out to somebody, I'd feel better, you know?"

"And do you?" I said hopefully.

"Kinda, yeah. I don't know. Maybe I just wasn't cut out for a major university. I probably should have stayed home and gone to community college."

"No, I taught at a community college. They're nothing but high schools with ashtrays. Look, this is a big adjustment—"

"Did you have a big adjustment when you went off to college?"

"Well, I was—"

"Where did you go?"

"Princeton."

Her gray eyes widened. "Wow. You must have been nervous."

"No more nervous than somebody coming here. This is a high-pressure place, too. But you're smart—you'll adjust."

"You really think so? You don't think I should just quit now and save my parents a lot of money?"

The word *quit* was not in my vocabulary growing up. I couldn't help making a face.

"Quitting is not an option," I said. "Look, the thing is that you've got to sort out your life."

"What do you mean? Like into piles?"

"Yeah, piles. You've got your classes pile, your social pile, your whatever-else pile—"

"God pile."

"Okay, whatever. And then you prioritize your piles and you deal with the most important things before you worry about the rest. You're still struggling with the academic adjustment, so just don't worry about the social thing. Trust me, it isn't what it's cracked up to be anyway."

She looked at me wistfully. "I bet you have a great social life. I mean, you're, like, so gorgeous."

"The best relationship I have is with my laptop," I said. "I'm focusing on getting my degree...which isn't going to happen if I don't get to work."

She sagged a little, but I didn't have time to pump her back up. I'd already spent ten minutes more than I had to spare. Besides, I'd run out of advice.

"I'm sorry," she said, jumping up with arms askew. "I didn't mean to take up your whole morning, but, gee, thanks, you really helped me. I feel like I could maybe get through the day without bursting out crying in the middle of a class."

She stuck out the Kleenex package, but I shook my head.

"Keep them," I said. If she had an attack during *my* class, I wanted her equipped.

I handed back first exams that day in Math 19, which meant the rest of the day was tied up with students coming in to complain, negotiate, and make appointments for help when I refused to participate in either the complaining or the negotiating.

"It's the freshman freak-out," Jacoboni said when one of them was barely out of earshot. "They were all valedictorians in their podunk high schools, then they come here and freak out when they find out they have to, oh, I don't know, *open a book.*"

"They can't freak out in here more than three hours a week," I said, "because I have other things to do."

"Like what?" Jacoboni said. He was obviously up for a protracted conversation.

I could have kissed my cell phone for ringing just then. I

didn't even mind that it was Max.

"How was Liz?" he said when we'd gotten the hellos out of the way. "When you didn't call me—"

"It was interesting."

"Did she talk to you? Did you find out—"

"No, I'm still clueless."

I could hear him sigh heavily into the phone. "What are we going to do, Jill? I'm out of my mind here. I lie awake all night—"

"Relax, Max," I said. "I'm working on it."

When I hung up, Jacoboni looked up ultracasually from his computer monitor and said, "Max, huh?"

"Yes, Jacoboni, Max. He's my mother's significant other, but he and I get together and make mad passionate whoopee whenever possible. Right now we're planning a tryst in the Caribbean over Thanksgiving break. Any more questions?"

If there were, I didn't give him a chance to ask them. I left the office in search of Nigel.

Dr. Frost wasn't available the rest of the day, so I had a head full of stuff from other compartments when I set out on the Loop that evening. The air was nippy and the wind was stronger than usual, so I wore sweats. By the time I got up the first hill, I stopped to strip them off. The harder I thought, the harder I ran, and the perspiration was out of control.

I was trying to maneuver the ankle elastic over my Nikes when I heard somebody talking. Why couldn't people just put on a Walkman and shut up while they were jogging? Some of us were trying to concentrate up here.

"It's Jill, isn't it?"

My head jerked up, and I had to hop on one foot to stay upright while I attempted to extract my foot from the other pant leg. I thrust out an arm for balance and nearly popped Sam Whatever-His-Name-Was in the jaw.

"Do I know you?" I said.

He grinned. "I can see I made a heck of an impression. Sam

Bakalis. Do you need a hand?"

"No," I said, though I now had my foot completely caught in the elastic. I gave it a yank and pitched forward, headed straight for the ground. Sam grabbed my elbow.

"That's funny," he said. "I could have sworn you were about to fall on your face."

He let go of my arm immediately, before I could even have the satisfaction of glaring at him.

"Thank you," I said and turned my attention to tying the sweats around my waist.

"So, what's new in vector bundles?" he said.

I couldn't help looking surprised. "You were paying attention."

"You were compelling."

Now *there* was a line I hadn't heard before.

"The vector bundles are fine," I said.

"You aren't going to ask me about Pascal?" he said. "I mean, since we're making small talk."

"Who?"

He grinned yet again. "I guess I wasn't as compelling."

No, pal, I wanted to say. *As a matter of fact, you were downright disappointing. If I recall correctly, you were trying to convert me over the carrot cake.*

"Right," he said. "Well, nice to see you again. Have a good run."

He adjusted his glasses and deftly sprang over the fence and loped off the path, right past the sign that read Please Remain on the Paved Pathways. For a guy in his mid-thirties he still looked lanky—yet comfortable in his own body. With those narrow shoulders he was no Arnold Schwarzenegger, but he was lean, sinewy, in a John Cusack kind of way.

I nearly slapped myself. Time to slip back into the proper compartment.

Which turned out to be my mother. By the time I finished

the run, I was so frustrated with thinking about her that I called her up and asked her to meet me for lunch again the next day. It was time to confront her, explosion or no explosion, so I could get on with my own problems. Remembering how late she'd been last time, I told her I'd pick her up at her office.

"You can meet me there," she said. "But we'll take my car. I need a chiropractor every time I get into that thing you drive."

The one *time you ever rode in it,* I thought. But it felt rather good to be irritated by her instead of dumbfounded the way I'd been recently. It was a more familiar sensation.

Just as I was leaving my office the next day at 11:50, Nigel appeared.

"Do you have a moment, Jill?" he said. He was the only person I knew who talked more properly than my mother—used to.

"Sure," I said. "I'm meeting my mother for lunch, but I can be a minute or two late."

"No, you absolutely cannot be late for lunch with your mother," he said. "Just see me this afternoon."

He turned and proceeded back down the hall, pace conspicuously unhurried amid the manic movements of the freshmen who'd just bolted from Deb Kent's tutorial. I almost ripped through them to catch up with him and find out what was going on with my thesis. But if I didn't get this taken care of with my mother, I was never going to be able to concentrate anyway.

I'm just going to see that she gets some professional help, I told myself as I pushed the speed limit on Campus Drive toward Stanford Hospital. *Then it's up to her what she does with it.*

The corridor leading to the hematology lab was bustling with its usual atmosphere of urgency when I got there. No one wearing a white coat ever *walked* anywhere; these people seemed to think that if they didn't run where they were headed, something catastrophic was going to happen. But I was oblivious to it, since I was busy considering the possibility that I was now trying to control my mother's life the way she'd always controlled mine. But I dismissed that the minute I got to her office door. It was cracked slightly, and somebody inside was doing the controlling for me.

"Liz, you aren't hearing me," he was saying. It was Ted Lyons, head of hematology. "I am not going to attribute this to an oversight on the part of one of the techs. This is your signature, your recommendation."

"Made on the basis of test results," I heard my mother say.

She didn't sound the least bit shaken. At the tone of Ted's voice, even I would have been. Every word was being punched at her like she was a leather bag. I leaned against the door jamb and waited for her to throw her next punch. I'd watched her many times discover a weakness in an opponent's case and magnify it to the point of ridicule. I glanced at my watch. I'd give it five minutes before poor Ted would be slinking out of there.

"The patient's first test for rubella was negative," Ted said. "So she didn't receive the vaccine."

"You've said that four times now," Liz said.

"But a subsequent test showed her to be rubella-positive."

"How many times are you going to go over this?"

Ted plowed on, his voice rising with each punch. "When you saw that, why didn't it occur to you that it was going to create a cascade of concerns for the fetus? The possibility of cerebral palsy alone is—"

"The sample was repeated—on my orders. It came up positive again. That is defini—defini—"

"Definitive," I whispered.

"It is *not* definitive!" Ted said. "It was completely uncharacteristic for you not to recommend a referral to the Infectious Disease people. Or at least to consider a false positive. You advised on the basis of low probability of the infection."

"I didn't want to put off the inevitable."

"Inevitable? That couple had a decision to make. Only

because the ID docs saw inconsistencies—inconsistencies you should have caught—did they send a sample to another lab."

"I know. It came back negative. Bravo for the couple."

"Why did another lab beyond Stanford have to find our mistake, Liz? It's unconscionable. What if that couple had elected to terminate the pregnancy? They would have done it on the basis of your report. We'd be responsible for the abortion of a perfectly normal baby."

Here we go, I thought. *She's going to get him on improper terminology or something—*

I waited. It didn't happen. There was a killing silence in the office.

"It's not the first major mistake that has come out of this office in the last two months, Liz," Ted said finally. "My question is this: Is it going to be the *last?*"

"You'll have to answer that one," Liz said. "I'm going to lunch."

I didn't even have a chance to back away from the door before she pushed it open. She didn't look at all as if she'd just lost an argument—probably the first one in her professional life. She just appeared puzzled to see me there.

"Oh," she said. "Oh, yes. We're having lunch."

She headed off down the hall at a stiff march, and her petite form was immediately lost in the sea of white coats. I got to her just as she was about to step into the line in the cafeteria. I looked at the myriad of shoulders in surgical scrubs and shook my head.

"Come on—let's get out of here," I said. "It's way too crowded." And too public. What I had to say, she wasn't going to want to hear amid her colleagues.

I had to move at a dead run to keep up with her as she turned abruptly and headed for the front entrance, lab coat flying out behind her. Was it me, I thought, or was she becoming more unkempt every time I saw her? She was wearing a pair of black slacks and the brown loafers she normally only put on to go out and get the newspaper off the front lawn.

Her Mercedes wasn't in much better shape. It was a cream-colored '85 she'd bought from one of the doctors when he retired. He reminded her of my grandfather or something; it was one of the few sentimental things I'd ever known her to do—that and the way she normally had the thing groomed every week. There was no evidence of that now. I had to move a pair of shoes and several empty Burger King cups before I could sit in the passenger seat.

Since when did you start drinking soda? I wanted to say. I managed to withhold comment, though. I had to stay in the right compartment—and that one was going to be hard enough. I'd be lucky if she didn't shove me out of the car the minute I started talking about it.

I tried for about the umpteenth time since last night to get my words organized, but it was pointless. The scene I'd overheard between her and Ted Lyons had given the thing a whole new twist. Other people *were* noticing—people who had a real impact on her career.

"Look, Mother," I said finally, "I heard what happened with Ted. The door was open, and, to be honest, I listened."

She looked at me vaguely and pulled the Mercedes out of the parking lot and onto Pasteur Drive. She didn't pick up any of the CDs in the console and stick them in the player as she was wont to do.

"And your point is?" she said.

"My point is, it sounds like things aren't going particularly well."

"Things are going perfectly fine. What are you talking about?"

I watched her closely. Her square face was as untroubled as ever.

"Ted doesn't seem to think they're 'fine,'" I said. "From the way he sounded, you could have caused somebody a personal disaster, not to mention the hospital a lawsuit."

"Ted Lyons has a strong sense of the—of the—the thing they do on stage, the theater—"

"The dramatic?" I said.

"He always imagines the worst possible impresario."

She must have meant scenario, but I didn't have the nerve to correct her. I just tried not to stare.

"Blood tests have a 99.9 percent accuracy rate," she went on, "but some of them are so sensational—no—so—you know, they detect every little—they're so—well, they're that way, and they can pick up a false positive."

She closed her mouth firmly, as if that should explain it all. I was groping.

"Yeah, but what does that prove?" I said.

She glanced at me coldly, which didn't surprise me, but I saw that she had a white-knuckled grip on the steering wheel. Maybe I should wait until we got to the restaurant to pursue this further.

"Where are we going, anyway?" I said. "You didn't like the food at Marie Callendar's."

"I liked it fine. I did a second test—"

At Marie Callendar's? No, she was back to the lab thing.

"The first one was just a—uh—you know, a test that rules things out."

"Screening test?"

"Screening test. The second one was to conform it."

She cocked her head slightly to the side. *She knows that wasn't the right word,* I thought. I was still considering whether to supply a quick "you mean *confirm*" when she continued.

"The second test was not as sensible but it was highly pacific. The first test was designated—determined—designed—*whatever.* It was supposed to pick up all cases but not all the people it would pick up would have the thing—the sickness—the—"

The skin between her eyebrows puckered, and she gave the steering wheel a soft pound with her fist. She had to suddenly slam on the brakes to keep from plowing into the back of the

BMW in front of us. I could see the driver staring into her rearview mirror.

"It's supposed to filter the false positives out. I guess it didn't."

Mother shrugged, but as we moved forward again she was still holding onto the wheel as if it were threatening to take on a life of its own.

"You guess?" I said. "I didn't think you ever *guessed.*"

"When did you get your medical degree, Jill?" she said.

"Mother, come on. You have always prided yourself on—"

"Ted goes off about the consolation—no, the comput—what the devil is the *word?*"

I never got the chance to answer. Nor did I have the opportunity to scream, "Mom! Stop!" I just saw the stop sign she was ignoring and heard the sickening squeal of brakes and screeching tires. The blue Jeep Grand Cherokee was just beginning its plow into my mother's side of the Mercedes as I was snapping my head toward her. The last look I saw on her face was one of complete bewilderment—before we were smashed into the street sign and came to a lurching halt.

FIVE

The next few minutes were a smear of Mrs. BMW peering into the Mercedes while chattering incoherently into her cell phone, and the driver of the Cherokee shouting over and over, "Didn't you see the stop sign, lady? Didn't you see it?" When the paramedics arrived, they added to it with a chain of increasingly pointless questions.

The only thing I remembered clearly—once I was piled into an ambulance I didn't need, ensconced in a neck brace I needed even less—was that my mother hadn't answered a single one of their queries. She'd just lain there in the front seat and then on the stretcher, blinking at them as they asked her to say her name and tell them if she knew where she was.

I slanted my eyes toward the paramedic in my ambulance, though I could only see half of him. The stupid neck brace prevented me from doing anything except stare at the ceiling. As far as I could tell, I had a lump on the side of my head and a gash on my right forearm. Why this necessitated traction was beyond me.

"Do you think my mother is in shock?" I said.

"Hard to tell."

"Hard to tell? Three paramedics and several thousand dollars' worth of medical equipment and you can't detect a simple thing like shock? Was her breathing shallow, pupils dilated? Isn't that basic First Aid?"

"Whoa, girl," the paramedic said. "Look at your blood pressure go up. She's getting good care. They'll fill you in at the hospital."

I gave the ceiling my blackest look. "No wonder you put people in these straitjackets—it's to keep us from smacking you when you make idiotic statements like that. My mother should have been telling *you* characters what her injuries were. Now, do you think she's in shock or has there been brain damage?"

"Brain damage? Now that's hard to say."

"Forget it," I said. "Just forget it."

"You need to try to stay calm. You've just been involved in a serious accident—"

"Ya think? What was your first clue?"

"She's a little cranky," he said to his partner as they were unloading me in front of the emergency room.

I wasn't any more cheerful in the ER when no less than six-teen people surrounded my gurney in the trauma room. I told them all in no uncertain terms that I had never lost consciousness and that I could have *walked* to the hospital if they hadn't strapped me to the stretcher like a mental patient.

"All I want to do is see my mother and have somebody tell me what injuries she sustained. I don't want stitches—I don't want a CAT scan—I don't want an MRI, for Pete's sake. I just want to know about my mother!"

I didn't calm down, despite the eye-rolling that was going on above me, until Ted Lyons came in. By then they'd determined that I had one subdural hematoma on my head—in other words, a bruise—and one laceration on my forearm that would require a few stitches.

"We'll get somebody in here to suture that up," a nurse said to Ted—not to me.

"I don't want sutures," I said through clenched teeth. "I want to see my mother, and if I don't, somebody's head is going to roll."

"She's already on her way to surgery," Ted said. He put a freckled hand on my shoulder and guided me firmly back onto the gurney.

There wasn't an inch on Ted Lyons that hadn't been liberally sprinkled with freckles. You could even see them up into the scalp of his thinning red hair. Though balding, he still had a boyish face that grinned down at me.

"You McGavock women are mean as snakes," he said. "Stay put and I'll tell you what's going on with your mom."

"And could you please take this thing off my neck before I go into some kind of meltdown?"

"No. I'm liable to get slugged by a nurse. They'll take it off. Just relax." Then Ted perched himself on a stainless steel stool beside my gurney. "Your mother has an open fracture of the femoral diaphysis—the large bone in the thigh—and the protective musculature is also displaced, which all means there's been significant bleeding and the potential for infection. Typically, patients with that type of injury heal well. These days they get them right up on their feet so they don't risk the complications associated with prolonged bed rest."

"So they're doing surgery just to set the bone?" I didn't even attempt to compete with the jargon he was throwing at me.

He nodded. "They're doing some intramedullary nailing—putting in pins."

"Ouch."

"She'll get plenty of pain meds, and they'll probably give her a sedative hypnotic, too, for the anxiety. That's pretty common. But there didn't appear to be any injuries to internal organs, no head trauma. The paramedics reported that she was verbally unresponsive, but apparently she was just stunned."

Ted stuffed his hands into the pockets of his lab coat and stared at the wall above me.

"What?" I said.

"The police officer told me the accident was Liz's fault, that she ran a stop sign."

I tried to nod and frowned as my chin collided with the overgrown collar.

"You don't have to answer this if you're not comfortable," Ted said, "but did she seem upset when she got in the car? I mean, upset enough to be driving erratically?"

"You mean upset over your conversation about the rubella test?"

"You heard."

"Yes. And, no, she didn't seem upset over *that*. I was more upset than she was because she *wasn't* upset. I am making no sense."

"You're making perfect sense. I had the same reaction."

He stared at the wall again, freckles folding around his eyes and mouth. "Do you mind if I speak frankly?" he said. "If you're not comfortable, I won't—"

"Say it already!" I said. "Just tell me what the *heck* is wrong with my mother."

He pressed his lips together. "You've obviously picked up on it—the language aphasia, the slurred speech, the errors in judgment."

"Just recently," I said. "But then, she's been avoiding me for the last six months. You're obviously way ahead of me."

"This whole thing with the pregnant patient and the rubella test—Liz knows that no diagnosis hinges on just one test. You use a constellation of findings. And this isn't the first time she's made that mistake in the last couple of months."

"I gathered that."

"About a month ago, apparently two patients' blood samples were switched in the lab. It happens once in about ten thousand lifetimes with the system we have, and that wasn't her fault—it was the technicians'. Anyway, the reports were given backward, and the doctor of the patient who received the positive result called Liz because the abnormal value didn't make sense with what he was seeing in the patient." Ted shook his head. "Liz didn't even look into it. She just told him the tests didn't lie—they were 99.9 percent accurate. She recommended the patient start treatment immediately. She said nothing about it to the techs, who then routinely disposed of the samples. The doctor had the patient retested and then called *me* to tell me the follow-up test was negative, which means we now have another patient out there who thinks he's disease-free because his results were negative. That shouldn't have happened, Jill. That and about a half-dozen other occurrences I could recount for you."

I closed my eyes and tried to compartmentalize. I couldn't. I didn't have a compartment for craziness.

"One of her friends thinks it's depression," I said.

"Could be. Depression presents itself in a number of different ways." Ted arched an eyebrow at me. "You're not buying that."

"I don't know. This is all so…weird. I don't have a scientific name for it."

"I don't either," Ted said. "But I think maybe somebody ought to find one."

I could feel my eyes sharpening. "What are you saying?"

"Why don't you see if you can talk her into submitting to a psychiatric evaluation while she's in here?"

"Sure. And while I'm at it, I'll also shoot myself with a large assault weapon."

Ted grinned. "I know she can be difficult."

"No, you haven't seen difficult until you see my mother's reaction to the suggestion that she go into therapy. I was just going to drop the hint today that maybe she ought to see a counselor, and I was sweating bullets over that. You'd better have those paramedics standing by when I drop this on her."

"Would you rather I did it?" Ted said.

"Yes," I said.

"Even though it would be in an official capacity?"

"As in, it would go in her file? You'd have to write her up?"

He nodded.

"If you'd suggested this to me a month ago, I'd have said *you* were the one who needed the psychiatrist."

He stood up. "Look, if you want to talk this through with me before you approach her, you have my number. Just call me—have my answering service page me if you need to. And you might want to wait until her orthopedic doc gives you the okay. We'll want to make sure she's strong enough."

Liz McGavock not strong enough for something? I thought when he was gone. Could the things I was now having to consider get any more outlandish?

It was another forty-five minutes before a resident who looked as if she ought to be skipping off to her Girl Scout meeting came in to stitch up my arm. When I was finally released to go to the OR waiting room, Max was there, pacing a path in the carpet.

When he saw me, he took the hall in two bounding leaps like he was going to scoop me up into his arms.

"Look at you," he said. "You're white as a sheet! Should you be here? Aren't they going to admit you?"

"They're going to have to admit *you* if you don't calm down."

"Where do you want to go? The recliner? The couch? Yes, lie here on the couch."

I sat down on a vinyl sofa, then Max took off his ankle-length black raincoat, rolled it into a ball, and put it behind my head.

"You need something to eat. The food here is for nothing. I could probably doctor up some soup for you—what can they do to soup?"

"Max, I'm fine. Stop it. Just sit here. You're going to drive me up the wall."

I patted the seat next to me and he sank into it.

"Have they told you anything about Mother?" I said.

"They put her under," Max said. He rubbed his hand over his face and looked at me, red-eyed. "They called down and said they were starting the operation. God forbid anything should happen to her."

"Something did happen to her," I reminded him.

"She may never walk again."

I snapped my head toward him. "They told you that?"

"No. But you know me, I always think the worst."

I sighed. "You don't have to think the worst, Max. The worst may already be happening."

I told him about my conversation with Ted Lyons. If anybody should be made aware of it, Max should. For reasons I could never understand, he was as loyal to my mother as a St. Bernard.

I could recall when Mother had first met him at some kind of university social soiree, though my memory was a little hazy. I'd only been about six. I knew I'd been smitten with him, though, probably because he came to the house every night after that for a while, bringing me a book or a puzzle for every bouquet of flowers or box of imported chocolates he brought my mother. Then there had been the period of time when we hadn't seen him at all. I remembered asking Mother why "Uncle Max," as he'd asked me to call him, didn't come anymore.

She'd been characteristically clinical about it. "He wanted to be my boyfriend," she had explained. "I don't want a boyfriend, or a husband, which boyfriends usually lead to. One husband was enough, thank you very much."

I'd known enough to realize she was referring to my father, whom I hadn't seen since I was eighteen months old and obviously didn't remember. Even by age six, she had told me that my father was a wealthy player who had preferred another woman to her, so they had divorced. We had left Virginia and never looked back. I didn't need a father anyway, she told me. I was doing just fine with her as my parent. I argued with her even less at age six than I did now.

But a few months after that conversation, Uncle Max had reappeared. He didn't bring flowers and candy and toys anymore. He just brought food and cooked it in our kitchen, at least once a week. And whenever there was a social event for which either of them needed an escort, they went together. We could expect Max for Thanksgiving and Christmas dinner, for birthdays and backyard barbecues, and as I'd grown older I'd just assumed that Max had decided friendship was good enough for him, too.

Now as I finished filling him in on Ted's recommendation, his soft eyes were troubled.

"This is going to hurt her—knowing we think she's cracking up."

"We don't think she's 'cracking up'!" I said. "We're not considering having her committed, for Pete's sake. Max, what?"

He was suddenly looking wilted, as if the St. Bernard had been caught with one of Liz's slippers.

I leaned closer. "You know something you aren't saying. What is it?"

"Nothing. I'm just so sad. How could it come to this?"

"Would you stop playing King Lear and tell me what you know! I can see it all over your face."

When he shook his head, I grabbed him by both lapels.

"This is not the time to be protecting Liz's dignity!" I said. "The woman is in trouble. I need every piece of information I can get before I go in there and tell her I want her to see a shrink so she won't screw up her whole life! Now talk to me!"

Across the room at the phone desk, a volunteer in a pink jacket cleared her throat. The other people waiting for word about loved ones were peering curiously over the tops of their magazines. I lowered my voice.

"You're not making it easier on anybody by keeping things to yourself."

Max looked wearily at the palms of his hands, which were sparkling with sweat under the fluorescent lights.

"These last six months," he said. "I've watched her change. It started with little things. You know, she would forget a word now and then—"

"A word?" I said. "Like what?"

"Like my name. Your name."

"Go on."

"She lost interest in music. She didn't want to go to the symphony, the opera—all the things she loved."

"You're talking about her like she's in the morgue," I said. "Look, I'm sorry I went ballistic on you, but don't do your pessimistic, this-is-the-end-of-life-as-we-know-it routine. This is data. I just need the data so I can formulate a plan. That's all."

He grabbed both of my hands and squeezed them between his damp ones. "You are so much like your mama—always a rock in a crisis. I never once, not in all these years, saw her shed a tear."

He went off down Memory Lane then, and I knew I'd gotten all I was going to get out of him. I half listened while I created a new compartment: the what-to-do-about-Mother compartment.

Later that evening, we finally saw her. She'd come out of the anesthesia—at least, that's what the nurses told us—and she was transferred to a private room. She did open her eyes, but she refused to talk to us, wouldn't say a word. I dragged a resident out of the room bodily and into the hall.

"Why isn't she talking?" I asked.

"That's hard to say," she said.

"What is it with you medical types?" I practically shrieked at her. "Just give me the possibilities!"

The resident, who couldn't have been as old as I was, straightened herself to a new height and said stiffly, "There is no evidence of brain damage from the accident, and she is fully responsive otherwise, so the probability of aphasia from the general anesthesia is very low."

"Which means?" I said.

"She's not talking because she doesn't want to," the resident said. "That's my educated guess."

"Thanks," I said. I waited until she was well down the hall before I went in and closed Mother's door.

"Mother, if you won't talk to us, we really don't have any

choice but to ask for a psychiatric evaluation," I said. "In fact, that might not be a bad idea anyway. What do you say?"

She didn't say anything. But she didn't pick up the bedpan and throw it at me, so I took that as a yes. I hailed a different resident and put in a request. Then I went back to Escondido Village and collapsed.

I woke up around three o'clock in the morning, still in my blood-stained top and skirt, riddled with anxiety. I didn't normally get nervous. Every time I heard of another grad student going on Paxil, I resisted the urge to say, "If you'd get your act together, you wouldn't have to pop pills just to function."

Right about then, however, I wouldn't have turned down a couple of Valium.

The only solution, of course, was to do something—anything. I tried grading homework, but when I found myself leafing aimlessly through the papers, I abandoned that. I thought about doing some of my own work, but that was pointless until I talked to Nigel. It occurred to me then that I hadn't even called anybody over at Sloan to tell them what was going on. Tabitha, I was sure, had folded when I didn't show up for her tutoring session. I could only hope Jacoboni hadn't been there to torment her, or she would be headed for the nearest community college.

This was getting out of hand. I turned on my laptop and logged on to the Internet.

"What do they call it when you lose your marbles?" I muttered as I stared at the cursor blinking *keyword*. "Wacko, nuts, section 8—no that's military. Think scientific—dementia!"

I typed it out, and then I hit the delete button.

What am I doing? She hasn't even had the evaluation yet and I've got her taking Quaaludes. Maybe she's just being stubborn. Maybe it's a mid-life crisis. Menopause?

No, she'd been through that. The way she told it, there was

nothing to go through. You just stopped having periods, and good riddance. These women with their hot flashes and hormone pills just didn't know how to let go of the reproductive years. She, personally, was concentrating on the most *pro*ductive years of her life.

I recalled all of that as I forced myself to type "Dementias" and waited for the computer to collect the data that was surely going to prove that I was wrong. The possibilities were more numerous than I'd expected—since I'd hoped for none. And they were all chilling.

I'd been right about her not having the symptoms of Alzheimer's, and depression seemed like only a remote possibility. But it could be a tumor on the frontal lobe of the brain. And it could be one of the few dementias that specifically affected language. Only one of them involved the area of judgment, however. Even the name needled me: Pick's Disease.

"Who came up with that?" I said to the screen.

It just blinked back at me and gave me a list of symptoms that could have been taken out of my diary entries about Mother—if I'd been keeping one. But what really shook me was the description of the later stages, given coldly, as if the writer were making out a grocery list:

Total loss of motor control
Total loss of all language functions
Severe dementia

There was no cure, it told me matter-of-factly. The progression couldn't even be slowed down. Its rate varied from a duration of less than two years to well over ten.

That's about the time I turned the computer off and made myself a cup of extra-strong Earl Grey. There was no way. We had to be talking at worst a tumor—which would more than probably be operable—or at best a case of severe mid-life crisis, which, knowing Mother, she could knock out of commission in about three sessions with a psychiatrist. Make that two.

By the time I finished deciding all that, the sun had long since come up and it was time to head for Sloan. I splashed some cold water on my face and threw on an outfit I wasn't sure was a whole lot better than the little number my mother had worn the day before.

The woman is haunting me, I thought as I headed across campus at a trot. *We have to resolve this.*

I was practically running by the time I got there, and I forced myself to slow down and get it together. Just because my mother was losing it didn't mean I had to. It was time to get out of the what-to-do-about-Mother compartment and into the what's-going-on-with-my-thesis slot. It would be bad form to actually look like I'd been up all night when I met with Nigel.

I fumbled in my bag for a clip and, using the front door for a mirror, organized my hair into some semblance of order. There wasn't much I could do about the bags, fully packed, under my eyes. For once I wished I *did* drink more coffee.

I closed my eyes, took a couple of deep breaths, and pushed through the double doors. They swung open into the cool, clean, orderly place that was my real world.

Except that Jacoboni was right there, leaning into the half-door on the department office.

"Have mercy, McGavock," he said. "I thought you looked bad yesterday."

I gave him a sour look and glanced at my watch. "What are you doing here at this hour? Am I that late?"

"No, the Arab terrorists roped me into meeting them for breakfast. Do people really eat at this ungodly hour?"

"The who?" I said. And then I put up a hand. "Never mind. I don't want to know."

"Actually it's Peter and Rashad, but—"

"Jill, I've been looking for you."

It was Nigel, emerging from the classroom across from the department office. It took a few seconds for that to register. My brain was like a 45 rpm being played at $33^1/_3$.

"I'm sorry," I said. "My mother and I had an accident yesterday on the way to lunch—"

To my utter amazement, Nigel put out a hand and curled it around my arm. "Come in here. We don't need to discuss this in the hallway." He drew me toward the classroom door, his eyes on Jacoboni. "Keep the noise to a minimum, would you, please, Alan? I have a class taking an exam in here."

I let him usher me into the classroom like I was some kind of bereaved mourner, but the minute we were in I managed to tactfully pull away. His eyes swept the room where ten students were hunched over their Scantrons and wiping away beads of sweat. Nigel motioned me toward one of the wide windowsills on the bowed window that overlooked Lomita Mall and the Science and Engineering Quad beyond it. I perched dutifully and tried to reclaim an aura of composure. Fortunately, I'd just clipped my hair back or I would've raked it.

"Have you had a chance to look at my new proposal?" I said.

Nigel gave me a long look.

Not a good sign, I thought.

"Is it a huge problem?" I said. "I felt confident about—"

"Were you hurt?" he said.

"By what? I haven't checked my mailbox yet this morning. Did you put some kind of reply in there? If the proposal is trash, I can deal with that."

"I'm talking about your accident." Nigel's normally impassive face was puckered. Was every middle-aged person I knew undergoing a personality transplant?

"I'm fine," I said. "A couple of stitches and a bump on the head. I'm ready to get focused on this issue."

"And your mother?"

She has nothing to do with this! I wanted to shriek at him. Only my reverence for all things mathematical reined me in. I explained my mother's injuries, leaving out the part about the psychiatric evaluation. Stanford was a mammoth community as universities go, but its grapevine was as efficient as any.

"It's nothing life-threatening," I said.

"But certainly enough to distract you." Nigel shook his head slightly. "We do not have to talk about this today. A couple of days for you to regroup and be there for your mother isn't going to hinder you that much."

If we don't talk about this right now, I thought, *I may explode.* That *would hinder me.*

"Look, Dr. Frost," I said evenly, "I don't mix my personal life with my academic life. Whatever needs to be done to get me back on track, I'd like to know now. Did I not go far enough with my thesis? Are you thinking I may be scooped again?"

I could tell I had Nigel a little unnerved, because he was patting his pocket for his half-glasses, which I spotted up on the overhead projector. Fine. Let him be unnerved. This wasn't about his life anyway.

"My notes are upstairs in my office," he said when he had given up the search for his specs.

"Shall I go get them?" I said.

"No," he said heavily. "I would prefer not to go into detail at this time. I will tell you, however, that in my view you may have gone further than you need to with the new thesis. There's a chance you won't be able to finish the necessary work on schedule, especially given your mother's injuries."

He apparently noticed my jaw tighten, because he continued.

"There are only so many hours in the day, Jill," Nigel said. "No matter how you juggle them, they still come down to twenty-four. Subtracting sleep, you're left with sixteen."

If I got eight hours of sleep a night I'd think I had narcolepsy, I thought.

"I see that you disagree," he said.

He was getting good at reading me. I didn't think I was so transparent.

"We will discuss this more thoroughly," he said. "At present, I think it's best you simply do what you can in your—" he paused—*"academic life."*

I heard his deliberate emphasis, and I resented it. My voice went cold as I said, "Do you have any objections to my continuing work on my thesis until we have a more in-depth discussion? I have to go in the same direction, no matter what is decided about the conclusion."

He absently patted his pocket again. "It would not be my choice, and I'm advising you against it. However, there will be no official consequences if you do. It is ultimately your decision how you integrate the various aspects of your life."

"Thank you," I said.

As I padded out of the room, I could feel him still watching me. He was "integrating" just a tad too much as far as I was concerned. My personal life was none of his business. Having him cross that line was worse than getting the once-over from Jacoboni. Who, I decided as I scooped the paperwork out of my mailbox, was going to get zero details about the accident. Nothing. Nada.

I headed down the hall toward the stairs, quickening my steps as I passed the break room with its odor of overcooked coffee. It was getting more tempting by the minute to take up the caffeine habit. Shuffling mail as I hurried down the steps, I stopped cold in front of the lecture hall at the bottom and stared at my mail. Stuck between the proclamation from American Express that I had qualified for a Gold Card and the latest plea from a distraught freshman to let him take his midterm late was a pink While You Were Out slip telling me to call a Dr. Fenwick at Stanford Hospital—re: Your Mother.

I took the rest of the turns at a near crawl as I studied it. It couldn't be an emergency or they'd have called on my cell phone.

I'd given the number to that second impertinent little resident. Of course, chances were he'd lost it.

When I got to my office, a dig through my bag revealed that I'd left the cell phone in my apartment. I went for the stairs again and climbed to the grad student lounge on the second floor. It was the only phone we had access to, though with everybody packing wireless it was always available.

I tapped the pink slip against the window as I waited endlessly for Dr. Fenwick to come to the phone. Who the heck was that, anyway? I'd talked to so many doctors the day before, I was surprised I remembered my own name. I stopped tapping and made a concerted effort to pull myself in. It was the crossover from mother-world into math-world that was stressing me out, and that was going to be my downfall if I didn't nip it in the bud.

"This is Dr. Fenwick," a deep voice said into the phone.

"Jill McGavock returning your call," I said. "Regarding Elizabeth McGavock, my mother."

"I know your mother well. We did some work together at UC San Francisco years ago."

I impatiently pulled the clip out of my hair and shook it out as I waited for him to cut the chitchat.

"We were able to schedule a psych consult last night," he said. "The psychiatrist on call was Dr.—"

"What did he say?"

"He was able to get your mother to talk—minimally— enough to conclude that this is not a psychiatric problem."

"So it's not depression, stress, schizophrenia, mid-life crisis."

"Right. Obviously those aren't things we can run blood tests for, but all the indicators rule those out."

"So she hasn't gone around the bend. What's next?"

"As her primary care physician, I'd like to call in a neurologist and have some tests done."

"For?"

"A number of possibilities."

"Name them," I said.

"I don't want to scare you."

"I don't scare. What are you looking for?"

"We'll want to rule out the possibility of a tumor. Then we'll look for evidence of brain disease, which can't be diagnosed with certainty, but we'll look for indicators and match those with her behaviors."

"Constellation of findings," I said. I didn't want him to think he was dealing with an imbecile.

"Correct," he said. I heard him chuckle. "You are your mother's daughter. You're not in med school, are you?"

"No. So let me be clear on this—you're looking for a tumor, brain diseases—dementias?"

"We'll consider that, but again, let's not jump to any conclusions."

Jump? Pal, the conclusions are standing there waiting to slap us in the face.

"How soon can they run the tests?" I said.

"Since she's already here, and because she's on staff, I think we can expedite the process somewhat. Say, results by day after tomorrow?"

Forty-eight hours. Could I handle that?

Of course I could handle it. Why shouldn't I be able to? Where the heck had that question come from?

"Fine," I said. "Should I call you or—"

"I'll catch up to you at the hospital. I'm sure you'll be there spending time with your mom."

"How long is she going to be in there, anyway?" I asked.

"You're looking at a good four or five days—and that of course is contingent on whatever we find in the neuro workup."

I hung up feeling something even my mother had never been able to make me feel: that my life was somehow not completely my own anymore.

SIX

The next forty-eight hours elongated themselves like a pair of stretch pants. I was so busy tearing from Stanford Hospital to Sloan and back to the hospital—barely touching down at Escondido for a change of clothes and a few hours' catch-up work—the time *should* have flown by. But the hours, I learned, tend to drag when nothing is as it's always been. And nothing was.

During the day, it wasn't too hard to keep my mind on teaching, tutoring, and making up for lost time on my thesis. When I didn't have to be at my desk for office hours, I worked in a corner of the computer room so I didn't have to put up with Jacoboni. My sessions with Tabitha were trying, because her inability to grasp derivatives seemed to be directly proportional to my need to get back to my own work.

But the evenings were decidedly more difficult. I spent them in my mother's hospital room amid the veritable jungle of flowers and potted plants that had been delivered. When she was awake, I sat next to her bed, across from Max on the other side, trying to get her to say something. It was a challenge I never imagined myself facing. Max was content to pretend Mother was participating. It drove me nuts. I hated small talk under the best of circumstances.

When she was asleep, I prowled the room while Max kept up a nonstop monologue.

"God forbid it's a tumor," he'd say. It can't be a tumor. She hasn't complained about pain. Although, you think she'd tell me if she were in pain? She wouldn't tell me. When she broke her arm skiing up at Tahoe, did she say a word? No. She's a martyr. She could've been in agony all this time and who would know?"

"She's not a martyr, Max," I told him. "She's a lot of things, but that's not one of them."

We must have had the same conversation about twelve times over those two nights, and we were launching into a thirteenth go-round the second evening when two men in signature white coats came in, looking doctor-grave. I glanced at the name tag on one of them: Carl J. Fenwick, M.D. The other one I couldn't see because the man must have been six foot nine. His head barely cleared the doorway.

"Jill," Fenwick said in his deep voice. He thrust out a meaty hand. "The last time I saw you, you were about five years old."

I nodded and looked quizzically up at Dr. Ceiling-Scraper.

"This is Dr. McDonald," Fenwick said. "He's chief of neurology. I wanted the best for your mother."

"Jill McGavock," I said, giving McDonald a nod. "You have results already?"

"Why don't we all go into the conference room down the hall and chat about this?" Dr. McDonald said.

He had a folksy way of speaking that made him sound more like the owner of the general store than a doctor. He seemed out of place at Stanford.

It was maddening to have to wait another five minutes while we all trailed down to a glassed-in room with plump couches and dim lighting, all of which I assumed was supposed to be soothing. They all sat. I stood against the wall, though Dr. McDonald could still look at me eye-to-eye. Dr. Fenwick glanced at Max.

"This is Dr. Ironto," I said. "He's a close family friend."

Max practically lunged at both of them, hands clasping theirs as if they'd already cured Mother and were about to sign her release papers.

"Thank you, Doctor," he said to each of them. "You don't

know how much we appreciate your time."

You think they're donating it, Max? I wanted to say.

He finally sat, perched on the edge of a chair, wringing his hands. I folded my arms and said, "What did you find out?"

McDonald tilted his head. "Well, now, in cases like this we don't have a lot of diagnostic tests. When we're looking at dementias—"

"Time out," I said. "You've ruled out a tumor?"

"That's right. There's no sign of any lesions."

"Thank God," Max said.

Personally, I wasn't at all sure thanks were in order—to anybody.

"Go on," I said.

"The results of the brain scan do show some shrinkage of the fronto-temporal lobe. You mind if I ask you a couple of questions about her symptoms?"

"You want symptoms?" I said. "I can give you symptoms."

I listed them for him, counting Mother's recent behaviors on my fingers until I ran out of digits. When I was through, Max forlornly reported his own observations. You'd have thought he was betraying a sacred trust. He couldn't even look McDonald in the eye, and he had to stop twice to blow his nose.

Through it all, Dr. McDonald nodded, his face sympathetic. Dr. Fenwick studied his palms as if they were signed death warrants. I looked from one of the doctors to the other until I felt nauseous.

When Max was finally finished clearing his nostrils into a Kleenex, Dr. McDonald stuck out his neck, cranelike, so he could look directly at me.

"Now, y'see, what happens in cases like this," he said, "is there's no way to be 100 percent sure of the diagnosis."

"How sure are you? Eighty percent? Twenty-five percent? Two percent?"

"About ninety," he said. "What happens is, we have to look at the test results and what you've seen and what I've seen. Looking at all that, I'm 90 percent sure your mother has what's called Pick's Disease. Now, it's a pretty rare condition—"

"I know what it is," I said. I gave him a litany of symptoms and prognosis, sounding more like a medical professional than he did. He just kept nodding.

"You know a lot about this already," he said.

"I try to be proactive," I said. "But I *don't* know what to expect at this point. How long until she loses her faculties completely?"

"Well, now, from what you've told me," McDonald answered, "she's been showing symptoms for seven or eight months. She probably knew something wasn't right several months before that."

"Whoa," I said. "Are you saying that she knows what's happening to her?"

"There's no way we can know that for sure—"

"Give it your best shot," I said.

"Pick's isn't like Alzheimer's, where they're unaware that anything's up. With this condition, the patient knows what's going on until the really severe dementia sets in. After that, who knows? When we catch them early enough, they can self-report, you see? They tell us they don't want to be around people anymore because they can't think of the right words." He crossed one endless leg over the opposite knee. "Some of them seem to know that their behavior is out of whack, but what happens is, they won't admit it to anybody. You see what I'm saying?"

I ignored the question. "Is she so far along that she *can't* talk?"

"Hard to say."

"Do you know how fed up I am with that excuse? Don't worry about covering your behind with me. Tell me what you think! This is my mother—I need to know!"

McDonald didn't even flinch, though Max reached for one of my hands. I pulled it away.

"I'll tell you what I think," McDonald said, "as long as you understand that it's just that—what I think."

"Go for it," I said.

"I think she's just decided she's not going to talk anymore because she can't completely control what comes out of her mouth. I don't know her personally, but Dr. Fenwick says she's a mighty proud woman."

"So how much longer before she actually *can't* talk?" I said. "Give me some kind of time line."

"Looking at the length of time she's been showing symptoms," McDonald said, "I'd say she's got to resign from the hemo lab immediately. And she can't live alone once she's discharged from the hospital."

"What does *that* mean?" I said.

"She's going to need a full-time caretaker," McDonald said.

"You can't be serious." I looked at Dr. Fenwick. "You know her. Can you just *hear* her reaction to that news?"

Dr. Fenwick took on a pained expression. "It isn't up to her anymore, Jill. It's up to you."

"Don't you have some family that can help you?" Dr. McDonald said.

"No," I said. "Her parents are both dead. Her brother was killed in Vietnam. Look, I can handle this on my own. I just need to know my options."

"Well, my secretary can fix you up with a good social worker," Dr. McDonald said. "We've got agencies, services, support groups—whatever you need." He fished in his pocket and produced a business card. "Just call my office when you're ready."

"You have a few days to decide," Dr. Fenwick said. "She won't be released for probably another seventy-two hours."

"One more question," I said. "Why did this happen? What caused it?"

McDonald put up a shielding hand. "When I say this, hold your fire," he said. "We just don't know."

"Is somebody working on it? Isn't somebody doing research, trying to find out?"

"Absolutely. There's a whole raft of docs in that field. But you see, it's so rare, we're behind where we are on Alzheimer's."

Dr. Fenwick looked up from his hands. "Jill, they're doing all they can. You need to focus on your mother's care."

I'm glad you know what I need to do, I thought. *Because I have absolutely no idea.*

My thoughts couldn't find a compartment to land in, and they were ramming into each other like bumper cars.

Dr. Fenwick stood up. "You know you can call me anytime. I'll continue to be your mother's primary care doctor if that's what you want."

"Sure," I said.

McDonald rose, too, and looked down at me from his other-atmospheric height.

"Now, you're going to have more questions," he said. "If you want to set up a time with me to chew on this together, we can do that."

"We appreciate that, Doctor," Max said. I could feel him groping for *something* to appreciate in this sea of information even he couldn't be thankful for.

Dr. Fenwick was already out the door, and McDonald was following him when he stopped and turned back to me.

"This is pretty hard to take," he said. "But I'll tell you one thing I've learned from families that have somebody with a dementia. They say the key to handling this is to believe that even though the mind and the body may be failing, the spirit is still in there."

I couldn't even respond.

"Thank you, Doctor," Max said for the umpteenth time.

McDonald left. Max sank back into the chair. I went out into the hall and leaned against the wall, where I could see Fenwick and McDonald retreating to the elevator.

Spirit? I wanted to shout after them. *That's very scientific, Doctors. Thank you.*

Then I marched to the nurse's station.

"Where can I get a coffee?" I said.

The *next* seventy-two hours made up for the slo-mo quality of the previous forty-eight and whipped past at breakneck speed. I attributed the racing in my veins to the amount of caffeine I had started consuming.

I called the social worker Dr. McDonald's secretary referred me to the next morning. Freda Webster-Claire insisted that we meet in person rather than do business over the phone. She was also adamant that we meet at Mother's house, since that's where she'd be going when she was released from the hospital.

"We'll want to look together to see if that's our best possible option," she said.

"There are no other options," I told her. "That's where she's going. All I want is the name of a decent caretaker."

"We'll go over all of that when we meet," she said.

I wondered if Freda Webster-Claire could hear my teeth grinding through the rest of the conversation.

We settled on that afternoon at two. That gave me five hours to get my academic life back on track. At that point, five uninterrupted hours sounded like a huge block of time.

I hadn't slept the night before anyway, so I'd used the wee hours of the morning to polish off some research and get caught up on paper grading. The big difference between teaching a class as a grad student and doing it as faculty was that staff members had graduate students to do their grading for them. I had to go over every muffed-up differential equation myself. It at least gave me a heads-up that Tabitha was making some progress—she was now up to C-minus level.

I handed back the papers at the end of class and then tried to beat it out of there so I could get organized for the meeting with Nigel that I was determined to have before the day was out. The students were so busy gaping at their papers that nobody—especially not Tabitha—seemed to be aware that I was leaping over vacant chairs to get to the door. She was engrossed in wiping tears off her upper lip as she sat slumped at her desk, looking at the paper as if it were written in Russian.

She's crying? I thought. *Nobody* cries *over calculus.*

I decided to leave her with a little dignity and pretended not to notice her as I proceeded toward the door. But one particularly large snort made ignoring her impossible. I looked right at her the very moment she tore her eyes away from her score and looked imploringly back at me.

I groaned inwardly and said, "You want to come to my office for a minute?"

She was out of her seat before I even finished the question, trailing down the hall after me like an abandoned cocker spaniel on roller blades.

She gets five minutes, I promised myself. *That's all I have to spare.*

The usual contingent of second-year males was in the hall as we passed, though they didn't seem to notice that Tabitha was now sniffing loudly enough to awaken Jacoboni over in Escondido Village. Just in case they did decide to do some kind of empirical analysis of Tabitha's behavior, I closed my office door behind us when we went in. She didn't even wait for me to clear off the chair—she just plopped right down on a stack of manila folders, dropped her face into her hands, and sobbed. All I could think to do was look for Kleenex, but since I'd started tutoring her, she'd pretty much cleaned me out.

She finally got enough control to paw through her backpack and produce one that was only semi-used. She blew noisily, reminding me of Max. I was going to have to start buying tissue in bulk.

"Look," I said, when I thought she'd finished wiping her nose, "you can't look at it as a C-minus. You have to view it as improvement. You flunked the first exam, right?"

She nodded miserably, hair spilling against her cheeks and sticking in strands to the leftover tears.

"We're going to have three more, and you have the option of dropping your lowest grade. If you keep coming in for extra help, I guarantee you at least a B for the quarter. I know it's not an A, but—"

"Why is it this hard?"

"I could give you a number of reasons," I said, "but you don't have that kind of time. Just for starters, it's a higher level of math than you've had before. It's college. It's Stanford."

"That's not what I mean," she whimpered. "This is—this is, like, what God has asked me to do. I told Him I would follow His will in everything in my life, and this is where He's led me. Only why is it still so hard? I mean, why isn't He helping me?"

"You don't even want to go there with me," I said.

She went anyway, dragging me right behind her.

"I always thought that if I was doing what God told me to do—if I was living in obedience to His will—He wouldn't let me fail."

"Look, if you're having some kind of spiritual crisis," I said, "maybe you ought to go talk to your priest."

"Pastor."

"Whatever. I don't think I can help you with this part. If you're struggling with the product rule, the chain rule, the quotient rule, I'm the one to talk to. But when it comes to God—"

"How did *you* know you were supposed to be a mathematician?"

"I was good at it, and I wanted to do something I was good at and something that made sense to me. Plus I didn't want to follow in my mother's footsteps and become a medical doctor."

She was blinking her enormous gray eyes at me as if she was

suddenly fascinated. I had to blink myself. Where the heck had that come from? I glanced at my watch. She'd already used up seven of her five minutes.

"Listen," I said, "if you're having this much trouble with math in your first college course, you probably ought to rethink your major. Who knows, maybe you heard wrong."

"It couldn't be wrong. My parents are so sure of it."

"Your parents?" I said. "They picked out your major for you?"

"Well, yeah. Not, like, totally. I mean, we all three sat down and went through my grades and my test scores and tried to figure out where God was leading. They figured God was pointing me to something like math because otherwise He wouldn't have allowed me to be accepted at Stanford."

I stared for a moment. "Really? I didn't know God worked in Admissions."

She blinked again, as if it was finally dawning on her that I hadn't been "born again." You'd have thought I'd slapped her across the face.

"Okay, look, we're getting off the track here," I said quickly. "I can't tell you why this is so hard for you. I can't tell you why things aren't working out the way you and your parents thought they were going to. All I can do is help you with the math. But whatever it is you do to make your decisions, do it again and see if some other major doesn't…what, present itself? However it is that works."

I stopped before I could offend her any further. The poor kid already looked as if she was going to need therapy because she'd just discovered everybody she went to for help wasn't going to quote the Bible.

"You're coming in tomorrow, right?" I said, standing up and reaching for the doorknob.

She nodded.

"Look over your test, write down the things you don't get, and we'll start from there."

She gave me one more long look before she slid for the door.

Then she looked over her shoulder and said, "So I guess you don't pray, huh?"

"I don't *what?*" The words were out before I could catch them, swallow them, or at least disguise them.

"Pray. I need to discern God's purpose in all this. Since you're so sure you're doing what you're supposed to be doing, I thought if you prayed…"

She trailed off. I felt as if I looked like her, mouth gaping, eyes blinking. It was one of the few times in my life I had ever been at a complete loss for words.

She just waited. Since it was obvious she wasn't going to leave until she got an answer, I finally said, "No, I don't pray. But how about if I hold a good thought for you?"

"Oh," she said. "Then I guess I'll pray for *you.*"

When she was gone, I shook my head to the empty room. *No wonder you're having trouble with calculus, honey,* I thought. *You're just a little dense.*

That was all the time I had for Tabitha's spiritual condition. I scooped up the now-warm folders from the chair and spread them out on my desk. My plan was to have my meeting with Nigel that afternoon, but I wanted to be able to hand him the work I'd already done on the new thesis at the same time, as evidence that this thing with my mother wasn't going to affect my progress or my performance. As a matter of fact, I decided as I pored over the work I'd squeezed in between grading papers the last three mornings from 4:00 A.M. to 8:00 A.M., I wasn't even going to tell him or anybody else in the department that Mother had Pick's Disease. The more separate I kept that from my real life, the better.

Besides, I wasn't even sure I believed it yet.

At noon, I was on my way out the back door to grab a bagel at the Terrace when Deb hailed me from the opposite end of the hall. I tried to pretend I didn't hear her, but Jacoboni poked his head out of Peter's office door and said, "Hey, Jill. Deb's calling you."

"Oh, really," I said.

"People are tryin' to work here, Deb," Jacoboni said. "You wanna hold it down?"

Deb blinked at him furiously and continued toward me, some kind of flowing, East-Indian-looking costume flying out behind her.

"Well, Deb, darlin'?" Jacoboni said, slanting casually in the doorway. "Do you plan to be functional as well as decorative today?"

"Jill, tell me you're on your way out to pick up three dozen cookies, and I'll kiss your feet," Deb said.

"Why would I be going out to—" It hit me like a freight train. "Is today that stupid tea?"

"Why, Jill!" Jacoboni said, his hand pressed to his chest in mock indignation. "Are you referring to an opportunity to meet with the best mathematical minds Stanford can bring together as 'stupid'?"

"You forgot?" Deb said. She tossed the unruly curly hair off her forehead with a jerk of her head. "I teamed up with you because you never forget anything. You have a mind like a steel trap. What happened?"

"Don't have a stroke," I said. I dug into the pocket of my jacket and produced a roll of ones. "I blew it. I'm sorry—just, here—take this and buy my share. I'll do all the legwork next time."

"Are you going to help me set up?" Deb said.

"What time?"

"The seminar's at four-thirty, the tea's at three-thirty—we ought to set up about three o'clock." She glared at Jacoboni. "If we set it up any sooner, the vultures will have the table cleaned off before the speaker even gets there."

Jacoboni shrugged. "I plead innocence."

"Tell me you can be there at three," Deb said to me.

I did a quick analysis in my head. I was meeting Freda

Webster-Claire-Smith-Barney or whatever her name was at two o'clock. If it took longer than forty-five minutes for her to realize that all I wanted was the name of a good caretaker, I was getting another social worker anyway.

"I'll be there," I assured her.

Then I skipped the bagel and went up to the first floor, poured myself a cup of coffee, which was now strong enough to stand a spoon up in, and headed back down to retrieve my folders and attempt to get a meeting with Nigel. Just then Nigel himself stepped out of the department office. For once something was going my way.

"Dr. Frost," I said. "Just the person I was looking for. Do you have a minute to talk about my new thesis?"

"Of course," he said. "We can go up to my office right now if that works for you."

I debated over whether to race down and get my folders but decided against it. A bird in the hand and all that.

Nigel led me unhurriedly up the steps to the second floor, nearly driving me crazy in the process. I had to force myself not to grab him by the arm and propel him forward.

"How's your mother?" he asked.

"What?" I said.

"Your mother. How is her recovery?"

"Oh. She's coming home in—" I glanced at my watch— "about forty-eight hours."

"She's doing well, then."

"Yeah," I said.

He didn't say anything else on the interminable remainder of the walk to his office. Except for my slight irritation with him a few days before, it was the first time I could remember feeling uncomfortable with Nigel. It had been apparent from the start of our advisory relationship that he wasn't going to intimidate me and I wasn't going to have to be Miss Congeniality around him. Since then, through the preparation for my area exam at the end of my third year, and through my research last year and this, we'd worked together like a well-oiled machine. Now I felt like the proverbial squeaky wheel.

But I didn't have much choice. If I didn't get this taken care of now, I wasn't going to be able to focus on handling Freda. And if I didn't handle Freda, Mother was going to come home to an empty house. Who knew what that meant at this point?

We were in Nigel's office before I realized he was talking again, glasses already in hand.

"Your new proposal is fine," he said. "As I mentioned the other day, if there is any fault at all, it may be overly aggressive."

I hadn't even sat down yet, and I stayed standing. "Could you flesh that out for me?"

He perched the glasses on the end of his nose, then took them off. With his usual maddening slowness, he sat down in his chair and folded one leg precisely over the other.

"I don't want to run the risk of being scooped again," I said. "I was merely—"

"Have you considered that you might be biting off more than you can chew?" Nigel said.

"No," I said. "I haven't considered that at all. If my approach is now to take someone else's work to a new level, I want to make certain that level is high enough to be considered original research in itself."

"Even a lower level than what you've proposed could be considered 'high enough.'"

"Maybe for the committee," I said. "But not for me."

He locked gazes with me for a moment, then returned his glasses to his face and flipped through my pages again.

"You realize, of course," he said, "that it is ultimately up to me to tell you when you have solved your problem."

I hadn't realized that. It had never been an issue, and I didn't see how it was now.

"At some point," he went on, "I may indeed feel that you have shown that something is *not* true, which is also interesting. Even being able to show a class of examples not previously known—"

"I know I can solve this problem," I said. "All I need to know is whether you have any doubts about my ability to do it."

"About your ability, no," he said.

"Then I'd like to proceed," I said.

The arm that reached out to hand me my proposal was stiff. I suddenly didn't want to leave it this way. I smiled at him as I took the folder.

"Just so you'll be reassured," I said, "I'll leave the work I've already done in your box."

He peered at me from behind his glasses. It wasn't the look of reassurance I'd hoped for. Whatever was there, I couldn't read it—and I couldn't leave it alone.

"You think I'm being too aggressive," I said. "But I don't see it that way. I hear graduate students reevaluating their commitment to their studies all the time. I don't do that. I know what I want and if I drive myself harder than anybody else to get there, it's because I know where 'there' is."

Nigel slowly removed his glasses and tucked them into his pocket. To my surprise, he smiled back at me in a wry way.

"My dear," he said, "if you always know where 'there' is, you possess a secret I'm not privy to."

For the second time that day, I was at a loss for words.

SEVEN

F reda Webster-Claire—the woman who was setting me up with a caretaker—arrived at Mother's house just as I was shoving the last of the dirty dishes into the dishwasher. As I opened the front door, I saw that she was one of those women who has enough hair for thirty-seven people and uses it as punctuation. She hurried up the front steps, hand already outstretched, hair in exclamation points.

"You must be Jill," she called. "Freda Webster-Claire."

"Come in," I said.

"Wonderful."

I led her through the foyer and into the living room, where I'd put a legal pad and a couple of pencils on the coffee table as a signal that I wanted to get right down to business. Freda was too busy saying how wonderful the décor was to notice. The minute we sat down, she reached over and squeezed my hand.

"This must be incredibly hard for you," she said. "How are you doing—really?"

"I'm fine." I withdrew my hand and reached for the legal pad. "Should we start with my questions or yours?"

Her smile didn't fade—I doubted that it ever did—as she folded her hands neatly around her knees and nodded, though at what I wasn't sure.

"Why don't we start with what's on your mind?" she suggested. "Then I think you'll feel more comfortable."

I wanted to tell her that I'd feel more comfortable if she stopped acting like *I* was the patient. Instead, I gave her my list of questions: What exactly does a caretaker do? How much was one going to cost? What accommodations did I have to make for her? Freda waited until I got through the entire list before she said, "Now, are you certain it's the best choice to have a caretaker here, as opposed to putting Mom in an assisted-living situation?"

"You mean a nursing home?"

"No," she said patiently, "assisted living is not a nursing home. We wouldn't recommend a nursing home for Mom unless she required bathing, changing, feeding—that sort of thing. As I understand it, she is still doing all those things for herself. In assisted living, Mom could continue to do that, but remembering to fix the meals and so forth would be left up to someone else."

"My *mother*," I said, "will be fine here. Dr. McDonald seems to thinks she needs a caretaker." I tapped the list of questions on the legal pad. "That's all I really need to know about."

Freda's smile went soft, and she patted my arm. "Wonderful. Let's focus on that for right now." She consulted her notes. "Her insurance will cover 80 percent for a full-time caretaker, and her supplemental policy will cover the rest. Your mom certainly had her affairs in order, which is wonderful." She cocked her head, creating a comma with her hair. "You know, I think it makes it that much harder when a bright, together person suffers from dementia."

I glanced at my watch. "And what does this caretaker do?"

Freda ran through the list of household duties, including dispensing medications, making sure "Mom" was bathing regularly and otherwise keeping up with her hygiene.

"She'll report to you daily any changes she sees in your mom's behavior," Freda said.

"Daily," I said.

"Yes. When you come in from work or after dinner when Mom is settled in for the night—whatever is comfortable for you."

"She and I can work that out, I'm sure," I said. "And she'll have my cell phone number."

"Wonderful idea," Freda said. "That way she'll be able to reach you at a moment's notice. What do you do, Jill?"

"I'm a graduate student."

"Wonderful," Freda said. "That's perfect. You'll have the time to spend with Mom, then. So many people have full-time jobs, and they're just overwhelmed when something like this happens."

"Right," I said dryly. "Well, that about covers it for me."

"My turn, then!" she said, hair in exclamation points again as she reached for her briefcase. "I just have a few things. I like to make sure my families know what may lie around the corner so they're not blindsided. You'll find out that I'm very protective of my families. I already consider you and your mom to be—"

I cut her off before she could say "family" again. If she'd uttered it, I probably would have ripped out a semi-colon or two.

"Wonderful," I said. "What things?"

There were more than just a *few*. She spent the next thirty minutes going over them. I was going to have to become acquainted with Mother's finances so I could take them over when she was no longer able to. There was a "wonderful" financial counselor available to assist me. I was probably going to have to handle her retirement from Stanford, and there was a retirement counselor at the hospital who could walk me through that. Then, of course, there were the family and friends to deal with who would have various reactions to "Mom's" changing behavior. Freda herself would be happy to help me through that, but I could also select my own therapist, whatever I felt most comfortable with.

Comfortable? If I made all the appointments with the people she suggested I talk to, I'd be wound up like a spring. But I took every business card she tucked into my hand—including the one with the name of the caretaker she was recommending—and continued to nod in hopes that full agreement would get her out the door sooner.

But even after she'd snapped her briefcase shut and appeared to be ready to leave, she leaned toward me yet again and put her hand on my knee.

"Let me just say this," she said. "You seem to be very capable and independent, and I think that's wonderful."

You think everything is wonderful, I thought.

"But the time is going to come when this is all going to seem like too much for you," she continued. "Promise me that you won't be too proud to give one of us a call. It doesn't have to be me."

Good thing! I thought.

Freda looked directly into my eyes, her own a practiced firm-but-friendly. "Now promise me."

I held her gaze and said, "Thanks so much for all your help. I'll call Ms.—" I glanced at the top card in my palm—"Rose right away and set things up with her." I shook Freda's hand solidly and couldn't resist saying, "You've been wonderful."

"Oh," Freda said as she stood up, "I never did have a chance to look around. Do we have time to do that?"

"Not really," I said. "What's to look at? My mother has lived here for twenty-five years, so it's not like I'm bringing her into foreign territory."

I could have bitten off my tongue. Freda's eyes lit up, as if she'd just hit pay dirt—some misconception I had that she could help me with.

"But you see, it is foreign territory to her now," she said. She walked briskly into the foyer and looked around. From there she could see Mother's study door and she made a beeline for it, with me trotting along behind. I'm sure my nostrils were flaring.

"This is obviously where she did her bookkeeping and such," Freda said. "And I'm sure at one time it was neat as a pin in here."

I had to admit she was right about that. I hadn't been in this room since before the accident, and it was currently far from pin-like. A drawer in the oak file cabinet was yawning open, exposing its untidy contents. A checkbook lay face down on the desk amid a jumble of papers, and a pile of unopened mail was spilling out of the In basket and onto the floor.

"The more cluttered things are, the more confused Mom will become," Freda said, "so you'll want to have this tidied up before her arrival, or she may think she can come in and pick up business where she left off. These things lying around will be reminders to her." Freda curled her fingers around my upper arm. "We can send someone over to help you get organized—"

"I'll be fine," I said.

"How about the other rooms? Where is her bedroom?"

"I think I have the idea," I said through my teeth.

"Wonderful. Whatever you're comfortable with." She at last turned toward the door, but her glance obviously caught the two photographs on the shelf, because she stopped. They were the only two pictures Mother kept in frames. One was of the two of us the day I graduated from Princeton, which resembled one of those Civil War era portraits of people who looked for all the world as if they were suffering from hemorrhoids. The other was of Mother with her father, the day *she* graduated from UCLA— after only three years, she'd told me at least a half dozen times. She and her father were shaking hands. He was looking into the camera with all the expression of a dial tone, but Mother was gazing up at him as if *he* were the one who'd just pulled off summa cum laude and she was bursting with pride at the feat he'd accomplished. I knew that photograph was one of her most prized possessions. There had been no photo of her graduation from medical school at Vanderbilt. Her father had died by then, and there was no one to make proud but herself.

"I know it's hard," Freda said at my elbow. "And I won't try to tell you that you'll adjust to the idea that she's not the same person she was before—"

"Good," I said. "Thanks again for coming."

She sagged ever so slightly, and she gave the stairs to the second floor a wistful look before she gave in and went out the front door.

I'm sorry you're not comfortable with that, I thought as I closed the door behind her. *Maybe there's a counselor we can set you up with so you can process it.*

I looked at my watch. It was ten till three. There was just enough time to race back to the math department and help Deb. I was turning out the light in the study, purse slung over my shoulder, when the phone rang in there, so softly I could barely hear it. Mother had obviously turned this one down instead of yanking it out of the wall completely. I pondered not answering it, but in spite of myself, I could hear Freda telling me all the things I was now responsible for. I picked it up.

"Elizabeth McGavock, please," a tired-sounding woman's voice said.

"She isn't here," I said. "May I take a message?"

"This is PG&E calling. To whom am I speaking?"

"If you're calling about a special offer, we're not interested," I said.

"No, I'm calling regarding her account," the woman said. "When is a good time to reach her?"

I had a sinking sensation. The power company didn't usually call to congratulate you on how beautifully you were handling your bills. I gripped the receiver.

"This is Jill McGavock," I said. "I'm her daughter. I'm handling her financial affairs now that she—while she—how can I help you?"

The woman then crisply informed me that Mother was two months behind in paying her gas and electric bill. She'd promised to make the payment last week, and she had, but the check had arrived made out not to PG&E but to herself. They were about to turn off the power.

"Don't do that," I said. "I'll get a check to you. How soon do you need it?"

"This afternoon by 5:00 P.M."

"What does she owe?"

"The amount is $456.17," the woman said.

I bit back a *You've got to be kidding!* and promised I'd have it there within the hour.

How I was going to do that, I wasn't sure. Mother's checkbook was there on the desk, but who could tell how much money she had in her account? She hadn't entered anything in it since August, as far as I could tell. The mail that was spilling out of the In basket included several bank statements, but until I could make some sense out of all that, I was hesitant to write any checks on it. And besides, what about a signature? I was going to have to get Power of Attorney. Of course, I could go to the hospital and ask Mother to sign a check, but the mere image of me telling Mother I'd been rummaging through her personal papers left me cold.

I dug in my purse for my own checkbook. I had about $1200 in my account, but that had to last me until the end of January. On the other hand, the reaction I could picture on Freda's face when she got word that I had taken my mother home to a house with no gas or electricity made me pick up a pen. Mother could reimburse me later.

By the time I got all of that taken care of, it was 4:15. The tea would already be winding down, and I wasn't in the mood to face Deb. So I went back to the house to look up the name of Mother's lawyer and get started on the Power of Attorney ordeal. His secretary promised she would have him call me as soon as he was free, so while I was waiting I attacked the unopened mail. I groaned with each envelope I opened.

PG&E weren't the only ones who hadn't been paid for several months. Pacific Bell was threatening to disconnect. The cable TV company had already discontinued service. American Express was "concerned" about her lack of payment since she'd been such a responsible customer for the last twenty years. The bottom line was, she was not to attempt to use her Gold Card until a full payment—of over five thousand dollars—was made.

Frantically I searched for letters from her insurance companies, but there were none. A hunt through the filing cabinet reassured me that both premiums came directly out of her paycheck. Which reminded me, her job was another thing I had to take care of and soon.

I called Ted Lyons and arranged to clean out her office the next day. Then I went back to opening the mail, only to find out that *all* of the checks Mother had written the week before to pay the bills had been made out to herself. They'd been returned with a variety of cryptic notes. I sighed and got out my checkbook again and paid all except American Express and the cable company. Nurse Rose didn't need cable as far as I was concerned.

The lawyer didn't get back to me until almost seven that night. He was sympathetic to the point of nausea—who wasn't?—and promised to have the Power of Attorney papers in order for me the next afternoon.

I tried to find something to eat in the refrigerator and after throwing away every container of leftovers I opened, I opted for a sandwich in the hospital cafeteria when I got there and took it up to Mother's room. Max, of course, was already there, pacing like a caged bear. When I walked in the door, he pulled me into his arms and broke into sobs.

Come on, Max, please, I wanted to say to him. *Can't we handle this like adults?*

But I could no more pull away from him than I could spit in the poor man's eye. I let him hold *me* until he got hold of *himself,* and then I gently pried myself loose. He went to the corner to blow his nose, and it was then I saw that Mother was in a wheelchair, leg stuck out in front of her like a cannon ready to fire. She was parked by the window, staring out.

She looked so little to me. It always struck me when I hadn't seen her for a while that she was so much smaller than I was. In one of the few references she'd ever made about my father, she'd told me I got my legginess from his side of the family. She was a petite five foot four with birdlike bones, and now, garbed in hospital attire that swallowed her, sporting a brace that tripled the size of her leg, she seemed tinier than ever. The confidence, the vitality, and the brilliance that had always given her stature were gone.

I stopped, frozen, at the foot of her bed. So what did that mean? If her mind was going, did that mean it would take her persona with it? Would she still technically be a person at all?

Even as I watched her, Mother's eyelids drooped and her head lolled to one side as she dozed off.

"They're still giving her something for the pain, thank God," Max said. "I keep thinking, ah, the drugs will wear off and she'll look at us and we'll have Liz back. I keep thinking it over and over."

I nodded toward the door and led him out into the hall.

"What?" he said. "God forbid you should hold something back from me, Jill. I know I'm not family, but I—"

"I'm not holding anything back, Max," I snapped, "if you'll give me a chance to get it out."

Lack of sleep and too much coffee were taking their toll. I could see the sting in his eyes, and I sighed.

"I'm sorry. It's just been a horrible day. I don't mean to take it out on you."

"Jill, no apologies. None." Max pressed my hands between his. His tenderness hurt, and I pulled them away.

"I talked to the social worker today," I said.

"Did you get a good caretaker? I've been trying to find a way to say this—if money is a problem, you let me know. Heaven knows we want the best."

"Insurance is taking care of it. The caretaker's name is Something Rose—I don't know. But Max, the social worker said we might want to consider assisted living. It's like a nursing home except—"

"No!" Max was shaking his head, and he reached out and

grabbed me by both shoulders. "Don't do that, please, Jill. She'd hate that. You know she'd hate it."

"I don't know what she hates anymore," I said. "That's the point. Just since the accident, it's like she's lost her entire personality. What if there isn't anybody in there anymore?"

"What are you saying? How can you ask that?"

"Because her mind was everything," I said. "Without it, she's gone."

Max wiped at his face. "I've been thinking—that's all I do is think now. But I've been thinking about what that doctor said—that neurologist."

"McDonald? About what?"

"He said we can find comfort in the fact that her spirit is still in there."

"What spirit?" I said. "I don't even know what that is. And if it's there, I don't see any evidence of it."

"I don't need evidence," Max said stubbornly. "I know there is an essence of a person—there is a soul."

"Soul."

"That's what goes when you die. As long as Liz is alive, that soul is still there. We can't put her away in some asylum. God forbid we should do that!"

"It's not an asylum," I said. "And that whole soul idea is a religious issue, as far as I'm concerned. You're not religious."

"I don't go to mass. If I went to confession, I would be there for days. But I know, Jill."

"Show me the evidence."

"I can't."

"Then there you have it."

Max stared at me. The softness left his eyes, and the lines around them hardened.

"'There you have it'?" he said. "This is your mother you're talking about, and you say 'there you have it'! This is not some mathematical equation! Not some science experiment!"

I put a palm up, and he lowered his voice to a hoarse whisper. "Do you know that through all of this mess—from the first signs, then the accident, then the doctor telling you that your mother has this horrible dementia—you haven't shed a tear. Not a tear, Jill. You don't even look like it bothers you—except that maybe it could, God forbid, interfere with your work!"

"I guess the apple doesn't fall far from the tree," I said.

His big head gave a violent shake, spilling hair down to his eyebrows. "No, you're wrong. Your mother has passion. She sees the value of life. She drives herself to save it, and she allows herself to relish it, to savor it. I swear I still see that in her."

"Max, you've always seen a lot of things in my mother nobody else could see."

"Then listen to me now. Give her the benefit of the doubt. Believe that she has a soul we have to protect until the day she dies."

I leaned against the wall and closed my eyes, which burned as if they were two lumps of smoldering coal under my eyelids. I felt Max's fingers under my chin. I opened my eyes as he lifted my face closer to his.

"If you don't believe it," he said, "then at least do your research and prove me wrong. Don't you owe it to your mother? You owe it to your mother. And I think you owe it to yourself, too."

His eyes misted over. I knew he wanted mine to tear up, too, but they only burned.

"I don't think this is the kind of thing you can research, Max," I said.

"But you can study it. Do you remember that young professor we met the night of your mother's dinner? The philosophy professor? Nice-looking man—"

"Yeah," I said. "Sam something. What about him?"

"Go over and talk to him. See what he has to say about the soul. Just talk philosophy."

"He'll try to give me a sermon, and I don't need that right now," I said.

"So you talk on your own terms. Just one time, Jill, go over and ask him what the thinkers really know about the soul."

"I'll find some way to read up on it, I promise, okay?" I said.

"No books—books are no good in this situation. Go see him. He's a good man—I could feel that. He has passion. You need to talk to someone with passion."

"I'll think about it, all right?" I said.

I turned abruptly to go back into the room. *Will I go talk to Professor Socrates in the philosophy department? No. There. I've thought about it.*

I pushed the door open, but I stopped dead in the doorway.

Mother was frantically wiping tears off her cheeks. She shifted in her wheelchair so her back was to me, and I saw her shoulders go up and down evenly three times. I didn't move. When she turned toward me again, her face was expressionless, her eyes flat. I groped for something to say.

"One more day, Mother," I said. "And then they're releasing you."

She nodded and held her chin up in that proud way she had.

"You can go home then," I said.

Behind me, I heard Max sigh.

EIGHT

I packed so much into the next day that I could feel the hours bulging at the seams. At least it wasn't a teaching day so I could get caught up on work in the morning—which I did hiding in the computer room so Deb couldn't find me. As it was, the minute I set foot out of there, she was the first person I saw, and she was already blinking furiously.

"About yesterday—" I said.

"All you had to do was tell me your mother's in the hospital, and I would have understood," she said.

I stared. "How did you know about my mother?"

"I heard it at the tea. And by the way, if anybody tells you I was using your name in vain, it's true, but that was *before* I got the word that she was in an accident—and you, too! Why didn't you tell somebody?"

"It's not a huge deal," I said. "Look, next quarter I'll do our tea solo. You won't have to do a thing."

"Sure, but if your house burns down or something, let me know, okay? I felt about an inch tall after I'd been griping about how you ditched the entire thing and then somebody says, 'Well, you know her mother's in the hospital.' I don't know how you do it, frankly. I'd have to take a leave of absence and check myself into the psychiatric ward. This place is so stressful to begin with—one more thing and I'd lose it."

"One has nothing to do with the other."

"Oh." Deb blinked several hundred more times. "Hey, I almost forgot—Nigel was looking for you."

"Thanks, Deb," I said and left her standing there.

All right, Jill, I told myself as I approached Nigel's office. *You haven't done such a great job of keeping Mother's situation separate from what happens here, but after today everything's going to be in order and it won't happen again. Just explain that to Nigel—promise not to miss another seminar.*

But the tea and the seminar weren't on Nigel's agenda. The minute I poked my head in his door, he handed me a folder. It was the work I'd given him the day before on my research.

"I know you suggested that I not work on it until you'd approved the thesis," I said. "But I felt that…"

I let my voice fade out as Nigel began shaking his head.

"I had no doubt you would go ahead with it," he said. "*That* isn't the problem. The problem is that you made an error in your second step of this segment of work."

"An error? What kind?"

"The simplest kind. I've indicated it there."

I took the folder and glanced inside. The inevitable Post-It note marked the spot.

"This means everything I've done since then will have to be adjusted," I said.

"I'm afraid so." Nigel took off his glasses and stroked his moustache. It was the first time I had ever seen him fidget in any way. It made *me* want to fidget. I willed myself not to rake my hands through my already finger-tousled hair.

"Jill," he said, "I am still concerned about the amount of work you are attempting to do while dealing with the stress of your mother's situation."

I watched him closely. Did he already know about Mother's illness? There was nothing on his face to indicate that the grapevine had already wound its way to him, but then, his face rarely showed anything. The fact that he had even wasted a gesture on his moustache, however, made me suspicious.

"It may seem like we care about nothing around here unless it can be put into an equation," he said, "but all evidence to the contrary, we are human beings, and we do not expect superhuman efforts from our students."

"But you do expect us to avoid making simple errors in computation."

"You would not have made those errors if you were not under a great deal of strain."

I could feel my jaw tightening. "What are you saying?"

"I'm suggesting that you go a little easier on yourself. Things like accidents and hospitalizations happen, and we can make allowances for those."

"I appreciate your concern, Dr. Frost," I said. "But don't forget that I'm older than most of the graduate students here. I don't let things throw me. I assure you, I'll be fine."

He opened his mouth as if he were going to comment, but then he closed it and nodded. I left, but all the way down the hall, I felt like I'd just left a chord unresolved on the piano.

Fortunately, there was enough crammed into the rest of my day to pretty much shove Nigel aside. I picked up the Power of Attorney papers at the lawyer's office, transferred money from Mother's savings account to checking and paid the American Express bill. I made a mental note to get the card out of her purse and shred it at the first opportunity. Then I tried to get in touch with Nurse Rose—whose first name, on close inspection of the business card, was something unpronounceable—but she wasn't in. I left a message for her to simply be at the house by one the next day, when I would be bringing Mother home. The message on her answering machine said something about "touching peace," which left me with a little creeping doubt, but my next item on the afternoon's agenda swept that aside for the time being.

I headed for Stanford Hospital armed with several large boxes, since I wasn't quite sure how many personal things Mother had in her office. As it turned out, I should have used them as shields against the barrage of people who came by while I was packing books and emptying drawers. The hematology lab employed more than a hundred people, and it seemed that most of them stopped in to ask about Mother. At least that was ostensibly their mission. I thought most of them were just plain nosy, or they wanted me to know that they had diagnosed her malady months ago.

Their remarks were largely variations on the same theme: "Jill, I am so sorry. When did you know? I'm sure you were in some major denial—we all were here. I didn't say anything, of course, but I noticed about six months ago that something was up."

The "something was up" list ranged from Mother standing in the middle of the lab wearing an absentminded expression to laughing at test results that inexplicably struck her as funny.

The conversations with Mother's coworkers generally ended with my not-so-subtle "Thanks for coming by," followed by their closing condolence: "She was a brilliant doctor. I'm so glad I had the chance to work with her." By the time the last of them left, I could hardly keep from screaming, "She isn't dead yet!"

Yet as far as they were concerned, she might as well have been. It was as if, since Liz McGavock was no longer of use to Stanford Hospital, she had ceased to exist. The thought stabbed at me, and then I chided myself for being annoyed. After all, hadn't I said the same thing to Max the night before? It brought back our whole conversation about the soul, and about Sam Socrates in the philosophy department. I could still vividly picture my mother trying to hide her tears from me. Last night had been the first time I'd ever seen her cry.

I dropped the last of the books into a cardboard box and stood up, dusting my hands off on the seat of my jeans. It was almost five o'clock, time to wrap up anyway. The phone was within reach. There was a Stanford directory right there next to it.

"I don't even remember his last name," I said out loud. Man. I was starting to talk to myself.

I flipped open the directory and turned to the philosophy department listing. Without even thinking about what I was going to say, I dialed the number.

"Philosophy. This is Petra," someone said.

"Uh, hi," I said. "Uh, I'm trying to locate a professor over there. He's not tenured and his first name is Sam—"

I couldn't have sounded more lame, but Petra was smooth. She said, "That would be Dr. Bakalis. Shall I transfer you?"

"Uh, no!" I said.

"All right," she said slowly. "Could I take a message, then?"

This was ridiculous. "You know, come to think of it," I said, "go ahead and transfer me."

"Certainly. May I tell him who's calling?"

"Jill. Jill McGavock. Tell him it's about K-theory."

"Certainly," she said.

At least that might eliminate a lot of awkward, "Now, who are you? Where did I meet you?"

"Jill! This is a surprise!"

It was Sam's voice. I recalled his sort of Midwestern twang.

"Hi," I said. "I was wondering if we could talk."

There was an ever-so-slight pause. I guess I couldn't blame him for being taken aback.

He handled it by half laughing through his next sentence. "Okay. You want to meet for coffee? Someplace on campus."

"Your office is fine," I said. "And no coffee. I just want to talk."

"You don't mind if I drink coffee while we talk, do you?"

"No."

"Maybe have a sandwich, too?"

"No." I gave the phone a bewildered look. "What time's good for you tomorrow?"

"I'm booked solid. Got any time today?"

I glanced at my watch. "In about an hour?" I knew if I didn't do this soon, I might change my mind.

"Excellent," he said. "I'll see if I can get a sandwich made by then."

Okay, so maybe I might change my mind anyway. I was still debating over that as I hung up and lifted the first of the boxes to haul out to the car. I had only taken about two steps outside the door when two facts struck me at once: I wasn't going to be able to carry the thing all the way to the parking lot without herniating a disk or something, and even if I did, there was no way the four boxes I'd packed were going to fit into my Miata. I was definitely slipping.

I set the box down and turned around to unlock the office door again, when a man called from down the hall, "Dr. McGavock isn't in. Can I help ya?"

He had a voice like sandpaper, and when I looked up I saw he had the face to match it. He wore a rather dour expression, and his once-bushy-now-thinning eyebrows hooded his eyes. His chin, which looked sharp to begin with, jutted even farther in my direction as he approached wearing a plaid flannel shirt, jeans, and a tool belt. Work boots completed the ensemble. The only thing missing was a hard hat.

"No, I don't need any help," I said as I clicked the door open. Not that it was any of his business.

"You takin' this in or out?" he said, nodding toward the box.

I was about to reiterate that I had everything under control when I saw the Stanford Hospital name badge peeking out from beneath one of the suspenders that held up his tool belt. Burl Vokey, it said. Lab Maintenance Supervisor. Okay, so maybe it *was* his business.

"I'm Dr. McGavock's daughter," I said. "She won't be coming back to work, so I'm clearing out her office."

The dour look disappeared and was replaced by the first expression of genuine concern I'd seen all afternoon. The cobwebs of tiny lines around his eyes deepened, and the blue in the eyes seemed to intensify.

"She's not comin' back?" he said, his words coming out in a clipped manner.

"No. She's retiring."

"That bad? I heard she only broke her leg or somethin'."

Evidently, the grapevine didn't extend to the maintenance crew. Too bad. This was one person who actually looked as if he gave a hang, although why I couldn't imagine. It was hard to picture my mother befriending someone on the janitorial staff.

Even as I was mulling that over, though, he was watching me intently. His face was deadpan, but his eyes wouldn't let me pull mine away.

"She's ill," I heard myself saying. "Something not related to the accident."

He nodded deliberately. "Thought so. She's been off her form these past couple months. Still, I was hopin' she'd pull out of it."

"Do you know my mother?" I said.

I thought one of his eyebrows twitched, but I couldn't be sure.

"Not that you wouldn't," I fumbled. "It's just that she never spoke of you—"

I stopped. I was only cramming my foot deeper down my throat.

"Fine woman, your mother," Burl said, still in that clipped tone. "She worked a lot of long hours, so she was generally still here when I started my shift. I'm the night supervisor for maintenance."

He folded his hands in front of his barrel of a body and stood very still. It occurred to me that there was something distinguished about the guy. Could have been the silver-gray hair, combed straight back and obviously held in place with some outmoded hair product. More likely it was the deliberate way he had about him—every move with purpose, none of them with haste. He was like a blue-collar Nigel Frost.

"We'd have a cup of coffee and talk now and then," he went on. "But the last few months, she'd kinda fade in and out. I figured it was only temporary because she worked s'dang hard."

I shook my head. "It isn't temporary. She'll just keep getting worse until...well..."

"I see," he said. He made a clicking sound out of the side of his mouth. "Doesn't that just jar your preserves? Fine woman. You tell her I'm thinkin' about her, would you?"

"Sure," I said, more out of surprise than anything else. "I'm not sure how much she actually understands, but I'll tell her."

"Oh, I'm sure she knows. It can't all go away that fast." He made the clicking sound again. "Fine woman."

He passed a hand briefly over his eyebrows, leaving a few of the hairs askew. Then he nodded at me, straightened his suspenders, and turned around to walk off. I was still standing there, staring like an idiot, when he turned back around and said, "I did little repairs for her now and then. If she needs anything like that, tell her I'm still around."

"Sure," I said.

We exchanged nods. Once again he turned to leave, and I looked down at the box.

"Uh, Mr.—" Shoot. I couldn't remember the name on the tag. He stopped anyway.

"I have four boxes loaded up with my mother's things," I said. "Could you keep an eye on them until I can arrange for someone to pick them up?"

"Consider it done," he said and gave me the final nod and walked off, slowly and deliberately.

Now that was a trip, I thought. *What other surprises am I going to discover about my mother's life?*

There was, of course, no time to ponder that. I had to go engage in serious dialogue with Socrates.

Exactly *why* I was doing it—now that was a question to ponder. And I did, all the way back to campus, all the way through the myriad of columned buildings that made up the most academic-looking part of the Stanford campus. It was all very Spanish-mission with its monastic arches and its stone walls cut out in simple rectangles of window-light. The math building—number 380 in the grand scheme of things—was part of it, but since I never ventured far from it, I knew it only as Sloan Hall. It always came as a surprise to me when I did go elsewhere on campus that Stanford was actually a beautiful maze of reverential architecture situated in malls and bordered with graceful palm trees.

The philosophy department was in Building 100 on the main quad, with a mosaic-covered drinking fountain just outside the door, compliments of the class of 1927. I stopped and took a long drink as I asked myself one more time what I was doing there.

Okay, this is going to be on my terms, I reminded myself. *We're talking philosophy, not theology—and I'm only doing that much to appease Max.*

And Mother's tears had nothing to do with it. I shoved my way through the door and scanned the directory.

What the heck was his last name again? Bacharach? No. Vitalis? Why did I have such a block with this guy's name?

Next to the directory there was a large group photo in a frame with the names, mercifully, printed underneath. I ran a finger across it, looking for the dark, curly hair, on the shaggy side, thin-rimmed glasses, thick eyebrows, olive skin, strong chin—

Good grief, girl! I chided myself. *What did you do, take an inventory of the man's facial features?*

I must have—unconsciously—because I knew the face as soon as my finger landed on it. It was sticking up above the crowd, and his arms were thrown lazily around the women on either side of him. He was grinning—not smiling, *grinning.* What was there to grin about while you were having your photo taken surrounded by Ph.D.'s in philosophy?

This is going to be the shortest philosophical dialogue in history, I thought.

I found the name that corresponded with the face. Bakalis. That was it. Second floor.

Registering the number, I headed up the stairs. Even before I reached the upper hall, I noticed something different about this place, compared to Sloan Hall. It was noisy in here. Except for the freshmen when they flooded out of our classes on roller blades, there wasn't continuous noise in the math department. In fact, that group of third-year guys could stand in front of a chalkboard for hours never uttering a word. They were a little extreme, of course, but even the rest of us weren't like these people. Every low-ceilinged room I passed was filled with chatter, and the very doors themselves were "loud" with bulletin boards plastered with cartoons. I glanced at one, but the caption contained the word *epistemology*. I doubted I would find it humorous.

Dr. Bakalis' door was open, but at first glance I didn't see him in there. It gave me a chance to give the place a quick survey.

That took about seven seconds. It was smaller than the office I shared with Jacoboni, or maybe it just seemed that way because three walls were completely lined with books and the one that wasn't had several stacks of files and books leaning against it. His desk was situated so that it peeked out through a small but welcome window. Above it, from the ceiling, hung the biggest kite I'd ever seen—a huge contraption in primary colors. Its juxtaposition with a bust of Plato placed precariously close to the edge of the desk made me smirk.

Having an identity crisis, Doctor? I thought.

"Hey," somebody twanged behind me. Somebody with his mouth full. I turned around to find Sam Bakalis holding half of a bulging submarine sandwich and chewing happily. There was a coffee mug in his other hand.

"Sure you won't join me?" he said, gesturing with the sandwich.

"Yeah," I said. "I had something a little less Neanderthal earlier." Might as well let him know I didn't find him amusing. It would save time.

He chuckled and continued chewing as he offered me a chair. Then he settled himself into one catty-corner from it, rather than retreating behind his desk. I was going to have to work a little harder to make it clear that this was strictly an academic meeting.

Sam set the sandwich on the desk and cradled the coffee mug

in his long, slender fingers. Where had I noticed those fingers before—was it at the dinner?

I snapped to and said, "Look, I won't take up much of your time. I just have some questions of a philosophical nature, and Max, I mean, Dr. Ironto—"

"I remember him. Great guy."

"Yeah. He suggested I consult you."

"Consult away," he said. If he was disappointed, he didn't show it. Behind his glasses, his hazel eyes kept their alert twinkle.

"All right. Well, uh—"

Great start. What the heck was wrong with me? I gave my hair a solid rake. "Okay, I have a decision to make, an ethical decision, and I may need a philosophical frame of reference."

He glanced around the room. "I might have one of those here someplace."

I looked at him, straight-faced. "Here's my question: Is there any real evidence that a person has a soul—something beyond the mind, the thought processes, if you will? Do the 'great thinkers' believe that if, say, the mind were to go completely, there is still something else there?"

This was sounding so ridiculous that I was sure I'd just answered my own question. If I couldn't even describe it, how could it be there? Sam, however, was processing it in his eyes, and he at least had the grace not to give me a condescending smile. I'd have popped him.

"Now, before you answer that," I said, "understand that I am not religious, and I know you are. I don't want the Sermon on the Mount, and I'm not interested in being converted. I want to keep this strictly philosophical."

He was nodding. "That's right. You practically waved your 'secular intelligentsia' membership card in my face that night."

"It was right up there with your born-again banner," I said.

"I'm surprised they didn't collide."

"If I recall correctly, they did."

I looked at him steadily. He looked back.

"So let me see if I'm hearing you right," he said. "You want to talk about the existence of the soul, but you don't want to talk about God."

"Right."

"So let me ask you this: What exactly do you mean by God?"

"I mean whatever it is you seem to believe it is. Some all-powerful force that controls my life. Nothing controls my life but me."

"So why are you here?"

"Excuse me?"

He set the coffee mug on the desk beside the half-eaten sandwich and formed his fingers into a pistol point, which he rested under his chin.

Some kind of philosophical pose, I told myself.

"If you control everything in your life, why are you struggling over this decision?"

"Who said I was struggling?"

"You look like you're struggling."

"I do not!" I was gripping the arms of the chair. I let my hands go slack and regarded him coolly. "Did I mention that I wanted to keep this impersonal as well as academic?"

"No," he said. "I must have missed that. Look, I didn't mean to offend you. I was just trying to get clear on where we're going here. Have you engaged in much philosophical discourse?"

"No," I said coldly. *Have you computed many derivatives?*

"One of the things it's really important to do is clarify your terms. All philosophy does, really, is seek to clarify so you can get to something richer, better, deeper."

"And all I want is to know if those richer, better, deeper people think there's a soul. Yes or no?"

He looked at me almost longer than I could look back. "I'm sorry. That's not a yes or no question. In fact, I'm not sure I can help you."

"Fine." I started to get up.

"Don't you even want to know why?" His hazel eyes were glowing. I'd never seen eyes with so many different looks. "I'm disappointed."

"Okay," I said. "Why?"

He resituated himself in the chair so he could lean toward me. I didn't give him the satisfaction of moving away.

"I can't possibly talk about the soul without bringing God into it, and not just *a* God, but the Christian concept of God—Father, Son, Holy Spirit—the whole ball of wax."

"You're telling me that you expound on this 'whole ball of wax' in your classes? Here at Stanford University? Where did they find you?"

I could see him stiffening. "First of all, this isn't one of my classes. You came to me with a spiritual question, and I can only give you a spiritual answer. And secondly, are you perhaps casting aspersions on my intellectual ability?"

I couldn't tell whether he was putting me on or not.

"You're right," I said. "You can't help me. Is there somebody else in the department I could talk to who isn't fresh out of Sunday school?"

Now I could read him. His eyes narrowed—yet another look—and he shot his glance around the room at sharp angles. One hand came up and rubbed the back of his neck, as if he were smoothing down his hackles.

"I'm sure if you look long enough, you'll find somebody who will tell you what you want to hear," he said. "But it won't be the truth."

"I'm thinking maybe in this situation, I need to find my own truth," I said. I groped under the chair for my purse.

"My experience has been that people who are afraid of the truth never do find it," he said.

I froze, still half leaning out of the chair. "If I were afraid of the truth, I wouldn't have come here. If anything, I was *stupid* to think some Jesus freak would even know what it is I want!"

"Then I guess a little of that stupidity rubbed off on me, because I thought for a minute I could crack that modern-pagan façade you're wearing."

"No, the stupidity is in calling yourself an intellectual and simultaneously espousing some faith mumbo-jumbo that belongs in the Dark Ages—"

"I think you'd better go."

He stood up, his taut frame towering over me. His eyes were showing me their final look of the day—they were smoldering. If I hadn't been smoldering myself, I would have been unnerved.

As it was, I stood up, too, and I didn't dodge him, so that my face came close to his.

"Not a problem," I said. "I was leaving anyway."

Neither of us said another word as I marched to the door. The only sound as I left was a stack of folders cascading across the floor, jarred by my exit.

You might as well toss that whole mess into some boxes, Dr. Socrates, I fumed as I headed for the stairs. *You won't last long around here anyway.*

NINE

Fortunately, there wasn't much time for me to fume about my little confrontation with Dr. Socrates. Although, the way the next week went, I'd have opted for fuming.

Max and I took Mother home the next afternoon. She wandered through the rooms on her crutches as if she were trying to remind herself what she was supposed to do in each one. After pulling out boxes of crackers, pawing through CDs, and picking up pens, she yawned and headed for the stairs. When Max and I jumped in to help her maneuver the crutches up the steps, she batted them at both of us and tried to make it on her own. After three frustrated tries, Max just picked her up bodily and hauled her up to her bedroom. When she pointed to the bed, he put her there, which was no small feat considering the size of the contraption on her leg. Once settled, she slept for several hours.

In fact, she slept for most of the day—that day and every day after that—which meant she rammed around most of the night, knocking things over with those infernal crutches, leaving lights on, and letting the refrigerator door hang open by the hour. I knew, because I wound up sleeping at her house every night.

I had to. The caretaker was a disaster.

She informed me on arrival when I introduced her to Mother as Nurse Rose that she was a home health aide, and that she preferred to be called by her first name, which was Shakti-Shambhala or something. I took several stabs at it and then gave up and resorted to referring to her as Freda II.

She wore what looked like surgical scrubs in a flowered print, but all resemblance to anything medically professional ended there. Her earrings were always made of some combination of beads and feathers, and they hung down to her shoulders. Mother stared at them oddly every time Freda II leaned over her. Which was often. She was constantly pressing her hands in Mother's and looking deeply into her eyes. Then she'd close her own eyes and sort of moan. When I asked her what the heck she was doing, she told me they were communicating.

Frankly, I didn't think Mother was communicating a thing. She'd deteriorated so much since the accident it was eerie. She didn't speak a word, and the only real sound she made was when Freda tried to give her the pain medication—then she fought like a tiger, sort of growling deep in her throat. It was too much for poor Max. Every time Freda announced that it was time for "meds"—and stood moaning over the pills, eyes closed, before she tried to get them down Mother's throat—Max left the room, or even the house entirely. Often he would go off to purchase yet another kind of pasta to tempt Mother with.

Eating was another source of frustration. Freda cooked, Max cooked, I even made a few feeble attempts—but Mother usually sat staring vacantly at her plate until one of us fed her the first few bites. Then she seemed to get the idea and started in—though she was apt to stop abruptly, get up from the table, and take off on her crutches. Invariably she wanted to go upstairs to her bedroom, the worst possible scenario.

Yet every time Max left with Mother in his arms, Freda II would look at me and say, "She's an incredible person, isn't she? You look in her eyes and it's just…*intense.*"

After about the third time she said that, I tried looking into Mother's eyes myself. I saw nothing. It was the most frightening nothing I could imagine.

I wasn't accustomed to being frightened, so I buried myself in research, teaching, tutoring Tabitha, and generally maintaining the separation between the walking nightmare of my personal life and the only thing that made sense to me—my work life. But at night I went back to the house and slept on a cot just outside Mother's bedroom door. That started the very first day, when Freda looked at me blankly as I started to leave after Mother was in bed and said, "Who's going to stay with Liz? I'm off at eight."

That was one detail I'd missed in my discussion with Freda I. Max offered to alternate with me, but I could only imagine him sitting up all night fretting, and I declined the offer.

At the end of the first week, as I dozed at the dinner table while Freda II was upstairs coaxing Mother into her pajamas, Max said to me, "Why don't you just move in here with your mother?"

"I thought I already had," I said.

"I don't know about this girl," Max said, nodding toward the ceiling. "She asked me today if I thought you'd mind if she burned some incense."

"Absolutely not. Next thing you know she'll be dragging crystals into Mother's bedroom."

"You didn't see them? She has them hanging over the bed."

"No, she does not!"

"She does. I just saw them." Max shrugged. "Who knows, maybe they'll help. How do we know?"

"It might also help if we made a little Pick's Disease doll and stuck some pins in it, but we're not going to do that either."

Max focused on his water glass.

"What?" I asked.

"Nothing."

"You're thinking something. What is it?"

By that time I was having trouble keeping the sharper side of my tongue from lashing out, even at Max.

"You want to know what I'm thinking?" Max said, his voice thick. "I'm thinking Liz needs you with her, as much as you can be. You're the only one she follows with her eyes when you walk across the room."

"No, she doesn't."

"You don't see these things. I do. If you could be with her more, I think she could hang on to…something."

His voice broke. I put my forehead on my fingers, elbows propped on the table. *Max, please, no crying*, I thought.

I smeared the annoyance off my face and looked up at him. "Okay," I said. "If you think it'll help, I'll move some stuff over here and I'll be here as often as I can. But Max, I have to keep up with my research or I don't graduate. I have to teach or I don't get paid."

"I know, I know, and I'll be here to help you. You think I'm going to leave you alone to handle this by yourself?"

I could sense the hug coming. Mercifully, the doorbell rang, and I leaped up like I was off to do the broad jump. When I threw open the front door, a silver head peeked at me over the top of two large cardboard boxes.

"Brought her things by," said a sandpaper voice.

"Burl," I said, because that was all I could remember of his name. "Come in, please."

Max presented himself, still stuffing his handkerchief into his pocket, and the two of them exchanged introductions and hauled the rest of the boxes into Mother's study, which I had been keeping closed since her second day home when she'd gone in and pulled everything out of the drawers.

"This was really nice of you," I said to Burl.

"How is she?" he asked.

Max sighed heavily.

"Not good, huh?" Burl said.

"No, she's not doing well," I said.

"Can I say hello to her?"

This man never ceased to surprise me. "Uh, well, you could, but she's already gone to bed." I said lamely, "But some other time—maybe during the day when you're not working. Of course, she sleeps a lot, but, you know, maybe between naps."

NANCY RUE

"I'll call first," he said.

After I let Burl out, Max gave another weighty sigh.

"That was a genuine human being," Max said. "That was a beautiful thing he did."

"You know something?" I said. "He's the first person who's been here to see Mother since she came home from the hospital."

The next day, after my afternoon tutoring session with Tabitha, my plan was to hightail it over to Escondido and pack a small bag so at least I wouldn't have to run back and forth so much. It was the closest I could actually bring myself to moving in.

I couldn't even handle Mother when she was in her right mind, I thought as I went up the stairs in Sloan Hall to pick up my mail and messages before I left. *How am I supposed to deal with her now that she doesn't even know what to do with a fork unless somebody puts it in her hand?*

"Jill."

It was Nigel. I hadn't checked in with him all week, but I wasn't due for a meeting with him until the following day. Still, I suddenly felt like the kindergartner with telltale chocolate all over her face.

"Meeting tomorrow, right?" I said. "And I *will* be at the seminar. And I put fliers in everybody's boxes about the teaching seminar November 10 and…I think that's about it."

"How are things going at home?" he said.

Did the man never give up?

"They're going as well as can be expected," I said. "We're all adjusting."

He patted my arm and moved on. I had the urge to resolve a chord again.

I went on to my box and found a pink While You Were Out slip on top.

Sam Bakalis called, it said. *Please call him back at—* There was

130

a number, but I didn't read it. I crumpled it up into a little pink ball and tossed it into the trash can on my way out.

It was a particularly rough night at Mother's. She was already asleep when Freda and Max left, and I propped myself up in the chair in her room with a stack of student homework papers and tried to concentrate on the polynomials that swam before me. No sooner had I actually maintained some kind of focus than Mother suddenly sprang up out of bed as if she'd had a nightmare— except that her eyes were expressionless. I would actually have loved to see some terror in them, or even some contempt. I'd have given a week's worth of research if she'd just said, "What are you doing here, Jill? Do you think I'm an invalid?"

But she just hauled her leg out of bed and started to stand up.

"Mother!" I said, lunging for the crutches. "You need these. Where do you want to go?"

As if she were going to tell me.

She brushed the crutches aside, face still stony, and tried to dodder in the direction of the door. Two steps and she was headed for the floor, with me hanging on to her from behind, barely able to keep either one of us upright.

"If you'd just tell me where you want to go, I'll help you get there!" I said. "You have to work with me here!"

Slowly, she turned her head to face me. Her eyes searched mine, and her lips moved. I hardly dared breathe.

And then she opened her mouth, and she laughed. It wasn't Liz McGavock's low, throaty chuckle. It was some kind of giddy, childlike gurgle that clutched at me.

"What?" I said. "What's so funny?"

The laugh disappeared as abruptly as it had come, and Mother held out her arms for me to prop the crutches under them. I followed her to the bathroom and waited outside the door. At least she could still do that by herself. Nobody had mentioned when we would be moving on to diapers, and I sure wasn't going to bring it up. In fact, when it came to anything related to Mother, I wasn't looking any further ahead than the next hour.

I finally got her back into bed, and I turned out the light in hopes that she'd drift off again. But we went through the same routine about four more times. I vowed the fourth time I was putting her back into bed that if it happened again I was going to insist on knowing whether she had diarrhea. I couldn't ever remember my mother and I discussing our bowel habits before. I was so groggy by then, I found myself wondering if she had ever deigned to change my Pampers when I was a baby or if I'd been forbidden to ever wet them.

This time she appeared to be exhausted and finally fell into what seemed to be a deep sleep. I curled up in the chair and was out myself within seconds. The next thing I knew, the sun was streaming through the front window.

I bolted up on the chair, knocking homework papers across the floor. Mother was still in her bed, but there was an eerie sound coming from her direction. It sounded like she was wheezing.

I slipped across the strewn papers and leaned over her. She *was* wheezing, and her chest was heaving as if every breath was a struggle.

"Nobody said anything about *this*," I said. "Mother, wake up. Are you okay?"

I shook her gently by the shoulder, but she didn't stir. The next shake was harder, and the third was strong enough to have rattled her teeth. I grabbed her by both shoulders and tried to sit her up. When I did, something tumbled off the bed and rolled across the floor.

I looked down at it in horror. It was a prescription container—empty.

I already had one hand on the telephone when I snatched up

the bottle. Lortab. The pain medication.

My trembling hands probably would have registered on the Richter scale as I dialed 911.

Freda II arrived about the same time the ambulance did, and I met her on the front lawn.

"How many of these were left?" I said, waving the prescription container in her face.

"We only used about half of those," she said. "Ever since I started giving her ginger and turmeric and that pineapple enzyme, she hasn't needed those."

"She took half a bottle of Lortab!" I said to the paramedic who was running toward me.

He snatched it from me and followed his partner into the house with me on their heels.

"Where were you keeping them?" I yelled over my shoulder at Freda II.

"I put them in the medicine cabinet."

"Right where she could get to them."

"I didn't think she'd want to get to them. You remember how she used to fight me when I'd try to give them to her."

"She doesn't know what she wants!" I said, tearing up the stairs behind the paramedics. "Can't you get that through your head?"

"You know, your hostility doesn't work for me, Jill," Freda said.

I stopped so abruptly on the steps that she ran into me.

"And my mother taking an overdose doesn't work for *me,*" I said. "You better start swinging your crystals and hoping she doesn't die."

It was iffy for the next few hours. I paced a path in the floor of the ER until Dr. Fenwick came out to tell me Mother was finally stabilized.

"Can I take her home?" I said.

"After I convince psych that it wasn't a suicide attempt. I think we ought to give it twenty-four hours anyway." Fenwick was watching me. "Jill, do you think it's wise for you to try to keep her at home? If she's a danger to herself, you almost have no choice."

Don't tell me I have no choice, pal, I thought. *That's the worst thing you can say to me.*

"You need a ride home?" he said.

I glanced frantically at my wrist, but I hadn't even put my watch on.

"She's going to sleep for a while," he said. "Why don't you go home, get cleaned up. I'll have someone give you a lift."

"No, I'll just catch the shuttle to campus," I said. "I've got to get to work."

Mindless that I'd thrown on sweats over my pajamas and had shoved my feet into a pair of sandals, I thanked Dr. Fenwick and ran for the parking lot. I arrived just in time to see the shuttle pulling away.

The idea of standing there waiting for the next one was unbearable, so I started to jog for the next stop. That lasted just long enough for me to realize that it was pointless to try to run in sandals, and I reluctantly slowed to a walk and tried to sort myself out.

Okay, Mother's fine. We'll lock up all the medicine. We'll put a padlock on the bathroom door. That's all I can do for now.

Think work. I can get some of my own work done this morning, then run home and shower before class at eleven. No, all my stuff's over at Mother's. Okay, I'll drive there.

In what? The Miata's already over there—

"Need a ride?"

My head jerked up, mouth ready to snap out a refusal. It was Sam Bakalis, peering out of the window of some foreign-made Jeep wannabe.

"Are you okay?" he said.

I wanted to say, *I will be when you move on,* but I just didn't have the energy.

"I've been better," I said. "I'm trying to catch the shuttle."

"Why don't you let me give you a lift? It's the least I can do."

I don't know whether it was because I was stunned or because I already had a large blister forming on my instep, but I nodded. He pushed the passenger door open for me and dumped a stack of folders into the backseat so I could sit down.

"Car trouble?" he said.

"No."

As he eased back into traffic, his glance went from the rearview mirror to me. "Look," he said, "I don't know if you got my message. I tried to call you at the math department because I didn't know how else to get in touch with you."

"Uh-huh," I said.

"I wanted to apologize."

I had to stare at him. He did look slightly droopy—shoulders curved, eyes not quite so bright behind his glasses.

"For what?" I said. "You have a right to your opinion."

"But I don't have the right to insult you with it."

"I wasn't insulted," I said.

"You don't do this often, do you?" he said, laughing through the words in that way he had.

"Do what?"

"Lie."

"I wasn't—"

He was grinning.

"Okay, I was insulted," I said.

"So was I."

"Why? What did *I* do?"

The sparkle was back in his eyes. "Actually, you started the whole thing," he said, grinning. "But that didn't prevent me from being the bigger person and calling to apologize first."

I wanted to put him in his place. I really did. But I was just too tired. All I could do was halfheartedly tousle my hair and sink back into the seat.

"You're not okay, are you?" he said.

"No, I'm not," I said. I pasted on a smile. "I will be as soon as I can get organized, but right now, I'm in a bit of a muddle."

He didn't say anything, which I appreciated. At least, until he had to ask me where I wanted to be dropped off.

"I'm going to the math department," I said. "Sloan Hall."

"Sure you don't want to go somewhere and have a cup of coffee first, before you get organized?" he said.

I shook my head, and for some reason that I still can't figure, I started to talk, my voice wooden. "My mother was recently diagnosed with Pick's Disease. It's a rare dementia—it'll take away her mind and everything else with it," I continued, voice toneless. "In the wee hours this morning, when I was supposed to be watching her, she got into her pain medication and overdosed on codeine and had to be rushed to Stanford Hospital, where they pumped her stomach. Now I practically have to have a court order to get her out of there. Meanwhile, I have just enough time to decide whether to continue this fiasco of taking care of her at home. Just drop me off at the corner there—" *Because I feel like a complete idiot. Why did I just dump all of that on him?*

Sam pulled the car up to the curb and turned to look at me. There wasn't a trace of pity in his eyes. He merely looked sad.

"I'm sorry," he said. "You must be in a ton of pain."

"I wouldn't call it pain—" I started to say.

He put up his hand. "Look, I see why you came to me with questions. Now that I have more information, I get it." He reached inside the tweed blazer he was wearing over a knit shirt and pulled out a card and a pen.

"I want to give you my home phone number," he said. "So in case you want to start that conversation over again, you know where to reach me, day or night."

I didn't have the urge to toss it back in his face when he handed it to me, so I took it. "Thanks," I said.

"Just call me if you want to talk."

For lack of anything better to say, I muttered another thanks and climbed out of the car. As he drove off, I crumpled up the card. After all, what was the point? We had tried to carry on a discussion twice, and we'd ended up at the same place both times—in the pulpit.

I looked around for a trash can, but I didn't see one, so I stuffed the crumpled card into my purse.

The first person I saw when I got to my office—avoiding the front desk altogether and going in the back door—was Tabitha. There was no eluding her. She was leaning against my office door.

"Uh, hi," I said.

I barely looked at her as I drove the key into the lock. She was very definitely looking at me, however.

"Hi," she said. "I know I don't have an appointment, but I thought if I caught you early enough—"

"Tell you what," I said, "we'll go over the homework in class today before you turn it in so you don't have to worry."

"It's not about that," she said. She tilted her head sideways, hair spilling over her cheek. "I just wanted a chance to thank you for everything you've done for me. I told my parents all about you, and my mom sent this for you."

I was so preoccupied that I hadn't noticed she'd been holding something behind her back. She presented it to me with a flourish, face beaming. I half expected a bouquet of dandelions or a drawing for my refrigerator door. But it was a box, and whatever was inside emitted an incredible aroma.

"Oatmeal raisin," Tabitha said. "They're the best. You like raisins, don't you? I mean, some people don't, but I thought since you came from California you probably did. But if you don't like them you can pick them out—"

"I have no intention of doing anything of the kind," I said. To prove it, I stuffed half a cookie into my mouth and closed my eyes as I chewed. It was so moist and flavorful that I knew it had to be made from scratch. I had experienced enough of Max's cooking to know homemade when I tasted it.

"You like?" Tabitha said, her big eyes shining.

"Oh, yeah," I said.

I reached for another one, and her face broke open into a wide smile.

"Come on," I said, motioning toward the box. "Take one. I hate to eat alone."

"No, these are for you."

"Take one. I'm your teacher. I'm ordering you to. Your grade depends on it."

She snatched one up and sank into the chair I pointed to. I sat on my desk and munched.

"Ms. McGavock, could I ask you a question?" Tabitha said. She was nibbling daintily—in sharp contrast to my gluttonous consumption.

"Yes," I said. "That's why they pay me the big bucks."

"This isn't a math question. It's a personal question."

"Oh," I said. "You can ask it, but I can't guarantee I'll answer it."

"Well…are you okay?"

"Yes," I said. "Particularly since I'm on my third one of these. Doesn't your mother just want to come here and live?"

"I just thought…you look way tired."

"It's the outfit," I said. "I haven't showered yet. That'll teach you to come in here without an appointment."

"I just thought the last couple times I've been in here—"

"That I've been a witch. Sorry."

"No, it isn't that," she said.

Okay, time to nip this little bleeding-heart session in the bud.

"Why don't you tell me what it is, then?" I said.

"It seems like you're upset—only you don't want anybody to know it. I don't think that many people around here care what their teachers are going through, just as long as they get the grades, but, like, I can't help seeing stuff, you know?"

"You know what, Tabitha?" I said. "You really ought to reconsider your major. I have just the department for you. Why don't you check out philosophy?"

The concerned expression she always wore transformed into bewilderment.

"Forget it," I said. "Bad joke. Thanks for the cookies and for the concern. But I'm fine. A little stressed out, but nothing a hot shower won't cure."

She seemed reluctant to accept that. In fact, I wasn't sure she was actually going to get up and leave, even though I had the door open for her and was all but waving her out of the room. She did finally stand up and roll her way slowly toward the exit. But she stopped in the doorway and looked back at me.

"I'm going to pray for you anyway," she said. "God knows what you need."

It's an epidemic around here, I thought when she was gone. *Is this still Stanford, or did we turn into Notre Dame when I wasn't looking?*

They released Mother the next day. Fortunately, it wasn't a teaching day for me, so I could take her home. Freda II was there waiting for us, earrings in full bobbing mode. When she'd gotten Mother settled in the downstairs guest room, I summoned her to the kitchen. "Look, uh—" I blanked on her real name and went on. "I bought a lockbox to put all Mother's meds in. You and I will be the only ones with keys, and we'll keep them on us while we're in the house."

"That's an incredible idea," she said, "but—"

"Can I finish? I also think it's ridiculous for us to keep her on the second floor when getting up and down the stairs is such a huge ordeal. I suggest you move her things into the guest room. She might fight you at first—"

"She won't fight me because—"

Because you'll be chanting the entire time, I know.

"Don't let her out of your sight, even when she's asleep during the day. I was in the same room with her when she overdosed, so we just can't be too careful."

"No, *you* can't be too careful," Freda said.

I finally stopped, and I could feel my eyes narrowing as I looked at her.

"We can't be too careful," I said.

"Not me anymore."

"What are you saying?"

She closed her eyes and took a deep breath. If she went into some kind of transcendental moan, I knew I'd lose it for sure. But she opened her eyes and focused them on me in a way so deliberate that I thought she was going to attempt hypnotism.

"I can't work here anymore, Jill," she said. "I'll try to say this as gently as I can. I love Liz. I think she's incredible, I think we're kindred spirits, and I think I could have had a tremendous impact on her healing. But you—" She closed her eyes again and shook her head. "Your energy and mine just don't mix. I leave here with my whole aura so disturbed. I think you're toxic for me."

"Uh-huh," I said. "So you're giving your notice."

"No, I have to leave now, before my psyche is poisoned any further."

"You're leaving *right now?*" I nearly shouted. "You're not even going to give me twenty-four hours to find somebody else?"

"I'm sorry." She pressed her hand to her chest. "I feel it in here. I won't have any peace unless I leave immediately."

"You're right about that," I said. "Nobody's stopping you. Leave."

"I'll just go in and say good-bye to Liz."

"Fine, and don't forget to collect your crystals while you're at it," I said with more than a hint of sarcasm.

Her "aura" was noticeably ruffled. "Do you see what I mean?

You have no respect for other people's beliefs. I encourage you to find healing for that."

"Thanks for the tip," I said.

Then I stared her down until she retreated from the kitchen. When she was gone, I leaned back in the chair and gazed at the ceiling.

"Okay," I said to it. "What do I do now? Just *what* am I supposed to do now?"

TEN

After Freda II left, there was nothing else to do but call the social workers' office and get another Freda. There was no telling how long it would take, so I phoned Deb and asked her to spread the word that I wouldn't be in until late afternoon.

"Don't sweat it, Jill," Deb said. "Jacoboni never comes in before noon and nobody says a word, so why should it be a problem?"

If you're lumping me in with Jacoboni, I'm doomed already, I thought.

Doom was a word I thought about a lot over the next few days. It took that long to interview enough Fredas to find one who didn't show signs of overdosing on the Zen lifestyle or who spoke a little English. I had grown up in a multi-cultural society, but I drew the line at having to use sign language when it came to my mother's care.

Finally—after having Max bail me out to watch Mother while I taught a class and rescheduled my office hours and Tabitha-tutoring sessions so I could conduct interviews—I found a Freda III I didn't think would burn down the house. She was middle-aged and motherly, and she patted my arm at every possible opportunity and called me "hon," but I was beginning to prioritize what I couldn't deal with, and that was falling to the bottom of the list.

It wasn't until I felt sure Mother was once again taken care of and got myself back to my office that the sense of doom really settled over me like a layer of smog. I did everything I could to diffuse it.

I redoubled my efforts on my research, spending so much time in the computer room that Jacoboni threatened to sublet my side of the office. I focused on the teaching seminar I was giving, talking it up so much that forty-five out of the fifty grad students in the department showed up for it. I threw myself into teaching my class. I even held a review session before the November exam and gave Tabitha a double dose of tutoring. But nothing I did blew the smog away.

About three weeks after the pill incident, when we were well into November, I was feeling like a piece of frayed rope. As she was leaving one night, Freda III gave me the inevitable pat on the arm.

"You get some rest tonight, hon," she said. "Mother should sleep through. She was awake most of the day today."

"Really?" I said. "What did you do, slip her No-Doz?"

"No, she had a visitor. He stayed quite a while."

"He who?" I said.

"Burl somebody. Nice man, about my age. Gray hair. He said he worked at the lab with her, and she seemed to recognize him."

"Really?"

"He fixed the back screen door and those broken stepping stones that go out to the koi pond." Freda III shook her head. "Then the two of them sat in the living room for the longest time."

"I hope that does mean she'll sleep tonight," I said.

She patted my arm yet again. "Now that she has that cast off, I think things are going to be much easier."

I took her suggestion and headed straight for the cot I had set up for myself in her room. I woke up once to the thought that I hadn't put the usual barricade in front of the steps, but I sat up and looked over at my mother, and she was sleeping soundly, so I flopped back down and conked out myself.

I was awakened later by a hard thudding sound. Who, I wondered, was dumping a bag full of watermelons down the staircase?

I rolled over, intent on going back to sleep, when it struck me. I bolted up. Mother's bed was empty.

The stairwell was not. There was a pile of books there, and several more on the steps as if they hadn't quite made the tumble to the bottom. From above, I could hear rustling around.

Tripping over several volumes as I went, I tore up the steps and looked around frantically. Mother's bedroom door was open, and the light was on. There was my mother, leaning out the front window from the waist down, with one knee hiked up on the sill.

I bit my lip so I wouldn't yell and startle her. When I got to her, she jumped back, and then she put her hand over her mouth and giggled.

I grabbed her by both shoulders and yanked her inside. The air was chilly and damp, but she wasn't even shivering. She was just giggling.

"What the heck were you doing?" I said. "Do you want to break your neck, too? What do I have to do, tie you to the bed?"

For a moment, her eyes flickered. It was the first emotion I'd seen her show in weeks, and it was fear. I felt a rising wave of nausea.

"Look, I'm not really going to do that, all right?" I said. "All right, Mother? I wouldn't do that. You just—come on, let's go back to bed."

The fear left her eyes, and she began to giggle again. She chortled like a five-year-old all the way down the steps. I found myself tucking her into bed like she was about that age.

"Get some sleep," I told her.

She nodded, and then proceeded to sit up and try to throw off the covers.

"No! Mother, it's night. See—darkness? Time to get some good REM sleep. You lose all perspective without it, remember?"

She settled back onto the pillows and watched me. There was nothing in her eyes, but she kept them focused on me.

"Okay," I said. "See, we're talking sleep deprivation here. I'm referring to myself. If I don't get some sleep, I'm not going to finish my dissertation."

She didn't move, didn't make a sound. But she watched me. Her eyes went from my lips to my eyes and back again. As long as I talked, she did that. When I stopped and tried to go back to the cot, she was immediately up and scrambling out of bed.

So I sat there and rambled on until four in the morning when she finally drifted off. Even then I couldn't let myself sleep. She was likely to shinny up the chimney or something if I did. But if I just sat there, I would either tumble off the bed into a coma or smother in the cloud of doom.

I got into a comfortable sitting position beside her and kept talking. I rattled on about K-theory and vector bundles, coefficient functions and Tabitha's mother's oatmeal cookies. I'm sure I fell asleep midsyllable.

When I woke up around seven, I could feel something warm pressing against me. I had to pry my eyes open to see what it was. Beside me, Mother was still asleep. Her head had lolled to the side and was nestled against my arm.

I closed my eyes and didn't move. I couldn't move. I was paralyzed with grief.

When Freda III arrived, I forced myself out of bed and avoided her eyes as I got dressed and headed for Sloan. I got as far as the coffee hut between two of the libraries, and I knew I couldn't go to the math department that day. I couldn't do anything. I sank into a wrought-iron chair at an outside table and stared at the fountain.

"You want coffee?" someone called from the counter.

I shook my head.

"Sure looks like she needs coffee," I heard her say to her coworker.

I didn't need coffee. I didn't need work. I didn't need to get organized. What I needed were answers—and who was going to give them to me?

Interesting, I thought vaguely. I'd always thought the only person who helped me was *me*. Maybe I did need a coffee.

I opened my purse and dug through it for money. There were a couple of dollars hiding in the bottom under a crumpled-up card. I pulled it out and smoothed it on the tabletop. *Samuel Bakalis, Ph.D., Associate Professor, Department of Philosophy, Stanford University.* The phone numbers swam in print too small to read in my present condition. I turned the card over, and there was a bigger number scrawled with a pen.

Call me anytime if you just want to talk, he'd said. And then there had been something about apologizing and hoping I would want to start the conversation over.

I stuck my hand back in my purse and fished out the cell phone.

"I *will* have a Café Borgia," I called to the girl at the counter. I was probably going to need coffee after this phone call.

At least his voice didn't ice over when I identified myself, and he didn't make a joke about wearing armor if I wanted to get together. He was, in fact, warmly calm, as if he'd been expecting my call.

"We've had a couple of false starts," he said. "They say insanity is doing the same thing the same way and expecting different results, so why don't we practice some sanity here and not try to just sit down and have a conversation. You want to meet on the Loop? About four? We could run and talk—then maybe grab some juice someplace. By that time we should be too worn out to argue."

I want to talk now, I almost screamed into the phone. But the gal behind the counter was waving to let me know that my Borgia was ready, and I was already feeling a little more in control, so I said, "Okay, but under two conditions."

"One."

"We stay on the legal paths."

"Fine. Two."

"No God talk."

I held my breath. To my surprise he didn't even hesitate.

"Deal," he said. "I'll meet you at the guard booth at four. If we can get past the Gestapo, we're good to go."

I actually almost laughed.

That evening, I timed myself so I wouldn't show up at the guard booth early. Looking as if I was too anxious would get us off on the wrong foot. He was there when I arrived, arms crossed lazily over his chest as he chatted with the Deputy Dog on duty. She was laughing with him.

So he's used to being Mr. Charming with the ladies, I thought. *I hope he's not expecting that kind of response from me.*

Sam looked up just then and saw me. "Hey, you!" he said. "Jill, did you know there's actually a new rule up here that you can't leave the paved paths?"

The guard threw her head back and howled. "Try to keep him under control, would you?" she said to me.

"Don't worry," I said to her. I nodded to Sam. "You ready?"

"You're gonna run me into the ground, aren't you?" he said.

"You're the one who wanted to do this here. I came to talk."

"All right, then, let's go."

He took off, leaving me standing there for a moment. *The arrogance,* I thought. *I can't deal with the arrogance.* I considered getting back in my car and going home. But I'd come this far, and besides, I needed answers.

I caught up with him and made sure I had about a stride and a half on him before I said, "You sure you can run and talk at the same time?"

He grinned. "Who's running? First question."

"You already know the first question. What is the consensus in philosophical thought—do we have a soul or not?"

He considered it for a few more strides. I noted that he was barely breathing hard, and we were halfway up Killer Hill. I willed myself not to breathe hard either, though I wanted to chug like a tractor.

"I'll stick with the philosophical tradition since that's your ground rule," he said. "So the question isn't 'Does your mother possess a soul?' but 'Does she possess the kind of soul that can transcend death or, in this case, a serious illness that takes away what has always been her life force?'"

"All right," I said. "So why is that?"

"When we're talking about soul, we're actually talking about what the Greeks called the psyche. It's the life principle, and in the Greek tradition, anything alive had a soul."

"That's the Greek tradition," I said. "What about now?"

"In today's society, a lot of people say only humans have a soul, which means they live in accordance with reason."

I only nodded until we got to the top of the hill, because, frankly, I was dying.

Sam looked at me and said, "I lied."

"About what?" I said.

"About talking and running at the same time." He grinned. "I thought we'd be starting off discussing the stock market or something. You like to get to the point."

"I do," I said.

He grinned again. "Okay, then we better walk."

We set off at a brisk pace. I still had to half run to keep up with his long strides.

"Where were we?" he said.

"You were admitting that the rational self is actually the life force of the person," I said. "It makes sense—I mean, that's observable, measurable."

"Is it?" Sam said. "If you open the brain, you won't find ideas in there that you can count and categorize."

"But the brain has a chemistry that enables the person to *have* ideas. As we now know, my mother's ability to have ideas has been curtailed."

I was surprised at the bitterness in my voice. It didn't escape Dr. Socrates.

"I wouldn't throw up my hands yet," he said. "If you're asleep, or you're unconscious, you still possess a rational soul."

"I do, because when someone wakes me up, I can think again."

"But while you're asleep, it's just inactive. Inoperative, if you will—impeded—"

"All right, I get it. What's your point?"

"The same thing is true of your mother. Because of whatever damage was done as a result of her disease, her rational soul has been impeded. That doesn't mean it isn't there anymore."

"It doesn't mean that it is."

"So who bears the burden of truth?"

"In my view, you do," I said.

"Then let's ask the real question," he said. "Is there a spiritual principle that says the soul transcends a muting illness?"

"Great. We have the question," I said. "Now answer it."

"I can't," he said. "You won't let me."

"What?"

"You said no God talk. This question—the question *you* are asking—is directly linked to a belief in God—or a disbelief, depending on how you look at it."

"Then let's look at it from the disbelief standpoint."

He slowed his pace a little. "Take Epictetus." Then he grinned. "Please."

"Very funny."

"He felt that there were gods who were immortal, but that we as humans are not."

"Hence, no soul that transcends death."

"Right. Now, the New Age movement—you know what I'm referring to?"

"Uh, yes," I said dryly. "I know exactly what you're talking about."

"The New Age belief is that there is a spiritual energy but that it is not necessarily God. Or they're pantheists and think *everything* is God."

"Yeah, God hangs out in crystals, incense, earrings—"

"Earrings?"

"Never mind. You had to be there. I just know everything is 'incredible' to them."

"And everything is 'wretched' to you."

"At the moment, yes. That seems a lot more realistic to me."

"The more common belief is that *either* there's no spiritual principle and everything can be reduced to the material and there is absolutely no God—*or* there is a spiritual principle and because of that, there is a God who infuses us with the immaterial."

I gave him an incredulous smirk.

"What's that look for?" he said.

"For laying your little trap."

"If I'm trying to trap you I'm doing it unconsciously—I swear it." Sam put both hands up in a gesture of innocence.

"I don't believe that," I said. "You tell me all this stuff in the guise of philosophy, and then you cop out by informing me that philosophy doesn't know any more than you do."

"It's not a cop-out," Sam said. "My belief goes beyond philosophy. I don't just believe in *a* god or *an* energy. I believe in a specific God—as incarnate in Jesus Christ—who actually intervenes in the world."

"Great. Can you get Him to do a little intervening on my mother's behalf?"

He smiled at me slyly. "We're making progress."

"How do you figure?"

"You just asked me to go to God for you. Hence, there is some degree of belief in you."

"It was a joke!" My voice had gone from bitter to sour. It was probably time to end this conversation, but I didn't. If I dropped out now, he'd think he'd won, and I suddenly couldn't stand the thought of that.

I stopped in the middle of the path. He stopped, too, still breathing hard. I had to shade my eyes from the sun with my hand to see him silhouetted.

"Let me ask you this," I said, "and don't get offended. How can a well-educated man possibly buy into a belief system that has no basis except in myth?"

"You're referring to the stories in the Bible."

"Isn't that where your credo is?"

"It is. But I didn't just read the Bible and decide I believed. I've lived what I believe and so it seems reasonable to me *to* believe it."

"And I'm living what I believe and that seems reasonable to me. Aren't we at an impasse, then?"

"No, because right now you're struggling with a question your belief system can't answer."

"And yours can?"

"As far as I'm concerned, it can. My own experience living my beliefs has taught me the answer to your question. Your mother has a soul that is still alive in her. That's my answer, based not on my education in philosophy, but on my education in life."

I didn't answer. I suddenly felt heavy.

"You okay?" Sam said.

"No," I said. "I'm not. If I go with what I honestly believe, then I have to think my mother is totally gone. She can't think straight anymore, she can't talk, she can barely feed herself—so she's gone. The essence of her has disappeared."

He didn't say anything, which was fine. I wasn't really talking to him anyway.

"I thought that would make my decision easy," I said. "Once I knew whether there was anything really left of her, I would know whether to keep beating my head against a brick wall and keep her at home, or to put her in a nursing home and let people who know what they're doing take care of her until her body dies, too."

"But it's *not* easy for you, even now," Sam said.

"No. Imagine that. I do know that there's no point in fooling myself any longer. It's clear-cut. It's simple. But I—"

"It's only clear-cut from the standpoint of your belief system."

I put a hand up. "That's against the rules."

"It's not against the rules for me to tell you not to give it up yet. You haven't explored all the angles. Look at it as a mathematical theory. You wouldn't consider it disproven just by looking at it from one point of view, would you?"

"What angles?" I said.

He looked me in the face as if he wasn't going to stop until he saw whatever it was he was looking for.

"What?" I said.

"This is huge," he said. "It affects your whole life to know whether the soul is mortal or immortal. You sure you want to continue this discussion tonight?"

"No, I don't," I said. "But I really don't have much choice. Last night, my mother tried to climb out the second-story window. Next thing you know she'll be swinging from the chandelier. I either have to put her in an assisted-living facility or put my life on hold until—who knows when."

"You want some advice—not philosophical, not religious— just an objective observation?"

"Sure," I said. "Go for it."

"You're seeing it in black-and-white, and there's a lot of gray area here." He grinned. "I've got gray areas I haven't even used yet. Look, there's a whole lot more we can talk through that might get you where you want to be. Meanwhile, don't jump ship one way or the other. Just stay put while you explore the rest of your options."

I hated to admit it, but that actually made sense. Why hadn't I thought of it? Probably because I was strung out on coffee and sleep deprivation, I told myself. I was in fact so wearied and muddled that I couldn't even think of a way to make Sam think he hadn't won the entire round.

"I'll think about it," I said.

"Good," he said. "And now let's think about something to drink."

"That's okay," I said. "I've got water in the car. But we can talk again—once I get my head straight."

"Sure. You say when. I'll say where."

"Why do you get to say where?" I said.

"Because I'm one for one," he said. "We just got through an entire conversation without drawing our weapons. I'm on a roll."

"I'll call you," I said.

He didn't push it. In fact, he walked me to the car in soft silence and patted the roof of the Miata as I slipped inside.

"Take care," he said. "I'm going to go soak in a whirlpool, rub on some Ben-Gay—"

"Wimp," I said.

He pretended to act wounded and grinned as I drove off. In the rearview mirror I could see his long, olive-skinned legs gleaming in the golden half-light.

I forced myself to stop looking.

ELEVEN

I took Sam's advice—grudgingly—and called McDonald's office and asked for a different social worker who could list my options for me. They referred me to a Paige Hill, but she was on vacation and couldn't see me for two weeks. Maybe that was good, I decided. It would give me time to "explore the angles."

So I met with Sam several more times—purely for that reason. And he followed the ground rules nicely, both the spoken and the unspoken ones. We carried on our discussions in some fairly bizarre venues—while throwing darts at the Rose and Crown, while eating peanuts and tossing the shells on the floor at Antonio's Nut House, and after running each other into the ground up on the Loop and then dialoguing over Gatorade. In spite of all the distractions, I was determined to keep the conversations academic.

One afternoon at the Rose and Crown—a student hangout in Palo Alto—I pushed it until we established the fact what we were actually doing was searching for truth. He insisted that we first had to define truth. His classes, I thought, must be a real snore.

I played along and defined truth as "life's inward reality." It was about as philosophical as I could get and still not stray too far from being rational about the whole thing.

Sam defined it as "God."

I wanted us both to continue to refer to it as truth, but he couldn't quite bring himself to do that, so I had to compromise.

That only gave me the motivation to beat him in darts that afternoon.

At our next off-the-wall meeting, he flew a kite out on the Oval while I watched. I asked pointedly how we were going to *get* to the truth. Maybe he had time to just toss it around between picnics, but I didn't.

"So you're asking what our guide is," Sam said.

"Yeah," I said. "In my view, it's science."

"It's faith," he said. "Have I ever told you about my friend Pascal?"

"Who?" I said innocently. "Is he on faculty?"

He looked intently at his kite. "I've got to give this some more string. Yes! See that thing bobbing and weaving up there? Check it out!"

Only because I knew he wouldn't let it go until I did, I glanced up at the sky. The red-and-white fish-shaped kite was indeed "bobbing and weaving," as if it were dodging a barrage of something. I decided I knew how it felt.

"Where was I?" he said.

"Your friend Pasquale," I said, tongue firmly in cheek.

"Blaise Pascal. Seventeenth-century mathematician."

"Right. The guy who bases his belief on flipping a coin," I said. "That's very mathematical. Although what can you expect from someone with a name like Blaze?"

"B-l-a-i-s-e."

"Blaze," I said. I sat down on the grass and leaned back on my elbows so I could look up without getting a crick in my neck. Sam looked away from the kite, his face lit up as if he'd just had a scathingly brilliant idea. I groaned inwardly.

"Tell you what," he said. "Come to my nine o'clock class tomorrow morning. We'll be discussing Pascal."

"You want *me* to sit in on your class? Will I be able to stay awake?"

He grinned. "Count on it."

I slipped into the back of the room in building 100 the next morning, cardboard coffee cup in hand and a thousand questions in my head, not the least of which was, *What in the world am I doing here?*

Sam barely nodded to me when he strode in, his eyes already on fire. The students settled down around the big conference table, most of them looking at him expectantly. One guy still had his head in a book and was gnawing on a fingernail, but when he found Sam cocking an eyebrow at him, he slammed it shut and gave Sam a sheepish grin.

"I trust you're just reviewing, Mr. Evans," Sam said.

"Of course," the kid said.

I was sure, though, that he turned a shade or two paler. *Huh,* I thought, *so Blaze is as much of a taskmaster as I am.*

"All right," Sam said, when he'd checked the roll. He actually checked the roll? Maybe he was *more* of a taskmaster. "Let's pick up where we left off yesterday. Pascal said faith is the one sure guide to reality. Any rebuttals?"

A boy's hand shot up. "Doesn't sound like much of a mathematician to me," he said. *"Science* is the one sure guide to reality."

You go, kid, I thought.

"But Pascal said science is man's quest for power, not truth. Any response?"

A girl's hand went up this time. I was getting the impression that they knew better than *not* to have a response.

"What about Descartes, though?" she said. "'I think, therefore I am.'"

"Excellent!" Sam said. He leaned across the table. "But Pascal said, 'I look for God, therefore I have found him.' So did Pascal prove that there is a God?"

Yeah, that was what I wanted to know. I leaned forward a little myself.

"Yes?" one girl said.

"Is that an answer or a question, Miss Robbins?"

The girl grinned. "It's an 'I don't know.'"

"Good. An I-don't-know is always preferable to a guess. No, Pascal did *not* prove that there is a God—not proof the way you see it. What did he say?"

No hands went up. Sam leaned toward "Mr. Evans" like a large praying mantis. I cringed for the kid. "Mr. Evans?"

"Uh—" Evans grinned. "I don't know?"

"Ah, but you should know, Mr. Evans." He made a buzzing sound. "Thanks for playing. What did Pascal say?"

Miss Robbins raised a timid finger. "He said it's the heart that's aware of God."

"Yes! Correct! That's what faith is: God perceived intuitively by the heart, not by reason. Hence, if a person can no longer reason—or at least express reasoning—that doesn't mean he or she is not still perceiving."

He didn't look at me, but I could see the glow in his eyes. He was talking to me. I talked back, under my breath. *I can tell you this much—my mother isn't looking for God.*

"Let me quote some Pascal for you," Sam said to the class. "'There is nothing which is so much in conformity with reason as the rejection of reason. The very reason on which man prides himself leads him to conclude that there are an infinite number of things beyond it.'"

Still another hand went up.

"Mr. Davis."

"Can you give us an example?"

"Death." He watched Mr. Davis' expression. "You don't buy that?"

"Well, what could be more measurable than death? You stop breathing. Your heartbeat flatlines. Your brain waves stop—"

"But why do we die?"

"Because the parts wear out. Because if no one died, it would get a little crowded."

Sam leaned back, hands behind his head. "If you had a terminal disease, Mr. Davis, would you be doing everything you could to recover—go into remission?"

"Of course."

"Good answer!" Sam narrowed his eyes at Davis. "But why?"

"Because no one wants to die."

"Why?"

"Because death is the unknown. We don't like the unknown."

"You mean, reason hasn't figured it out yet?"

"No."

"Then death is beyond reason."

Miss Robbins gave a groan. "Could you go over that again?" she said.

Sam grinned at her. "Are we moving a little too fast for you, Miss Robbins? Let me just say this: Pascal said reason's last step is the recognition that there are an infinite number of things that are beyond it. And if natural things are beyond it, what are we to say about supernatural things?"

"Supernatural—as in the spirit world?" Davis said.

"The spirit world, the afterlife, the soul," Sam said. And this time he did sneak a glance at me.

"So, Dr. Bakalis," said a young man who up until that point had been quiet.

"Mr. Francis. I wondered when we'd hear from you."

There was a bit of eye-rolling and exchanged glances among the students.

"So," Mr. Francis said, "Pascal didn't try to give reasons to believe there's a God. He was just trying to make it reasonable."

"And is it?"

"It's reasonable…but I don't believe it."

Sam leaned so far across the table this time that I thought he was going to jump up onto it. "Yes, but, Mr. Francis, the more reasonable it becomes, the less reasonable it is *not* to believe it." And then he did practically mount the tabletop. He was like an excited little kid who's going to tell you the amazing thing that happened on the way to the playground. "If there is a God, He's infinitely beyond our comprehension. So who can condemn any believer for not being able to give rational grounds for His belief?"

He looked around the table. Several hands shot up.

"Mr. Evans."

"I can," Evans said, "because I'm a skeptic. A true skeptic."

"There's no such thing. Tell me, Mr. Evans, do you doubt everything?"

"Not everything—"

"Do you doubt whether you're awake?"

"No."

He reached over and lightly pinched the young man's arm. "Do you doubt whether you're being pinched?"

"No!"

He wrapped his fingers around Evans' wrist. "Do you doubt that I'm touching you?"

Evans shook his head.

"If you really doubted everything," Sam said, "you'd go stark raving bonkers. You would doubt whether you were doubting, doubt whether you exist. A perfectly genuine skeptic has never existed."

Hands went up all over the place. It was all I could do not to raise mine.

"What about Nietzsche and Sartre?" one of the girls said.

Yeah! How about it, Sam?

"Ah, that whole crowd," Sam said. "I think Nietzsche and Sartre have driven more skeptics screaming into the arms of God than the Billy Graham Crusade. If you're going to call yourself a skeptic, perhaps you should qualify your definition. Is that not what we do in philosophy?"

He let them think about it for a minute.

Mr. Francis raised his hand again. "I consider myself a skeptic to some degree," he said. "I don't just accept everything at face value."

"For instance?"

"For instance, I question whether people who believe in God possess the truth."

"You're right. That's the whole point. The truth isn't in us believers."

"It's in God. Is that what you're saying?"

Sam nodded. "As a believer, that's what I'm saying. The question before us is, 'What did Pascal say?'" He pointed at Evans. "Mr. Evans?"

Come on, Evans, you can do it.

But Evans had to shake his head.

"We know what Mr. Evans is going to be doing before our next class," Sam said. He was grinning, but the kid squirmed.

Huh. I'd been wrong about Sam's classes. This one at least was far from tranquilizing.

They went on to discuss the fact that Pascal wanted Enlightenment thinkers to get away from science, calculation, and problem solving at times and get back to wisdom, understanding, and exploring mysteries. Nobody, Sam said, could know God through pure reason.

That pretty much left me out, then.

Sam ended the class with an assignment: "A belief in God has to come from something not simply human. That's where Pascal's famous wager comes in. Study that for tomorrow—eh, Mr. Evans?"

After the class had filed out, some of the students stopping to banter with Sam before they left, Sam came over to me and sat on the edge of the table.

"Did you get that assignment?" he said, eyes twinkling behind his glasses.

"Study the wager," I said.

"Wrong! *Your* assignment is to *take* the wager."

I shrugged. "You flip the coin. Heads says there's God. Tails says there's not. I pick tails."

He cocked his head at me. "Would you, though, if you considered it reasonably?"

"What's to reason? The odds are fifty-fifty. Of course, that changes with the number of times you flip—"

"There's only going to be one flip. Suppose you pick heads and you live as if there was a God—if it actually comes up heads, you've won. Suppose you pick heads and you live as if there was a God—if it comes up tails, you haven't lost a thing. But suppose you pick tails, you will either win or lose."

"Fine. I'll admit it's reasonable, but not reasonable enough for me to believe it. I'm just being rational here."

"Nah. You're being irrational."

"How do you figure that?"

"Reason is rational. Fear is a passion."

I shook my head at him. "How is it that you can infuriate me? One minute I'm thinking you're an amazing teacher and the next I want to wring your neck."

"Okay, forget the wager for the moment," Sam said, laughing through his words. "You up for some experiments? Purely scientific, of course."

"Right."

"This isn't a trap. I'm clean. See, nothing up my sleeve."

I actually glanced at the slender arms before I checked myself and said, "What's the design for these experiments?"

"For the next twenty-four hours, examine your thoughts. See how many of them are about the past, how many are about the present, and how many are about the future. You don't have to graph it or anything—just get a general idea."

"I'm not a general idea kind of person," I said. "Now, why am I doing this? What's the projected outcome?"

"I don't want to give you any preconceived notions. Just do it."

"What does this have to do with my mother?" I said.

"Everything," he said. "Do you tell your students everything you know about K-theory and expect them to understand it, or do you give them their own vector bundles to play with first?"

"You don't know what you're talking about," I said. "You realize that, don't you?"

"Yeah," he said. And then he got me with a grin.

But the next twenty-four hours were filled with more than me categorizing my thoughts. In the first place, it was obvious I was going to have to give up the pretense of only staying at Mother's house temporarily.

Still, I thought I was holding my own in keeping up with things at school, but when a memo appeared in my box reminding me that I was to maintain a minimum of nine office hours a week, the adrenalin started pumping.

Can I actually keep up with all this and take care of Mother, too? I thought. *Should I just be considering what's going to happen if I don't finish my dissertation in time to graduate instead of trying to read my mother's soul? Maybe I ought to explore those angles, too.*

That wasn't the only time anxiety reared its ugly head. That night when Freda III left and Max finally finished saying his good nights to Mother, a silence fell over that house that was so heavy I was convinced I was in a funeral parlor. I couldn't stand it, so I sat beside Mother while she stared out the back window of the guest room at the koi pond, lit up by pathway lights, and I droned on about anything that came into my head until she climbed into bed.

I continued looking out the window myself—taking stock. Ninety percent of what I'd thought about all day was the future. I hadn't lost my grip as much as I'd thought.

Why, then, did I feel like hurling myself *into* the koi pond?

Mother was asleep by then, and the silence was maddening.

I went to the phone and dialed Sam's number—all but the last digit—and hung up.

What are you doing? Are you getting attached to this character?

"No," I said out loud. "He's just somebody to talk to so I won't keep talking to myself!"

I dialed the whole number the next time. He answered on the first ring.

"The future," I said.

There wasn't more than a fraction of a pause.

"Wow," he said. "Okay."

"What do you mean, 'okay'? Those are my test results. What are they supposed to tell me?"

"Well, let me ask you this." His voice grew warmer. "Did you think about the past at all?"

"Yeah. I thought about how simple my life was before all this happened."

"So you were still thinking of the past in terms of what light it might throw on your plans for the future. It's probably the same with the present. Am I right?"

"Well, yeah. I live proactively."

"If you want to call that living."

"Don't disparage my lifestyle, Blaze."

"Sorry, sorry, I stand corrected."

He was laughing through his words, but I had to hand it to him—at least he knew when he was being arrogant.

"All right," I said, "I'll play along. Why don't you think making the future my end is actually living?"

"Because everything is about tomorrow or the next day or six months from now, so basically you're only hoping to live." He chuckled. "Everything you do is so that someday you'll be happy."

I thought about it for a second. "Yeah," I said. "Although until this Pick's thing happened, I thought I was already happy."

"What is happiness, do you think?"

It wasn't a professorial question. He sounded like he actually wanted to discuss it, as if he wasn't sure himself.

"I never had to define it before," I said. "I guess it's a state of being where everything is going well and your mind is at ease."

"Using that definition, how much of your life would you say you have been happy? What percentage?"

I tapped my fingernails on the desk. He began to hum the theme song from "Jeopardy."

"Forget the 'going well' and the 'mind at ease,'" I said. "Just stick with the state of being. Peaceful being."

"Okay." His voice was warming up more, and I could picture his eyes lighting up. "If happiness is a state of being, you could, theoretically, be happy right now in spite of everything that's going on in your life."

"Theoretically," I said slowly.

"You want to try another experiment?"

"Sure," I said. *Please. Just give me something to keep me from climbing the walls.*

"Do you have an hour?"

"Depends what the experiment is."

"Sit in a room there in the house—alone—for an hour. Don't do anything. Don't read or turn on the radio or compute logarithms in your head or whatever else you would normally do for fun." The laughter was seeping through. "Just sit—for one hour—and do nothing."

"Are you nuts?" I said. It slipped out before I could bite it back. I went for a lighter tone. "All right, I think I can do that. Then what?"

"Then call me if you want. Or you don't have to. Depends on how you feel."

"What does that mean?"

"No preconceived notions. Talk to you later."

He hung up first. I sat there with my hands on the desktop until I realized I was leaving sweaty handprints on the finish. I couldn't think of anything more unbearable than sitting there for an hour and doing absolutely nothing. The thought sent me straight up out of the chair and charging for the door.

I stopped with my hand on the doorknob. It was shaking. I was panicking, and that in itself was terrifying.

I don't panic! I thought—frantically. *What is wrong with me? I'm freaking out over nothing!*

I kept my death grip on the doorknob for another couple of seconds, and then I took a deep breath, straightened my shoulders, and marched back to the desk chair as if I had an audience to perform for. It *was* a performance, a complete act, because my heart was pounding hard.

Finally, after several minutes, I could sit down in the chair. I could breathe evenly and close my eyes without the certainty that I was at any moment going to have a psychotic episode. I was calm. Okay, I was *relatively* calm, in comparison to my former urge to run down the street in my pajamas.

I looked at the clock: 10:16. I rested my spine against the chair back and concentrated on my breathing. In through the nose, out through the mouth. Inhale. Hold. Exhale.

Wait. Did that constitute—what had Sam called it?—something I normally did for fun?

No, breathing exercises couldn't actually be defined as fun. What was fun? Fun was making Jacoboni's mind spin without him knowing it. No, that was triumph. Fun was standing at a chalkboard with Rashad and Peter. No, that was, I suppose, satisfaction.

What did you do when you were having fun? Laugh? Mother laughed. Well, now she did. She didn't used to. She would smile—charmingly in social situations, ironically when it was just the two of us. Now and then she would let out a deep, throaty chuckle that practically sent Max off into spasms. But now she laughed—giggled like a little kid. Giggled like she had probably never even done when she was a little kid. All I heard about was how she worked her tail off to get her father's approval and—how the heck did I get here?

I'm supposed to be thinking about fun. No, I'm not supposed to do anything fun—I'm just supposed to sit here, in this house, doing nothing, until my own thoughts drive me completely around the bend. Do not pass go, do not collect two hundred dollars, go directly to the loony bin because if you aren't doing something, Jill McGavock, you don't even know who you are!

"Yes, I do!" I said out loud.

I stopped. Had Sam said anything about talking to yourself? I was pretty sure that wasn't allowed.

I looked at the clock: 10:18. I shook my head and squeezed my eyes shut.

Thinking had to be allowed. Nobody could be expected not to think for an hour. Although Mother probably did it by the dozens of hours, by the day. No wonder she slept all day. Who could sit around with not even her thoughts to occupy her? But what if she didn't know she wasn't thinking? How could she think that she couldn't think? Did she just feel it? Did she just have some sense that something that used to be there wasn't anymore? Was that why she couldn't stay in bed when the house was completely quiet? She couldn't stand herself?

I looked down at the desk. There were two splashes of something wet on the cherry finish. I stood up. I realized then that I was crying.

"I don't cry!" I said out loud. "What is this? All I wanted were some real answers, so I could make one simple, stupid decision. What happens? I turn into a basket case—and I still don't know a thing!"

I shoved the emotional outburst back into my chest, where it stuck like an impaction. I wasn't shaking. I wasn't crying anymore. And I did know one truth, one real thing.

I knew that I, calm, svelte, driven-but-stress-free Jill McGavok, was unhappy. Unhappy to the very depths of my being.

TWELVE

I slept that night, though fitfully, and I woke up mad. *All right, so I'm unhappy,* I thought en route to the campus the next morning. *I was happier not knowing I was unhappy!*

That, I knew, made no sense. It was apparent that I'd been living under some kind of illusion, and that was what had my emotional hackles standing up. How had this misery crept in on my watch?

I hadn't called Sam the night before, but he called me that morning, right before I left the office for class.

"Hey, you," he said. "You okay?"

"You knew what was going to happen when I tried your little experiment, didn't you?"

"Haven't had that second cup of coffee yet, huh?"

"What do you *want,* Blaze?" I said. "If you just called to take some perverse kind of pleasure in my current state of wretchedness—"

"I'm sorry, Jill," he said in a soft voice. "I really did want to see if you were okay."

I softened my tone too. "I can't even tell you how *not* okay I am. I've got to get to class."

"Why don't you meet me for lunch, over at Tresidor? I'll even let you buy."

"Oh, no, you'll buy," I said. "You owe me."

"Twelve fifteen. That give you enough time?"

"Enough time to work up a good head of steam? Oh, definitely."

He was chuckling when I hung up.

I was headed out the back door after class when I ran into Jacoboni. Literally. He was backing in while watching a pair of coeds in tight jeans next to the planter and plowed right into me.

Run for your lives, girls, I thought as I passed them. Then another thought occurred to me. *Am I always that sardonic?*

I checked out my thoughts the rest of the way across campus to the student union.

When I passed one of those kiosks plastered with fliers for everything from tutors to vans for sale, I spotted a brochure beckoning students to come work for Maytag. I thought, *Oh, can I? Please?*

When I stopped at the corner and found myself surrounded by people wearing lumpy backpacks, I thought: *They all look like Quasimoto gone Gap.*

When I got to Tresidor, I thought, *This doesn't look like a student union—it looks like a shopping mall! We've got a credit union, even a travel agent, for Pete's sake! We're all yuppies in training.*

Yeah, I was always that sardonic. It was suddenly depressing.

Sam was already there, parked casually at a table outside, reading the *Stanford Report* amid the murmur of varied accents around him. Although it was almost Thanksgiving, it was still fairly warm even in the shade. There was a slight breeze blowing, but Sam seemed oblivious to the shower of tiny yellow elm leaves that floated down on him with every new gust. One leaf in particular had settled itself on a wayward dark curl. He looked up expectantly from the newspaper and grinned when he saw me.

"The laurel leaf in the hair look definitely works for you," I said. "Nice touch."

I reached over to brush the thing out of his curls, just as he put his hand up to do the same. I pulled my hand back so fast that you'd have thought he had leprosy. I groaned inwardly. What was this, junior high?

"Hungry?" Sam said. "I went ahead and got us a couple burritos. The lines are unreal in there already."

I looked doubtfully at his plate, where two suspiciously soggy tortillas lay with some kind of bean concoction oozing out of either end. I shook my head.

"I'm not that hungry," I said.

"Do you mind if I—"

"Oh, please, go ahead. Knock yourself out."

I watched with a mixture of horror and fascination as he deftly maneuvered one of the burritos into his mouth and took a squishy bite.

"You sure you don't want some?" he managed to say through a full mouth.

I shook my head. I was feeling heavy again. I wanted to throw my arms down on the table and bury my head. Not a good choice out here in wide-open academia, however.

"I really did want to make sure you were okay," Sam said. "You're not, are you? You haven't made any deprecating remarks about my lunch choice. Evidence of preoccupation."

His eyes were twinkling, but not teasing. I put my hand up to rake my hair, but I didn't even feel like doing that.

"Sam?" I said heavily. "What is this that you set me up for?"

"'This' meaning what?"

"This feeling."

"Despair?"

"No!" I looked at him. "Yes. Where did it come from?"

"It's probably been there all the time. You just always had plenty of diversions to keep you from noticing it."

I grunted. "You're calling working on a Ph.D. a diversion?"

"Not completely, but maybe it was part of it."

"Yeah, well, it isn't working anymore, so try again."

"It makes sense that it wouldn't work now. Your mother's illness has hit you pretty hard. I mean, it's huge. It would knock anybody down. There is no diversion great enough to keep you from mourning over it. Although, I have to hand it to you, you tried to create one."

"Work isn't a diversion, it's a necessity."

"I was talking about me. Wasn't I something of a diversion?"

I laughed. "Don't flatter yourself, Blaze!"

"I didn't mean me personally," he said. Two red spots appeared on his face, one on each cheek. He had actually embarrassed himself. "I just mean this whole business of talking to me about the soul—that in itself was a diversion of sorts, kind of a sedative that deadened your spiritual nerves. Except you woke up."

"I'm not diverted right now," I said.

"I'm thinking that's good," Sam said. He took another large bite out of his burrito.

"What are you, a sadist?"

This time he had the grace to swallow before he answered.

"I'm sorry you have to go through this, but in my view—and this is just my opinion, I have no way of knowing exactly what's going on in your head, but as I see it—"

"Oh, for Pete's sake, say it!"

His face sobered. "I think that before, you had no other way of overcoming fear except with indifference, and now indifference no longer works. It may be painful, but I think it's good." He abandoned the rest of the burrito and leaned across the table toward me, his eyes bright. "You finally had no choice but to look at yourself—the way we all have to sooner or later—and listen to your heart and see the great, gaping hole inside you and be terrified."

"And this 'great, gaping hole' is good?" I said.

"It is when you realize that nothing but God can fill it."

"I haven't realized that," I said. "Let's make that clear. I found a pit, I'll grant you that, but I will not concede that I have to fill it with 'God.'"

"Then what are you going to fill it with? You only have two real choices, as I see it."

"Which are?"

"God or yourself. And I'd be willing to bet that's the one person, next to God, you currently fear the most, the one person, next to God, that you're always trying to escape by not being alone with her in silence. And I *know* this: she's the only person, next to God, that you can never escape."

He searched my face for a few seconds, and then he rubbed the back of his neck and surveyed the tabletop. He seemed to realize he'd come on strong.

"I didn't mean to get in your face," he said.

"Get in my face?" I said. "You tried to crawl inside my brain. I really didn't want this. I just wanted some…knowledge to help me make a decision. Suddenly, I'm in the middle of psychotherapy. I didn't ask for this. I don't want it. This was a huge mistake, and I'm sorry I've wasted your time."

I hadn't meant to get that carried away, and now the only thing I could do was leave. I scraped the chair back, colliding with a student's tray and splashing the soup of the day down the front of his shirt.

"Sorry," I said to him. "Sorry."

He gave me a disgruntled nod and moved off toward another table. I looked back at Sam, who was by now standing up.

"Look at me," I said. "I'm a mess! I was handling things better before!"

"I'm sorry—"

I turned to leave, this time checking for oncoming traffic first. I felt a warm hand on my arm.

"Jill, don't go," Sam said.

I looked down at his fingers, but he didn't let go.

"Let me at least walk you back," he said. "Let's not leave it like this." He let go of my arm and followed me down the steps.

"I accept your apology," I said. I stopped several yards from the steps and faced him. I was beginning to sag. "Look, Blaze, I admit it's really hard for me not to like you. But I feel like you're pushing me."

"I'm sorry," he said again. But his eyes were light. "Still, I have to push it just a little further."

I closed my eyes and sighed. "Go ahead."

"I know you're unhappy," Sam said, "and now *you* know you're unhappy, and it stinks. But at least now you're being reasonable because you're seeing things as they really are. And isn't that what you value the most—your intelligence?"

I slowly shook my head. "You are the most infuriating human being I have ever known. The other day being reasonable was bunk, and now you're congratulating me for it."

"I never said being reasonable was bunk. I said you can't base absolutely everything on reason. You have to use your heart in some cases—and now we know you have one, because it's spitting nails!"

His eyes were alive.

I was trying not to smile. "You're enjoying this, aren't you? You are getting a big kick out of proving to me that I'm miserable."

"I'm not enjoying it, but it's satisfying to see that you're sane."

"Was there some doubt about that?"

"You'd call yourself an atheist, right?"

"Yes."

"A happy atheist is either a liar, a fool, or a nut case. You are now none of those."

I motioned in the direction I'd been walking, and Sam nodded. He fell into step beside me, and I continued in a calmer voice.

"I tell you what," I said, "if I go home this afternoon and my mother is completely cured of Pick's Disease, I'll believe in God."

Sam was quiet for a minute. I sneaked a sideways glance at him. Was he stuck? I felt strangely disappointed.

"No, you wouldn't," he said finally. "Not on that alone. A miracle would convince your mind, but if you're determined not to believe in your heart, you'll figure out a way to discredit it."

By then we'd reached the patio just off the back door to Sloan.

I dropped to the bench, and Sam propped his foot up on it.

"I'm going to give you a list of phrases," he said. "'Invite Jesus into your heart.' 'Repent and be saved.' 'Accept Jesus Christ as your Lord and Savior.' 'Let go and let God.'" He cocked his head at me. "Any of those mean anything to you right now?"

"No. They're clichés. I can turn on any religious station and hear them coming out of the mouth of some TV evangelist before the next commercial."

"Exactly. Subtract the heart knowledge, and that's all you have left. A bunch of platitudes that set your teeth on edge."

"So what's your point?"

"You're peeved at me for making all this too much about you, and I might have pushed you too much. I'm sincere when I say I'm sorry."

"Okay," I said.

"But if you really want answers about your mother, they have to be answers about you, too. You can't know what's going on with her, but you can know what's going on with you, and that's going to lead you to the right place."

"And how do you know this?"

He paused a second, and then sat down beside me.

"Because I've lived it. That's all I can tell you. Have I used a single one of those catchphrases on you?"

"No," I said.

"I never will. But I can give you options, and you can feel for yourself. From here on, it's just options. No more psychoanalyzing."

"Then be honest with me," I said. "You're trying to convert me, aren't you?"

He widened his eyes innocently. "Why do you ask?"

"Because otherwise, why would you be persisting?"

He grinned. "Am *I* the one who's persisting? I thought it was you."

His arm came around me and pulled me into him as he

laughed into my hair. I let it go just long enough to feel the warmth before I pulled away.

Sam was straight-faced, but he couldn't disguise the smile in his eyes. "You know, I really should pattern myself more after Pascal. Did you know—"

"If it's about Blaze, I'm sure I didn't know," I said. "I doubt the man ever actually existed."

"No, I'm serious. He was so on fire with the idea that he shouldn't cause another person to sin that he actually wore a belt with steel points on it to keep people from getting too close to him."

"No, he did not."

"Would I lie to you?"

"I have no idea."

"No, I wouldn't."

He grinned at me, and I had to grin back. I found myself leaning toward him.

Then I stood up. "Just give me some time to process all this. If I feel like I need to, I'll call you and we can talk some more."

"Sounds like a plan." He stood up, too. "Thanks for the lunch." Then he sauntered off, lanky arms dangling comfortably at his sides. He hadn't tried to hug me again.

And I'd wanted him to.

No, I told myself sternly. *You cannot go there.* I might not be able to control a lot of other things in my life, but I could control that.

It was a good try. I don't know that I was entirely persuaded.

I wasn't in my office ten seconds when Deb poked her head in.

"You got a minute?" she said.

"Sure."

She closed the door behind her, and when she turned back to face me, I could see she was struggling. If she wasn't careful, she was going to pop those contact lenses right out.

"What's up?" I said.

"Did you get that memo about office hours?"

"I did," I said, rolling my eyes.

She plopped down in the chair and tapped her lips with her finger. "Look, Jill, there's talk. I've tried to defend you and tell everybody it's because your mother's recovering from an accident—"

"What exactly are you defending me from?" I said.

"People talking about how you're never here anymore. How you don't hang out with anybody. You dash out the door after class like there's somebody chasing you." She lowered her voice as if the place were bugged. "It's going to get back to Dr. Ferguson. I mean, he *is* the head of the department, Jill. You don't want that."

As a matter of fact, I didn't.

"Thanks, Deb," I said. "But don't worry about defending me. I'll get it worked out."

"It's just that you work so hard. Who wants to see all that go down the drain?"

Certainly not me. The minute she was gone, I marched upstairs to Nigel's office.

"I won't take up much of your time," I said as I closed his door behind me. "I just want to know one thing: Is there a problem with my performance around here?"

"Why don't you sit down, Jill?"

"Because it can't take that long to give me a yes or no answer!" I said—a little too forcefully.

And then I stopped. I had a flash of my mother, standing in front of me in the kitchen, finger pointed at my face as she told me just how it was going to be. Whoa. Where had that come from?

I sank into the chair. "I'm sorry."

"You're under a great deal of strain."

"That's no excuse. I'm sorry." I wanted to look at him and say,

"Am I always this way? Have I turned into Elizabeth McGavock?" But I raked my hair instead. I suddenly didn't care if he thought I was stressed out or not. Hadn't I just made that painfully apparent anyway?

"Dr. Ferguson did remark to me that it appeared you were out of the building more frequently than you have been known to be in the past," Nigel said.

"How would he know that? Am I supposed to be punching a time clock? Sorry—"

"I'm not sure how Dr. Ferguson got his information," Nigel said, "and I assured him that you are fulfilling all of your requirements and then some. However, he did ask me to make certain that you knew how many office hours you were supposed to be keeping."

"He did that himself," I said. "Via a memo."

"And are you maintaining your office hours?"

I nodded, but the reassurances I would normally have given him in no uncertain terms didn't even make it to my lips.

"I don't know how much longer I can do it, though," I said. "My mother is requiring a lot more care than I anticipated, and although I'm exploring other options for her, it's going to take some time."

"Then *you* take some time, Jill."

"On top of Dr. Ferguson's comments? I don't think so."

"Keep your office hours, teach your class, do what you absolutely have to do here in this building, and do the rest of your work at home. Work on your research there, your class preparations. Those don't require your physical presence."

"Isn't that going to raise some eyebrows?"

"I will take care of the eyebrows. If I thought there was any reason for them to be raising in the first place, don't you think I would have come to you?"

I looked at him. He would have. He was a decent human being. It was as if I were seeing that for the first time.

"Just let the ladies at the front desk know where you're going to be in case we need to reach you, then go and be with your mother," Nigel said. "Go."

It was as close to an order as anything he had ever given me. I left dutifully. But somehow, the chord was still unresolved.

Freda III looked surprised to see me when I walked in the front door at one-thirty in the afternoon. She and Mother were sitting in the den with the television on, deep in the throes of *The Bold and the Beautiful*—or at least Freda was. Mother appeared to be dozing while sitting straight up.

I set up my stuff in Mother's study and left the door open a crack, although the argument some couple was having about whose baby was whose made it slightly more difficult to concentrate on K-theory. I was about to go ask Freda to turn the volume down when the phone rang. I snatched it up.

"McGavock residence," I said. "This is Jill."

"I'm so glad it's you," a husky, timid voice said. "When they gave me this number, they said it was your home phone, but I was afraid somebody else was going to answer and then it would be like I was bothering them and—"

"Tabitha?" I said.

"Uh-huh. Is this okay?"

"Where did you get this number?"

"They gave it to me at the math department. I didn't ask for it. I just asked them if they knew where you were, and they gave it to me. Is it okay that I called?"

I reigned in my bark. "Yes. What do you need?"

"Some extra help. I don't understand this new stuff at *all*, and I'm starting to feel like I did at the beginning of the quarter, and—"

"Jill! Jill, help! Come here! Quick!"

It was Freda III, squalling from the den. There was an edge in her voice that went right up my spine.

"I have to go," I said.

I dropped the phone on the desk and ran.

THIRTEEN

I careened around the corner into the den just in time to see a rather macabre sight.

Freda III was in a half-reclining position at one end of the couch. My mother, on all fours, had her pinned down like a large cat, and she had one of Freda's eyelids lifted with her finger and appeared to be peering intently into it.

"Get her *off* me!" Freda III screamed.

Her cry went up my backbone, but it didn't even faze Mother. She was moving methodically to the other eyelid.

"Make her stop!"

"Mother!" I snapped. "Get off her! Come on!"

I took Mother by both shoulders from behind, but I couldn't budge her. For a petite thing, she was wiry—like a deceivingly strong wrestler in the flyweight division.

"You push while I pull," I said to Freda III.

She did, but even at that it took several attempts before Mother finally let go, sending the two of us tumbling backward off the couch with her on top of me. I rolled her off and scrambled up to check out Freda III's condition. Mother wandered wordlessly to the TV and turned up the volume.

"Are you okay?" I shouted.

"I don't know," Freda shouted back.

She sat up and brushed at the sleeves of her sweater as if Mother had deposited lice on her.

"What happened?" I said. I picked up the remote and muted the TV. Mother just blinked at me.

"We were just watching our show," Freda III said, "and she nodded off and I guess I did, too. There wasn't that much interesting happening on there today—"

"What *happened?*" I said.

"I woke up and she was on top of me, just like you saw her, pulling up my eyelid and staring in there like she was looking for something!"

"Did she hurt you?" I asked.

"No, but she scared the daylights out of me. What the devil do you think got into her?"

"Equal and reactive."

Freda III and I stared at each other. Those words had come from my mother.

I whipped my head around. "Did you say something, Mother?"

She just put her hand over her mouth and giggled.

"She thinks it's funny," Freda III said. "She's losing all sense of judgment now. She's really failing fast—"

"Why don't you go in the kitchen and put on a pot of tea?" I said. "I'll talk to her."

Freda III patted my arm and shook her head. "When are you seeing that social worker?"

"Why?" I said.

"Because I think it's time to consider other arrangements."

"Make sure you use the caffeinated tea," I said. "No sugar in mine."

When she was gone, I turned the TV off altogether and squatted in front of Mother's chair. She had stopped giggling and had returned to her usual flat expression.

"You were looking at her pupils?" I said. "Why?"

She didn't answer.

"You just talked, Mother. We both heard you. You can still do it. Why won't you just talk to me?"

She did nothing but blink.

"You want to look at *my* pupils?" I leaned close. "Go ahead.

Peel these babies back. Tell me what you see."

This time she shook her head, and I rocked back on my heels. There was no way I could know what was happening in her head, and Sam was right. I was terrified.

Max came over to cook dinner about four o'clock, and we let Freda III go home early.

"I hope she comes back tomorrow," I said to Max. I joined him at the sink, where he was pulling the tentacles off some poor former sea creature. "What is that?"

"Squid," he said.

"What are you doing to it?"

"Cleaning it. They'll clean it for you at the fish market, but they never do a thorough job—and heaven forbid I should bring any more germs into this house. My mama, she's the one who taught me how to clean squid." He stopped and looked at me. "Why wouldn't she come back tomorrow?"

I stepped away from the sink and went for the sack of fresh peas on the table. One more moment of squid cleaning and I was going to gag. In fact, everything was making me want to throw up.

"Tell me she didn't bring in crystals, too," Max said. "She did, didn't she?"

"No," I said, and then I gave him a rundown on that afternoon's episode.

When I was through, Max laid a paper towel over the wet mess on the counter and came to the table where I was shelling peas. He moved them away from me and took my hands. The odor of raw seafood was nauseating.

"Jill," he said, "maybe we've made a mistake. Do you think?"

"What—hiring Freda? Max, I didn't have many good options."

"No, I mean trying to keep Liz here."

"You were the one who talked *me* into it."

"I know, I know, heaven forgive me. I just couldn't stand the thought of somebody else taking care of her. Who was going to make her calamari the way she likes it? Who was going to buy fresh squid and clean it right there in the sink?"

"Oh, I'd say nobody."

"There's more to it than squid—"

"I certainly hope so."

Max's deep, dark eyes looked absolutely tragic. "I'm not kidding with you, Jill. I think maybe it's not safe here for her—for anybody. I think I was wrong."

"So you're saying put her in a home?"

"Am I saying that? I don't know what I'm saying!"

Max pulled his bear of a body out of the chair and lugged it back to the sink, where he leaned over the squid with his back to me.

I stayed in the chair, staring miserably at the unshelled peas, having yet another epiphany—about my fourth of the day.

"Max," I said. "You're in love with her, aren't you?"

He moaned as if he were in physical pain. "I've been in love with her since the first day I saw her. I settled for a friendship— that was all she would have—but I never stopped. Not from here." He pounded a fist on his chest.

Maybe he was right. Maybe it was time to seriously consider moving Mother to a home—social worker or no social worker, truth or no truth. But knowing what had been right there in front of my eyes for over twenty years, that Max was hopelessly in love with my mother, it was clear he was the least reliable person to help me make this choice. All he wanted was to stop hurting, and that didn't require any rational thought. I wasn't sure he even had any rational thought *left*.

I wasn't sure I did either, for that matter. All I could do at the moment was *feel*—feel heavy, feel nauseous, feel like my chest was going to contract completely if it got any tighter.

"Max," I said, "can I pass on the squid? I need to go out and get some air."

"Sure, sure, you go. You're going crazy here, huh? This thing, this tragedy—it could drive a person mad."

"Something like that," I said.

I went upstairs, pulled on some running clothes, and called Sam. I kept my voice controlled. I knew if I didn't, I'd probably throw up on the cell phone.

"Can you meet me on the Loop?" I said. "In about twenty minutes?"

"Absolutely. Thought you'd never ask."

His voice was light and happy, and that was good. So far I'd disguised how much I wanted to vomit up everything I was feeling. Hopefully by the time I saw him, I'd have myself calmed down.

When I got to the Loop, Deputy Dog lowered her sunglasses, which were virtually pointless at that hour, and said, "He's not here yet."

"Would you just tell him I started without him?" I said.

"Sure," she said. "With those long legs of his, he should have no trouble catching up."

I skipped the stretching and set off at a jog for the first hill. It was going on five o'clock and getting chilly, so there was no one else on the path for as far as I could see. I tried to settle into the blessed solitude, just the way I'd always done.

Only it was no longer blessed. It wasn't even solitude. It was loneliness. I'd never been lonely in my life. I had always been enough for me. When I heard Sam calling my name from the bottom of the hill, I turned in relief. And then I stared.

What the heck was he wearing?

I shielded my eyes with my hand and peered down. Sam was charging toward me in his usual swishy running shorts and T-shirt that looked like it had been rescued from the bottom of the laundry basket. But there was something metallic around his waist, and as he drew closer, I could hear it making a sharp, wicked-sounding noise.

What on earth?

When he was within a few yards, I saw what it was—except that I didn't believe it. Why the *heck* was he wearing what looked like an oversized spiked dog collar around his waist?

"What is *that*?" I said.

He stopped in front of me, breathing only slightly harder than normal, and unhitched the contraption in the back.

"It's for you," he said, grinning. "A la Pascal. So you won't accidentally let somebody touch you—"

He stopped, the spiked belt in hand, and the grin faded. "This isn't the time for a joke, is it? Jill, I'm sorry."

"For what?" I said. "Very clever, Blaze. Very cute. But if you think I'm going to wear that thing—"

"Stop," he said. "Just stop." He tossed the belt off the side of the path and put his hands on his hips. "Did something happen? You look wretched."

"Thank you so much." I strained to keep my voice even. "Look, I just wanted to tell you that I've made my decision so we probably don't need to talk about this anymore."

"About your mother."

"Yes, about my mother," I said, teeth gritting.

"Okay," he said. "But can we talk about you?"

I started to say no. I wanted to say no. I wanted to fire off some sizzling retort and trot my way around the Loop and go back to the life I'd been entirely satisfied with before. Before I'd found out I was wretched.

Instead I said, "You know, I was perfectly content until you helped me see that I am a miserable, sarcastic—"

"Come here," he said. "I want to show you something."

He took me by the arm, looked over his shoulder, and pulled me to the waist-high fence that rendered the hill beyond the path off-limits. Before I could even protest, he picked me up lightly and deposited me on the other side of the fence and then followed, leaving the spiked belt hidden in some bushes.

"What are you doing?" I said.

"Breaking every rule you made," Sam said. He took my arm again. "Come on."

I let him take me down a partially overgrown sand path that wound up the hill and down its gently sloped other side. We stopped in front of the thick, gnarled remnant of a tree.

"What do you see?" Sam said. "Humor me. It's another one of my little tests."

I yanked my ponytail tight with both hands. "It's a tree."

"What's it doing?"

I titled my head. "It looks like it got broken off—probably in an earthquake or something—only it kept growing."

"Yes! Ten points! Now for twenty bonus points: *How* did it grow? Where? In what way?"

"Blaze, you're out of control. Okay, it continued to grow, but along the ground instead of straight up."

"Right again! You get the bonus points!"

He nodded again at the misshapen tree, which, as I'd described it, had grown a strong, thick trunk in a horizontal direction, not five inches from the ground.

"No earthquake is going to take this baby down again," Sam said, "because it's already down—and yet it kept growing. It's still alive. Playin' it safe but alive."

"Is there supposed to be some hidden metaphor here?" I said.

Sam sat down on the horizontal trunk and patted it with his hands on either side of him. "I think the tree's you," he said. "I think you've grown like this—safely, along the ground, where nobody can hurt you."

"And so far nobody has," I said, "so I guess it's working."

"Is it? You aren't feeling any pain right now?"

I folded my arms across my chest.

"You don't even have to answer that," Sam said. "I can see it in your face."

"But they're just circumstances, and I'm only trying to cope with them!"

"Like this." He patted the tree. "I can tell you why it isn't working for you anymore."

"You said no more psychoanalyzing."

"Options, then. I promised you options."

I considered it. Then I went to the tree and climbed onto a gnarled place just above where Sam was sitting. "Okay, options."

"Passion is an option," he said.

"*What?*"

"I'm not talking about sexual passion. Contrary to the picture society paints, there *are* other kinds."

"Name one."

"The kind of passion I see in you when you lose your temper and start beating me up."

"Well, you tick me off."

"But that isn't just anger—it's passion. You have a passion for finding out the truth. And not just so you can do the right thing for your mother, although that was the catalyst. I don't think anything else you've ever done in your life has aroused that kind of passion in you—no mathematical dilemma, no man—nothing until now. That's what has you torn up. You're finally finding out that you have this deep passion inside you, and you don't know what to do with it. I'm offering you the option of finding out."

I was still suspicious. "Why?"

"Because I love passion. I love to see its fire in someone."

I bet you do, I wanted to say. But I didn't. I just watched him closely.

"I don't like empty Christianity any more than you do," he said. "And there's a lot of it around, especially in intellectual circles. It's cold. What I like to see is real fire, real passion for God—somebody who *sees* Jesus Christ and is burning up with the vision."

Sam was doing a fair amount of burning himself. His eyes looked like they were going to ignite any moment.

"I know you think I'm obsessed with Pascal," he said, "but he's just so right in this situation. He was consumed by a divine fire, and I relate to that. And I want to see the passion of a direct, immediate experience of God. What I wouldn't give to see just a spark of that in one of my colleagues who calls himself a Christian."

"And you're expecting me to exhibit this passion?" I said. "For a God I don't even believe in?"

"I'm saying use your natural passion to help you where you are right now. Take the wager, Jill. Just act as if there is a God."

"You better spell that out for me," I said. "There is no Sunday school in my past."

"Do some research. That's your thing anyway, right?"

"Research. Like what, read the Bible?"

"Eventually. But for now, approach it scientifically. Observe and imitate the experience of people you know who have succeeded in finding God."

I grunted. "Except for you, that is exactly no one."

He slipped his hands easily into the pockets of his running shorts and lounged on the tree. "Try it for, say, a week."

"Are you going to leave me alone until I do?" I said.

"Probably not."

I pressed my hands into the bark. *What are you doing, Jill?* I thought. *What are you thinking?*

But I knew what I was thinking. For the first time in several days, my thoughts revealed a clearing in the smog. I was thinking if I didn't hang on to something, I was going to get lost in it—and I was never going to come out. If it had to be passion, then let it be passion.

I looked at Sam. He was watching me, intent on my face.

"On one condition," I said. "That I go at this as a theorem I can either prove or disprove."

"You can do that," he said. "Because in order to disprove a theorem, you have to apply it repeatedly until you find an instance in which it doesn't work."

I narrowed my eyes at him. "You play dumb when it comes to math, but you know more than you let on."

"Just enough to be dangerous," he said. And then he grinned at me.

Yeah. He was dangerous, all right.

All was quiet at home when I got there. Mother was sleeping, for the moment, and Max was watching her.

"Do you believe in God, Max?" I whispered to him.

"God?" He looked at me as if I'd grown an extra head out on the Loop. "Of course! Doesn't everybody?"

Somehow I was sure that wasn't the kind of belief Sam had in mind. But I did watch as Max leaned over and kissed my mother tenderly on the forehead.

"She would never let me do that before," he said. "Never."

It wasn't a bad night, and Freda III did reappear the next morning. I wrote down my cell phone number for her for the tenth time and pressed it into her hand as I was leaving the house.

"Call me if she even looks like she's going to do something weird," I said.

"All right, hon," she said and patted my arm.

I almost asked her if she believed in God, but I decided against it. I was pretty sure I'd get an answer like Max's, and that wasn't doing anything for my research.

No "test problems" presented themselves at all, in fact, until that afternoon when Tabitha came in for her tutoring session. Why, I asked myself, hadn't I thought of her before?

FOURTEEN

I coached Tabitha as usual that day, and then I watched her struggle with a problem, twisting her hair around her finger and silently moving her lips. It was enough to make me change my mind about Sam's proposed research, except that I didn't have a whole lot of other possibilities. None, to be exact.

"Oh!" she said suddenly. "So if you add the series in sixteen and seventeen and then divide by two, the even terms cancel."

"Right," I said. "You had it all along. You just freak out."

"It's like, I—"

I cut in or we'd have been there for days "Tabitha, you believe in God, right?"

"I do," she said without hesitation. "I couldn't even live my life without the Lord."

"Lord, as in…"

"Jesus Christ. He's God, only—"

"That's okay," I interrupted again. "Just let me ask you this: What does that look like in your life?"

"I don't understand."

"How do you live differently than you would live if you didn't believe in God?"

"Oh!" She frowned. "I can't even imagine that."

I groaned within. This had been a really bad idea.

But Tabitha's face smoothed over, and she looked at me straight on. "Yes, I can imagine it," she said, "because, like, at the beginning of the quarter when I was all messed up about everything—you remember that?"

"Vividly," I said.

"I would get this really empty feeling when I was wondering why God had me here when it was so hard, and I started thinking maybe He really didn't care, and whenever I started thinking that, I'd feel really mean toward the girls on my hall."

"I can't imagine you being mean, Tabitha," I said.

"I didn't actually *do* anything mean, but I wanted to."

I found myself being intrigued. "Like what?"

"Like this one girl came in and she was talking to my roommate and she was all going on about how they were out partying the night before, and I'm, like, trying to study, plus they were acting like I wasn't even in the room and I was thinking, *I hope you get picked up for underage drinking and have to spend the night in a jail so I can have some quiet to study!*"

I couldn't hold back a snort. "That sounds like a normal reaction to me."

"But it isn't God," she said. "See, with God—Jesus—in your heart—"

I stiffened at the cliché, but I let it pass and nodded.

"—you respond in love instead of hate. You show as much love as you can because you show God that you love Him by loving His people, no matter who they are. And if you love God, you'll see God and you'll know what He wants you to do and then you'll do it. So it's all about love, see?"

I wasn't sure I did see. In fact, it was all I could do not to go cross-eyed.

"Okay. Well, I was just wondering." I gestured toward her calculus book. "Why don't you try number ten?"

Tabitha turned happily back to the problem at hand, and I tried to sort it all out.

So you act like you believe in God by kissing up to everybody.

No, that wasn't what she said. You love people no matter who they are.

Jacoboni? I shuddered. She couldn't possibly mean that.

"So, Tabitha," I said.

She looked up expectantly. She really was a cute kid.

"This love thing," I said. "You just sit around thinking lovey-dovey thoughts about people?"

"No," she said. "It's more like you *do* loving things for people. You know, little stuff like let somebody in line in front of you or listen to somebody talk even if they're boring you to death—or it can be big stuff, like you making extra time to tutor me when you probably don't actually have to. You want to hear the really weird thing about it?"

"That's why I came in here today," I said.

She looked puzzled for a second, then grinned and went on. Where did this girl *come* from?

"What's really weird is that I have the hardest time loving the people I actually love. I mean, like my family sometimes or my friends. It's so hard not to take them for granted. Wow!"

She stopped, her eyes wide.

"What?" I said.

"I just thought of this!" she said. "Maybe that's why I've had to be so miserable here so far. Maybe God's trying to teach me not to take the people I love for granted. That is, like, huge! I've been trying to figure it out all quarter and then—bam!—there it is." She looked at me in awe. "It was a God-thing, you asking me all these questions today. I would have taken forever to figure that out."

"I did a God-thing?" I said. "I don't think so, Tabitha. I don't even—"

I bit my lip and nodded at her book. "Do one more, and I think you'll have it."

Then I watched the top of her head as she bent over the problem. I couldn't just out-and-out tell this kid I didn't believe in the God who *she* was obviously convinced ran her whole show. I might as well knife her as do that. Besides, I was supposed to be acting "as if."

Love. That was the ticket as far as I could tell from Tabitha, and since she was my only available test case, that was all I had to go on.

When she was gone, I picked up a pad from my desk and poised my pencil over it. In two minutes, I'd gone cold. The theorem was practically disproven already, because I couldn't think of a single name to write down.

Don't be stupid. You have friends. There's Max. That was a given. *Deb. Jacoboni.* Jacoboni? I could barely stand him. And what did Deb and I have beyond mutual complaining?

But if they weren't on the list, who was?

And where were they anyway?

It was unusually quiet in the halls, even for Sloan. I checked the schedule tacked to the wall above my desk.

Oops. There was a Kiddie Colloquium going on up in the grad student lounge. I was supposed to be there. I snatched up the pad and pencil and headed for the door. At least the KC gave me an excuse to suddenly spring myself on them after hibernating for the last month.

Kiddie Colloquiums, as we called them, were get-togethers the math grad students had every Friday. Somebody presented something to the rest of us and we responded—giving us practice in defending our dissertations or in lecturing. Our hope was always to become better speakers than most of the people who came from other universities to give seminars and who generally put half the audience into a coma.

When I got to the lounge, Rashad was standing at the overhead holding forth in his thick Israeli accent. There were about fifteen other grad students sitting on the motley collection of chairs and couches, staring at him with glazed eyes. I slipped onto a black vinyl sofa beside Deb and whispered, "What's going on?"

"He's just finishing up," she whispered back. "To what do we owe the honor of *your* presence?"

There was a sudden spattering of applause, and several people got up and scurried out the door as if they heard their pagers beeping. Rashad looked at the rest of us with raised eyebrows.

"Feedback?" he said.

Jacoboni sprang up from the nap he'd fallen into in the corner and said, "Hey, what do you say we give you feedback at Antonio's, eh, Rashad? It's Friday afternoon!"

"I *love* that idea," Deb said.

"Hey, is that Jill?" Jacoboni said.

"Yes, it's Jill," I said. "I still work here."

"But the question is, do you still party here?"

"Come to Antonio's with us," Peter said.

I agreed to go—but only because being alone suddenly felt threatening.

A dart game ensued almost the minute we arrived, and within about five minutes, Jacoboni had downed his first Heineken. I sat at the bar on a stool and ordered a club soda and wondered who I was supposed to reach out to in love.

It obviously wasn't this crowd. I'd been exchanging barbs with them for almost five years now, and I knew virtually nothing about any of them. Tabitha's advice notwithstanding, I didn't really *want* to know any more about them than I already did.

But that wasn't a satisfying realization. It was a lonely one. I was developing a cold ache I wasn't accustomed to.

I was already trying to figure out a graceful way to leave when my cell phone rang. It was Freda III, yelling into the phone.

"I think you'd better come home, hon!"

"*Why?* What's wrong?"

Her voice was breathless. "I just found Liz in the study. I don't know how she got in there—whether you left it unlocked or what. But I was fixing lunch and suddenly I heard all this noise—"

"What noise?"

"The paper shredder."

"Paper shre— What was she shredding?"

"I don't know," Freda said. "When I got in there, she was taking something off the desk and sticking it into the machine."

"Get her out of there!" I said. "I'll be right home."

I flung the phone into my bag, snatched out a handful of bills and slapped them onto the bar.

"Hey, Jill!" Jacoboni called to me. "Where you goin', darlin'? You just got here!"

"Party's over," I said and bolted for the door.

When I got home, Freda had Mother at the kitchen table with a sandwich in front of her, and she was standing over her with her arms folded.

"She hasn't moved since I called you, hon," she said. "But I don't know how much she destroyed before I caught her. I hope it wasn't anything important of yours."

I know it was important! I thought frantically as I hoofed it down the hall to the study. *There wasn't anything on that desk that wasn't important!*

Silently cursing Nigel for ever suggesting I work on my dissertation at home—and myself for listening to him—I got to the desk and froze. My binder was open, the one I used to do all my computations for my research. I turned pages like the Tasmanian Devil, first in one direction, then in the other. There was no way to know until I sat down and went through it step by step, but it appeared that everything was still there.

I lifted the top off the shredder and pawed through the confetti. That told me nothing, except that the stuff on the top all seemed to have been typed. There was nothing with pencil in any sizeable piece.

I put the lid back on and sank into the chair.

"Everything all right, hon?" Freda III said from the doorway.

"Yeah," I said. "I think so."

But I didn't. I didn't think so at all. It was the most—what was it Sam had called it?—passionate I had felt all day. It wasn't rage; it was fear that something I'd cared about for two years had almost become packing material. I hadn't been able to think of anyone to put on my "people-to-love" list, but I'd go to the guillotine for my work. I leaned down and yanked out the shredder's plug from the socket and then picked up the phone and dialed.

"Sam Bakalis."

"I have no passion for people."

"Hi, Jill. I'm fine, thanks."

"I'm serious, Blaze. Why do I have absolutely no passion for anything but this dissertation?"

"Personally, I think you do, but since we're sticking to options, here's the deal." I could picture him shifting in his seat, ready to weave the tale. "To be human is to worship. We do it whether we mean to or not, because that's what people do."

"You're saying I *worship* my work."

"I haven't finished yet."

"Sorry," I said. "Go on."

"If human beings don't worship the true God of love, sooner or later they'll find some false god to worship."

"Where's the option?" I said.

I could almost *hear* him grinning. "This might get a little heavy for the phone. You want to meet me somewhere?"

"No, I'm at Mother's house, and I'm going to let Freda go home soon. I need to stay here."

"I can come there."

"Okay," I said, "but no spiked belts, all right, Blaze?"

I spent the next half hour alternating between brushing my hair and putting on lip gloss, and chastising myself for feeling better because I'd heard Sam's voice, and for feeling even better than that because he was coming over.

By the time he got there, however, I had chewed off enough of the lip gloss not to look too terribly inviting, and I'd talked myself into believing that anybody's voice would have sounded good to me at this point.

Mother was sitting at the kitchen table when I let Sam in. When I introduced her to him, she covered her mouth with her hand and ran giggling from the room. I heard her slippers hit the floor in the guest room.

"She's going to take a nap. Probably number six of the day."

Sam looked at the doorway she'd just vacated. His eyes were sad.

"That isn't the same woman you saw speaking at that dinner, is it?" I said. "I thought she was acting strangely *that* night. I had no idea what she was about to turn into."

"She doesn't act like the same woman," Sam said. "But I'm still holding out for you to agree that she is."

"You want something? Tea? Soda?"

He shook his head. "Nope. I think we've evolved far enough that we can just sit here and talk. Unless you feel better pacing?"

"I'm not pacing," I said.

I stopped in the middle of the kitchen floor, and he grinned at me.

"I'm sitting," I said, and I dropped into the chair across from him.

He leaned toward me, eyes intent. "I knew you'd move fast, but I didn't think it would be this fast. You're already licking the earth."

"What?"

"That's what Pascal called it. He said something like, 'I conceive it to be the glory and the greatness of mankind to be able to look upwards from licking the earth to survey the destiny that awaits him beyond time.' Something like that."

"Nothing like that." I got back up out of the chair and opened the refrigerator and stood there looking sightlessly at Max's collection of Tupperware containers. "It took me twenty-four hours to figure out that I have no real friends. I don't call that 'licking the earth.'"

"You already said you feel wretched and miserable and that the only passion you see in yourself is what you have for your work."

"My little idol, as you called it." I picked up a container of ravioli, opened it, then sealed it back up and returned it to the shelf.

"You're not going to find what you're looking for in there," Sam said.

I closed the door and faced him. "Where are all these options you're supposed to be giving me?"

"That *is* your option. You either admit you're licking the earth—"

"Could you please choose another image?" I said.

"It's a riddle, or so Pascal says." Sam got up and hoisted himself onto the counter, where he sat swinging his legs. "You can either try to unravel it using human reason…"

"Or?"

"Or not."

"What do you mean, 'or not'? What's the alternative?"

"Silence."

"I tried that. Look where it got me."

"Pretty far, from what I can tell."

"Far?" My voice was rising to fever pitch, and no amount of hair-raking or furniture-clutching was bringing it down. I just stood there, hands gripping the back of a kitchen chair. "I'm in a worse mess than ever. I'm friendless, loveless, sarcastic—"

"And passionate. And real. And genuine." Sam stopped bumping his heels against the cabinets and slid down to come to the chair next to mine and lean on it. He looked at me with soft eyes. "This woman I'm seeing now is the real thing."

"If that's true, I'm not liking it."

"I am."

He tilted my chin up with the tips of his fingers. I didn't stop him, not until he had kissed me with a softness I didn't know a man was capable of, a softness that ached down into the very hollow of myself.

I think he pulled away before I did, and he was already rubbing the back of his neck.

"I *knew* I should have brought that spiked belt," he said. His grin was sheepish. "What were we talking about?"

"Me acting like there's a God," I said.

"And already being more real."

We were both talking too fast and avoiding each other's eyes.

"Believe that if you want to," I said, eyes focused on a splotch of tomato sauce on the table. "But so far, I can't see what difference it makes."

"Don't worry." He tilted my chin up again. "It'll happen."

FIFTEEN

I called Dr. McDonald's office again on Monday and asked for another social worker's name. I didn't have time to wait for Paige Hill to come back from Maui or wherever she was. I needed options now, and I asked for a list of good assisted-living facilities. The secretary said she'd fax one over to me where I worked.

That gave me pause. I thought I should probably just go over and pick it up rather than run the risk of somebody in the math department seeing it and wondering why Jill McGavock needed assisted living. And then I stopped pausing.

Who cares what they wonder? I thought. *The separation lines have gotten way too fuzzy to be worrying about that.*

"Do you have access to a fax machine?" the secretary said.

"Yeah," I said. And I gave her the number.

Of course, I hung around the math department office for the next twenty minutes waiting for it to come in, which caused a few puzzled looks among the secretaries, and I snatched it out of the machine almost before it was finished printing. Then I scurried to my office with it like I'd just staged a bank heist. I was poring over it—a thermos of coffee beside me—when my cell phone rang.

"Have I got a deal for you," Sam's voice said.

"I'm sure," I said. "So far your deals have done nothing but complicate my life."

"I'm about to uncomplicate it," he said. "You want to go to dinner tomorrow night?"

That didn't qualify as uncomplicating as far as I was concerned. Sam must have heard that in my silence, because he said, "You don't want to miss this. It promises to be upscale. My father is buying."

His *father?* Meet a parent? Good grief.

"He's going to be breezing through the Bay Area and wants to take me to dinner." It was Sam's turn to pause. "If you have any pity for me in your heart at all, you won't make me do this alone."

"He's that bad, huh?" I said.

He chuckled. "I don't want to give you any preconceived notions."

"If there's one thing I have for you, Blaze, it's pity. What time?"

"Hercules Bakalis always dines fashionably late. Will you be starved if we make it 7:30?"

"No way! Your father's first name is *not* Hercules."

"It is. I swear it."

"I'm going to want to see a driver's license."

"You know what?" Sam said, laughter weaving itself in. "If you meet my father and ask for his driver's license, I will lick the earth."

"That's really okay," I said. "Where am I meeting you?"

"The Iberia Restaurant in Menlo Park, right across from the train station."

"Swanky," I said.

I had to admit that conjuring up images of what Sam's father was going to be like provided the best distraction yet. By the time I parked near the Iberia the next evening—after leaving Mother under Max's watchful eye—I was convinced he was either going to be a paragon of the church with a heavily hair-sprayed do and the Ten Commandments engraved on his cuff links, in which case he would embarrass Sam right under the table with his clichés, or he'd be a long-faced Latin scholar of the old school, who would himself be driven under the table by his son's unseemly jocularity.

I was wrong on both counts.

In the first place, the man who stood up as I approached the table was the absolute spitting image of Sam, except that there were a few streaks of gray in his dark, curly hair, and he had a better haircut. In fact, his haircut probably cost him what I earned per quarter. Like Sam, he had thick eyebrows that were already expressing approval of the fact that I wasn't drop-dead ugly. His olive skin was only slightly lined with age, and a strong chin gave him a look of power, even though he had the Bakalis narrow shoulders and wiry build. He even wore glasses with frames similar to Sam's.

When Sam stood up, too, I was surprised to see that he was actually taller than his father. Hercules appeared bigger. It was probably the take-charge way he put out both hands, grabbed mine, and pulled me within inches of his face.

"She's incredible!" he said. "Marry her quick, son, before I take her for myself."

I turned to stare at Sam. His facial expression was a mixture of utter mortification and extreme delight. It was obvious he was enjoying my current state of speechlessness more than he was suffering from embarrassment. I turned back to his father.

"You're both out of luck," I said. "I'm not up for grabs."

I knew it was a poor choice of words before the sentence was even out of my mouth, but I didn't expect the leer that formed itself on the man's face.

"Now, that's really too bad," he said.

"So, uh, Jill—have a seat!" Sam said.

I practically dove for the one across the table from Hercules, but he was too fast for me and tucked me into the chair between himself and Sam with such deftness, I would have had to knock him, the table, and a nearby waiter down to avoid it.

"What does this gorgeous creature drink?" Hercules said.

Sam blinked at me. "I have no idea."

"I can see your social prowess hasn't improved any. What will you have, honey?"

"Club soda," I said.

"That's it? Are you a teetotaler like my son?"

"Something like that."

He gave an exaggerated sigh. "It's a shame when a beautiful woman like yourself falls into the clutches of the church."

"Dad—"

I put my hand up to Sam. "I have fallen into no one's clutches," I said to his father. "Least of all the church's."

A grin spread slowly across his face. "Well, then, this could turn out to be a very interesting evening after all."

While he ordered Scotch on the rocks—at least his second from what I could smell—I exchanged glances with Sam. I think he would have been savoring my annoyance more if there hadn't been something else going on with him. I could see it in the way he was running his hand up and down his water glass.

Interesting, I thought. *Sam in the hot seat instead of me.*

With drink orders taken and an appetizer both Sam and I had declined on the way, Hercules turned back to me and launched into a series of questions. They were the usual getting-to-know-you queries, but I had the sense that although I was grudgingly giving him information about the status of my dissertation and my plans for the future, he was reading my measurements into my answers. It was all I could do not to ask the waiter for a barf bag.

Sam only let that go on for a few minutes before he said, "So, Dad, what's on your plate these days?"

Hercules's eyebrows lifted. "You mean, besides trying to entice this woman away from you?"

"Yeah," Sam said.

"I'm trying to sell off those condos down in West Palm Beach," Hercules said. "Too much of a hassle. Interest rates are down right now—or did you notice?"

"I heard something about that, yeah," Sam said.

"You heard something about it," Hercules snickered. "You better get your head out of that ostrich hole, son. It's time for you to invest in a little real estate. You still living in a rented room?"

"I haven't changed my address, if that's what you mean," Sam said.

I looked at him. He was grinning. There was no gritting of teeth, no tightening of the jaw. If that had been my mother and me having that conversation—and it could have been a year ago—I'd have been clawing the tablecloth.

"My son has more money than he knows what to do with," Hercules said to me. "Did you know that?"

"I had no idea," I said.

"Now you do. Does that change your mind about being up for grabs? Because if it does, let me tell you about *my* financial status!"

He winked and took a swallow of his Scotch. I kicked Sam under the table.

"Jill grew up on a college campus," Sam said. "She knows non-tenured professors don't make a lot of money."

Hercules pretended to choke on his drink. "You're still not tenured?"

"No, Dad."

"What do you have to do to change that? Who do I have to call?"

Nobody if you ever *want him to be tenured!* I thought. *One conversation with you and the poor guy will be blackballed from academia forever.*

"I'm not trying to change it," Sam said.

"Yeah, well, that's no surprise." Hercules gave Sam a long look over the top of his glass, shook his head as if he'd just seen something disgusting, and drained half his drink. When he spoke again, it was to me, in a voice embittered by liquor and whatever old baggage he'd just opened.

"You probably don't know this, Jill," he said, "or maybe you do. You seem like a pretty sharp cookie yourself. My son is brilliant. Near genius, I'd say."

"Hardly," Sam said.

Hercules pointed his finger at Sam, though he was still talking to me. "But you see? You see what he does? He pretends not to recognize his own potential so he'll have an excuse not to live up to it. He's always been that way—incredibly intelligent and lazier than heck." He gave his head another derisive shake on the way back to the Scotch. "What a waste."

The only reason I didn't respond was that I was torn between anger *for* Sam that this man would humiliate him in front of someone he didn't know and anger *at* Sam for not reaching across the table and grabbing him by the chest hairs—which, I noticed, were peeking out of his too-far-unbuttoned shirt. I was growing more mentally nauseous by the minute.

"Sorry, Dad," Sam said easily. "This is where we agree to disagree, remember?"

Hercules looked at him, grunted, and shook his head.

"If we're going to do that," he said, "I'm going to need another drink." He looked at me. "You sure you don't want anything stronger, honey?"

"It's Jill," I said. "And no—thanks."

At that point, Sam steered the conversation back to his father's business ventures, during which there was a great deal of name-dropping, geographically speaking. We stayed on that somewhat safer ground until Hercules had polished off three-quarters of his next Scotch and said to Sam, "So, have you heard from your mother?"

"Yeah. We talk at least once a week."

"And? How is she?"

I assumed by this time that Sam's parents were divorced. I couldn't say I blamed his mother. Her husband had probably been running around on her for years—or maybe just trying to. I couldn't imagine any woman with an ounce of self-respect falling for a man who virtually drooled over his prey. He made Jacoboni look like a prude.

"Has Sam told you that his mother left me for another man?" Hercules said.

"Uh, no," I said.

"Nor does she want to hear it from you, Dad," Sam said. There was still no clear annoyance in his voice, but he wasn't thrilled with this line of questioning either, I could tell that by the way he was toying with the silver napkin ring.

"Up and left me after twenty years of marriage," Hercules said. "Is she seeing anybody now?"

"You'd have to ask her," Sam said.

"Not possible. She hangs up on me every time I call her." He looked at me. The whites of his eyes were turning into road maps. "Why would a woman you raised a family with do that to you? Why do you think?"

"What? Hang up when you call her?" I said.

"Yeah. You're a woman—and a beautiful woman. Have I told you that?"

"Several times, Dad," Sam said.

"So you oughta know why a man's ex-wife won't give him the time of day."

"I've never been an ex-wife," I said. "So I couldn't even venture a guess." *Besides, you don't* even *want to hear my theory on this.*

"How old are you?" Hercules said suddenly.

"Not that it's any of your business," I said, "but I'm thirty."

His eyes lit up. "I like this woman, Sam. Why have you been hiding her?" He looked back at me. "So, if you're thirty, why haven't you ever been married? I know it's a personal question. I'm just curious."

No, you're just nosy. And obnoxious. And smarmy. Sam must have gotten his personality genes from his mother.

The appetizer arrived—some kind of seafood concoction made with fish flown in from the Canary Islands. Max would have been in ecstasy. The server's arrival at our table created enough commotion to divert attention from Hercules's question, and Sam again jumped in to redirect the conversation.

"So, Dad," he said. "Have you been back to the cardiologist?"

"Are you kidding?" Hercules said. "I'm not going back to him. Why should I pay three hundred and fifty bucks to have him tell me to quit drinking and quit smoking and slow down, none of which I have any intention of doing?"

"Do you have any intention of living much longer?" Sam said.

I glanced at him. He was serious. He actually cared whether this man dropped dead or not. I had to give him the Compassion Award for that. If he'd been my father, I would have practically been *wishing* for a nice myocardial infarction.

"Don't start in on me with your lifestyle lecture," Hercules said. "I'm going to live my life to the fullest, and I'm going to die doing it. End of discussion." He shifted his focus to me, though by this point the word *focus* was an overstatement. "I had to end the discussion, because the next part is where he tries to convince me that I need to get religion before I keel over."

"I have never tried to convince you to *get religion,*" Sam said.

It was the first hint of real tension I'd detected in Sam's voice all evening. In spite of the subject matter, I wanted to say, *Atta boy, Sam. That's the spirit!*

"What do you call it, then?" Hercules said. "I have it memorized, Jill. 'I'm still praying for you, Dad.' 'Just hear me out, Dad, because I know you're hurting.' Oh, and here's my favorite—"

"That's enough, Dad."

Hercules grinned at me slyly. *"That's* not my favorite."

"This is where I draw the line," Sam said. "You can ride me about my financial status and my social life and anything else— but stay away from my spirituality. I mean it."

Hercules gave him another long look, but this time he didn't shake his head or grunt in disgust. I could see him having to force the grin onto his face.

"I'm in trouble," he said to me. "You think he'll ever speak to me again?"

"Not if he's smart," I said.

He threw his head back and laughed. I didn't.

The evening went downhill from there. Sam diplomatically suggested that Hercules lighten up on the Scotch, so he switched to brandy. With relative aplomb, over the lamb shank and the paella, Sam kept further discussion away from things spiritual and navigated us through politics, sports, and social issues. When we finally got through dessert—which both Sam and I refused, but found ourselves presented with anyway—Sam borrowed my cell phone to call his dad a cab.

With Sam otherwise occupied, Hercules grabbed my hand, and I didn't try to pull away. It was too much like being stuck in one of those Mexican finger toys.

"You're a beautiful woman," he said thickly.

"So you've said."

"You're not churchy, huh?"

"'Churchy'? I'd have to say no, I'm not churchy."

"Then it's a good thing you don't have your sights set on Sammy. He wants a church lady, you know."

We hadn't exactly discussed Sam's preferences in women, but I nodded.

"He's told me that himself," Hercules said. "It's a good thing you're not hearing wedding bells for you and Sammy, because he's definitely looking for a church lady." Hercules gave me a pull, bringing me close enough to see every turn of the ever-reddening maze of capillaries in his eyes. "Now me on the other hand, I'm looking for—"

"Dad," Sam said. He was standing behind him, hands on Hercules's shoulders. "The cab's on its way. Come on, I'll wait outside with you."

Hercules, of course, had to have the last word. He pulled my hand to his lips and gave it a wet kiss. I waited until Sam had him pointing in the other direction before I wiped it with my napkin.

"Wait for me, would you?" Sam said over his shoulder.

Only so I can get even, I said with my eyes.

But when Sam came back, the look on his face melted my resolve to lay into him for putting me through that. It had obviously been a whole lot worse where he was sitting.

"Your father's quite the character," I said.

Sam sank heavily into the chair next to mine. "I didn't know he was drinking that much now or I wouldn't have dragged you here. He's still obnoxious when he's sober, but he's not quite as sloppy about it."

"Don't worry about it, Blaze," I said. "I know why you had me come."

His eyebrows went up. "Why?"

"So I could see that things could be worse for me. I thought *I* had the parent from Hades—at least, at one time I thought she was."

Sam leaned back and toyed with his dessert fork.

"You handled it a lot better than I ever did," I said. "And I didn't even have the alcohol to deal with. How do you sit there and let him rake you over the coals?"

"I feel sorry for him."

"Why? He could get it together if he wanted to. He's obviously intelligent. He isn't unattractive. I mean, he looks just like you—"

Whoa. Had I said that? I longed for a delete button. Sam was looking at me oddly.

Here it comes, I thought. *He's going to say, "Oh? You find me attractive?"*

But he said, "You think we look alike?"

"Except for the age difference, you could be identical twins," I said. "Until he opens his mouth and lets his personality out. No offense, Blaze, but the man borders on loathsome."

"So we *look* alike, but we don't *act* alike."

"Are you fishing for a compliment?"

He looked at me with genuine innocence. "No, I'm not. I really want to know."

"You definitely don't act alike. In terms of behavior, it's hard to believe he sired you at all. Were you separated from him at birth or something?"

Sam laughed. "No."

"It's like he's you—only you with some ingredient missing."

"You're right about that. I was just like him until I added the 'ingredient.'"

"No way," I said.

"Yes way. I was going to follow in his footsteps—do the whole pull-yourself-out-of-the-blue-collar-pit, make-a-pile-of-money, take-charge-of-your-world thing."

"And then?"

"And then I found God."

"That's it?" I said.

"Well, God and a group of believers who help people shed their false skins."

"Explain," I said.

"Christianity is supposed to help believers get rid of the false self we start forming the first time we do a no-no and have to deal with it. Like about age one. By the grace of God, I fell in with a group of Christians whose main goal was to get every member stripped down to the heart."

"So you got stripped of everything on you that was your father. That's why you're different."

"Not quite. You can't just empty out without filling up with something else."

"You're going to say it was God, aren't you?"

"I'm going to say it was knowing God and discovering that Christ is the real center of me—not some self I created."

"So your father is you, only without the God."

Sam's mouth formed a smile. "You've got it."

"Yeah, but I know people who are nice, decent human beings, and they don't necessarily have God in their belief system."

"Like who?"

I pretended to have a sudden desire for my abandoned dessert so I could think of someone. That list was about the length of the one containing the people who *did* embrace God. Did I actually *know* anybody who was nice and decent?

"Max Ironto," I said.

"Max is an atheist?" Sam said.

"No, he claims to believe in God."

"But you're not buying it."

"Okay, not Max. Nigel Frost. My advisor."

"Nigel Frost?"

"You know him?"

Sam's grin got bigger, if that was possible. "He's in my men's group. We have a bimonthly prayer breakfast. I don't know a more godly man."

"Nigel?" I said. "He's never said a word about God to me!"

"Nigel comes from a more genteel background. He doesn't bulldoze like I do, and since I'm sure *you* never broached the subject—"

"It doesn't come up that much in K-theory."

"It could," Sam said. His eyes were sparkling behind his glasses. That was something old Hercules's eyes had not done.

"We haven't completely proven the theory yet," I said.

"We haven't disproven it, either."

"So for now I'll concede that I have seen what you would be if you didn't have God."

Sam leaned toward me. He didn't try to kiss me. He didn't touch me. But his voice wrapped itself around me and held me.

"Jill," he said, "you *are* beautiful."

He couldn't have sounded less like Hercules Bakalis if he'd tried.

SIXTEEN

The next day, I made an appointment to see the Hopewell Care Center on Saturday. Then I teetered on the edge of indecision for the next *three* days.

One minute I was certain I needed to just take Mother with me to the interview and check her in on the spot; the next minute I was picking up the phone to call and cancel. It was Mother herself, in a sense, who clinched it for me.

When I got home on Friday, Freda III was sitting in the foyer with her sweater on, purse in hand, looking like she was waiting for a bus. The instant I opened the door, she was on her feet, babbling out paragraphs she'd obviously been saving up for me all afternoon. It was such a muddle, I didn't understand a word she was saying.

"Wait. Time out," I said. "Let me just put my stuff down, and we can sit down and talk—"

"I'm through sitting and I'm through talking," Freda cut in. "After what happened today, I'm through with all of it."

My heart started racing, and I dropped my bag on the bottom step. "What happened? Where is my mother?"

I hurried toward the living room, but Freda said, "She's in her room napping. I've been sitting here ever since she laid down, staring at that bedroom door, so unless she's climbed out the window, which wouldn't surprise me, she's still in there."

I was inclined to go see for myself, but the way Freda III was heading for the front door, I didn't dare leave the foyer lest she bolt and leave me clueless. As it was she was red-faced and breathing hard. The next thing I knew she'd be having a stroke.

"I've stayed on, Jill," she said, "because I knew the fix you were in, but today takes the cake. I can't handle any more."

"What—"

"I'm standing in the kitchen. She's at the table. I turn my back for no more than fifteen seconds, I turn around again, and she's gone."

"Where?"

"After I nearly lost my mind looking for her, I found her out in the backyard."

"I thought we agreed that she wasn't to leave the house without someone with her."

Freda gave a grunt. "You and I agreed. We must have forgotten to tell *her*. I got out there, and there she was, *in* the pond, on her stomach, splashing all around."

"You're not serious."

"Hon, I am serious as a heart attack, and I had a devil of a time hauling her out of there, I can tell you that. It's a wonder we didn't both drown, but if *she* had, it would be my fault, and I can't take that kind of responsibility."

"But that's what you do! You take responsibility for sick people."

"Sick people who are in a bed—not ones I have to watch like a lifeguard."

I could feel my eyes narrowing. "When I interviewed you, I asked you if you'd had experience with dementia patients, and you said yes."

"Yes, with people who are talking out of their heads. She doesn't talk. She just goes!"

I pulled both hands through my hair. "All right, look, I'll call Burl and get him to come over and put some different bolts on the doors or something."

"You can do that, but don't do it on my account." Her face

was fading to a merely flustered pink, and she reached over and patted my arm. "It's not like I'm leaving you high and dry. You were going to put her in a home anyway."

"I'm considering it."

Freda III hiked her purse strap over her shoulder and set her face. "Well, then, hon, maybe now you'll just *have* to do it."

Lady, I wanted to tell her, *I don't have to do anything!*

But I couldn't say it, because I didn't believe it. It did seem as if all decisions were being moved just beyond my reach. Other people, on the other hand, were making choices right and left.

Freda III left, and Max arrived shortly thereafter. Over dinner, I filled him in on the afternoon's events.

"I guess we'll just have to take Mother with us tomorrow," I said. "She should be okay as long as we keep an eye on her so she doesn't wander into somebody's shuffleboard game. Can you be here at 9:15 so we can get to Hopewell by 9:30?"

Max didn't answer. He appeared to be studying his mortadella.

"You *do* support me on this, right?" I said. "You're the one who talked me into it."

"God help me, I did," Max said, but he still wouldn't look at me. "It's the right thing to do. I know it."

"Then what's wrong? Just say it, Max."

He set down his fork. "I can't go with you tomorrow. I can't go to that place and know that that's where we could be abandoning Liz."

"We aren't abandoning her. In the first place, we're just going to go look at it."

"I can't. I know I'm a coward, but I just can't. I'll break down."

He was about to break down already. What was I supposed to do—slap him and tell him to snap out of it?

I put my hand on top of his. "Okay, Max. You stay here with Mother, and I'll go alone."

He smothered both our hands with his other one, so that we

now had a large pile of fingers and palms on the tabletop.

"God bless you for that, Jill. I'll do anything else that you want me to do, so help me I will. But not that. You understand?"

"Yeah," I said. "There's Kleenex over there on the counter."

He untangled the hand pile and crossed the kitchen to blow his nose.

"I want to ask you something, Max," I said.

"Anything. You want more mortadella?"

"No. You've mentioned God a couple of times in this conversation. Have you always done that and I've just missed it, or is that a new development?"

Max stuffed the used Kleenex into the trash can. "He's in here." He tapped his forehead. "Lately He's in there more and more. I'm asking Him: What are you doing up there, huh? I mean, excuse me, but we got problems down here. What's going on?"

"Do you get any answers?" I said.

He came over and stood, hands pressed on the table. One lock of dark hair was falling over his forehead as usual, and his big chest was heaving under the silk shirt. He was like a character in a Brontë novel—and yet he was all too real.

"You are my answer," he said.

"Me," I said.

"You are the answer to almost every prayer I have prayed. You moved in with your mother like I wanted. You're taking care of her like I prayed for. The only thing you haven't done is take this whole nightmare away. You haven't done that yet."

"I don't think that's going to happen, Max," I said.

I didn't have the heart to tell him I hadn't been the answer to the rest of his prayers either and that, in fact, it had all been blind luck because I had no idea what I was doing.

That was blatantly obvious the next day when I went to see the Hopewell Care Center. I walked in, dressed in a black suit with my hair up, list of questions on a legal pad in hand so they would know I wasn't the type to be hoodwinked by appearances and promises. I had to pass through a large entry area to get to the office, which I did with an observant eye, hawkish in an effort to spot anything I didn't like.

On the left was an aquarium, which an old man was peering into, muttering under his breath and gesticulating wildly for the fish.

On the right were two women leaning on their respective walkers, white heads bent together as they talked, as if they'd just been lifted from the back fence and placed there in mid-conversation. Gossip was apparently what, in their opinion, women were born to do.

Straight ahead was a man of about thirty-five in a high-tech wheelchair whose face and body were so contorted that I had to look away to avoid staring at him.

I glanced down at my list of questions. I might as well scratch them all out and ask just one: *Does my mother really belong here?*

A blond woman poked her head out of a door farther down. "Are you Jill McGavock?" she called.

Only because I smelled coffee and thought she might offer me some did I say, "Yes. Are you Monique?"

Contrary to the message that her name—Monique l'Orange—suggested, Monique at least appeared to be sensible. I didn't see any crystals dangling from the ceiling, and she did not attempt to squeeze or pat any part of my anatomy. A few sips into a cup of coffee, I was describing my mother's behavior to her and asking her point blank: "Is this the place for her?"

"Let me show you something," she said.

What she led me to was a separate section of Hopewell, where no one was confined to a wheelchair or wandering aimlessly. This, Monique told me, was the assisted-living section, as opposed to the nursing home area I'd entered through.

The rooms had a relatively homey look. In the recreational

area ping-pong matches, card games, and communal TV watching were going on simultaneously. The crowd around the television was actually watching *Moonstruck* and nodding appreciatively every time Olympia Dukakis came on the screen.

"We don't park them there for the day," Monique told me. "We limit their TV watching and try to divert them into more stimulating activities."

I found myself wondering if my mother could actually be stimulated by a rousing hand of canasta. As we continued on toward the dining room, I said to Monique, "I've described my mother's condition to you, and I think I've made it clear that she's deteriorating rapidly."

"You have."

"So, do you think she can handle this atmosphere? I mean, these people all seem to be in their right minds—relative to her, anyway."

Monique stopped in the doorway to the dining area. "I know what you're saying, but I think when you see your mother with other people whose behaviors are similar to hers, she won't seem so strange to you."

I scanned the dining room. It was a cozy collection of tables, each one set with cloth tablecloth and napkins and a Christmas centerpiece.

"Wow," I said. "Did Thanksgiving already happen? I was only half kidding about that."

Monique smiled. "You're about to get your life back," she said.

I grasped at that like it was the last rope hanging. "When can you get her in?"

There was the rub. They had a room available in assisted living, but the paperwork was going to take at least five working days.

"It isn't like checking into a hospital or a hotel," Monique said. "You are basically turning all responsibility for your mother's care over to us."

"Five days?" I said. "I can handle that."

How, though, I hadn't a clue.

That day and Sunday were fine. Max and I took turns keeping what felt like surveillance, and Mother was cooperative except on Sunday afternoon when Burl came over to drain the koi pond and transfer Mother's fish to a neighbor's pond three doors down.

"You could sell these and get a good price for them," Burl told me as he cornered one with his net behind a rock.

"You're kidding," I said. "I thought they were just overgrown goldfish."

Burl shook his head and nodded toward the house. "She knows what I'm doing, too, and she doesn't like it. She's fixin' to have a hissy fit."

I looked at the house. My mother was indeed standing at the guest room window, overseeing the whole operation. Even as I watched, she brought up a hand and tapped sharply on the glass.

Burl turned toward the house. "I know, Doc," he said. "But you're gonna be movin' on and there won't be anybody here to take care of them the way you did. I got it covered—trust me."

Was it sheer coincidence, I wondered, that she then moved away from the window?

The next five days presented another set of problems, but I got them somewhat worked out. Burl, of all people, agreed to stay with Mother while I was teaching class. I tried to convince Nigel to let me do office hours at night, but he was concerned about my safety and suggested instead that I forget them for the week and just give my students an e-mail address and a phone number where I could be reached at certain times. He assured me he would handle it all with Dr. Ferguson.

My students took the news about my office hours with only mild interest. Except for Tabitha. She got a panicked look on her face, which remained there through the entire class.

I actually felt sorry for her. When she approached me after class, I said, "Look, I'll draw you a map. You can come over to my mother's place for your tutoring session."

"Are you sure?" she said.

"Yeah," I said. "Just don't wear the skates, okay?"

With all of that in place it was, to say the least, an interesting week.

Burl arrived Monday, Wednesday, and Friday precisely at 10:30 A.M. wearing his tool belt as if he hadn't been to bed yet. While I was gone, he trimmed the oleanders, fixed a couple of shutters that were threatening to separate themselves from the house, and unclogged the downstairs toilet.

"I didn't even know it was stopped up," I said when he told me.

"It wasn't till she tried to flush a pair of pantyhose down it." He gave a soft grunt. "That's one place I don't follow her."

Max came over every evening to watch Mother so I could run with Sam on the Loop and then get some work done. Every night Max cooked a dinner more elaborate than the one before it. I guessed that was to assuage his guilt, but I didn't mention it. I hadn't eaten that well, that consistently, in years.

Even though I didn't normally tutor Tabitha on a daily basis, she came every afternoon that week. The first day, I was lucky enough to get Mother down for a nap before she arrived, and then I whisked Tabitha into the study so fast that she didn't have a chance to ask where my "ill" parent was. We almost got through the entire session before I heard Mother get up and start rattling things around in the kitchen.

"Try number eleven," I said to Tabitha, and then I hurried in after her.

Mother was opening and closing cabinet doors and growing stiffer by the minute.

"What are you looking for?" I said. "Are you hungry?"

She nodded.

"Okay, what do you usually eat for a snack?" I opened the

refrigerator and peered in. "You want some…leftover mortadella?"

I pulled my head out of the refrigerator and looked around. She was gone.

With visions of her diving into the now-empty koi pond dancing in my head, I broke for the hall. From the study, I heard Tabitha's husky voice bubbling out a "Hi!"

This was going to be a trip.

I got to the study just in time to see my mother dipping her hand into the bag of Doritos Tabitha was holding.

"Mother, no!" I said.

"Oh, it's okay. She can have some," Tabitha said. She wrinkled her freckled nose at Mother. "Aren't they good? Sour cream ranch—they're totally my favorite."

I had never known them to be "totally my mother's favorite," but she was chowing down on them as if she'd been craving them all day. As far as I knew, she had never put a morsel of junk food into her mouth until that moment.

"I'm sorry, Tabitha," I said. "She doesn't know what she's doing."

Tabitha gave me a blank look and then looked back at Mother. "Well, she's not bothering me. Can she just sit here while we work? Or do you need me to go? I can go—"

I looked at my mother, too. She popped another chip into her mouth and then giggled at Tabitha.

"She's sweet," Tabitha said. "Can't she stay?"

"She'll probably only sit there for about two minutes," I said. "She doesn't stay put for long."

But Mother remained, calmly polishing off the rest of Tabitha's chips while I explained second-order equations. If I hadn't known better, I'd have said she did it just to make a liar out of me. When we finished, Tabitha picked up one of Mother's hands and pressed it between hers.

"It was nice to meet you," she said. "I know you've been sick, and I'm praying for you. God's with you, you know."

I watched my mother closely. If anything was going to stir her up, it was going to be a comment like that.

But Mother just watched Tabitha with that same flat expression she'd worn while I was rattling on about differential calculus. It didn't matter what we said. She was there for the Doritos.

It may have been my most profoundly disturbing thought yet.

That was all Sam and I talked about up on the Loop that week. It was no longer a question of *whether* my mother still had a soul. It was now a matter of my proving *that* she had one. Otherwise, she was on a par with one of the koi we had just transferred from one pond to another so somebody would take care of it.

"So, the Wager is working," Sam said to me late Friday afternoon. We'd slipped off the beaten path again and were perched on what Sam insisted on calling the Jill Tree.

"What do you mean it's working?" I said. "I don't see it working. In the first place, I don't even know *how* to act as if there's a God."

"You're doing it."

"How am I doing it?"

"You've turned your whole life upside down this week for your mother."

"Like I had a choice."

"You did. You could have hired a temporary caretaker."

"I couldn't face another Freda."

"Could you have a year ago? Six months ago? Even six weeks ago?"

"But what real difference is it making? Mother doesn't care who's there with her, as long as we feed her and keep her from flushing lingerie down the john. And you still can't answer this question: If there's a God, how could there possibly be this—this injustice—this brilliant woman reduced to a zombie stealing a kid's Doritos?"

Sam inched forward on the horizontal trunk. "Let's clarify," he said. "If we say that there is *in*justice, we can only be sure of that if we know that there is justice itself. Correct?"

"What do you mean? Like we can't know if we're unhappy unless we know what happy is?"

He grinned. "You should be going for a doctorate in philosophy. Forget all that math nonsense."

"Move on, Blaze," I said.

"All right, if there is injustice, then it must be that there is true justice for it to be a defect of."

I traced that knot mentally and nodded.

"Now, does true justice exist?"

"Theoretically."

"But in reality? In practice?"

"Not that I've ever seen," I said.

"And I'm sure most people would agree with you. Ergo, if there has to be true justice—"

"Did you just say *ergo?* Tell me you didn't actually use the word *ergo.*"

"Yes, I did. Now stop breaking my train of thought. If there has to be true justice, and this true justice is not found on earth or in man—" his eyes glowed—"it must exist in heaven and in God."

"You can't just take everything and turn it into God," I said.

"Sure I can," he said, "because God's already in it."

I didn't answer right away. I had a half-dozen sarcastic retorts just waiting to fire at him. But as I flipped through them, they merely turned over on themselves, like cards in a Rolodex file.

"You know what's really maddening?" I said.

Sam shook his head.

"That I have to admit that if I could see just one sign that 'God' was making any of this better, I would want it all to be true. I would want God to exist."

"Why is that maddening?"

"Because I hate to be wrong. I would have to admit that I've been wrong all this time."

"If you don't ever want to be wrong," Sam said, "then you *sure* don't want to be wrong about God." His grin widened and he got closer to me, so that I could almost feel the glow in his eyes. "What kind of sign are you looking for? What is it that you want to see?"

"I don't know."

"Then how will you know it's a sign when you see it? Maybe you've already had signs and you didn't recognize them."

"Do you seriously think that?" I said.

"Look, Jill," he said. "I can't talk you into God. Matter of fact, I can't talk you into anything. Nobody can."

"At least you know that much," I said, grinning.

"I know this, too: If you don't want to believe in God, you won't. But you want to—you said it yourself."

"I *might* want to," I said. "But wanting isn't getting. I'm thirty years old, Blaze—I've figured that out."

"And I'm thirty-five, and I've figured out two things." He raised a finger. *"Only* those who seek God find Him." He raised another one. "And *all* those who seek God find Him. Since the signs of God can only be seen by those who seek Him, He stays partially hidden."

"You're making this up as you go along!" I said, laughing.

But his face was sober. Only his eyes still danced.

"God doesn't want the seeing-is-believing approach," he said.

I could feel my face growing sober, too—and something like anger brewing in my heart.

"Then what the heck does He want?" I said. "I've just about given up everything that was important to me. I'm down to begging for answers—and for me that is rock bottom. I'm sick of these intellectual arguments and these faith experiments that tear me apart! What does He want me to do?"

Sam took me firmly by both shoulders. I was crying. I was

yelling loud enough for Deputy Dog to hear me. I was practically tearing my hair out by the roots. And I wasn't caring that I was doing any of it in front of him.

"You tell me what it is He wants me to do!" I cried again.

Sam put his arms around me and held me tight, so that no amount of fighting could push him away.

"He wants you to do what you're doing right now," he said into my hair. "He wants you to let Him have it. He wants you to let Him have it all."

SEVENTEEN

S am followed me home from the Loop in his car, just to make sure I was all right, he said. That was despite my protests that I had only lost it for a few minutes and I was fine now. We both knew I was lying.

He walked me to the door and stood looking down at me, hands lazily parked in his pockets.

"You going to be all right tomorrow?" he said.

"If tonight is any indication, probably not."

"So go ahead and cry through the whole ordeal. I'm sure they've seen family members do that before."

"No one but you has ever seen me do that or ever will," I said. "You tell anybody and I'll cut your heart out."

He didn't respond. In fact, he looked rather shyly at the toe of his running shoe, which he was using to guide a beetle away from the doormat. When he looked up at me, his smile was soft.

"Too late," he said. "I think you've already cut my heart out."

Then he took my face in both hands and kissed me, and I didn't push him away. I kissed him back until I could no longer breathe.

"I'll be praying for you tomorrow," he said.

I stayed on the front porch long after he was gone, mentally turning myself inside out trying to deny the potential for passion. I lost.

I took Mother to Hopewell the next morning. Burl followed in his pickup truck with suitcases, a box of decor I'd selected for her room, and the armchair from the guest room that she sat in at the window. Max had stood waving from the doorway, giving every indication that his heart was breaking in half.

I, on the other hand, was the picture of control. It was the first time I'd had Mother out of the yard since her last appointment with the orthopedic surgeon, and she'd definitely declined since then. My main focus was to keep her from stealing some poor unsuspecting resident's breakfast.

The focus shifted slightly when we pulled into the parking lot and I turned off the ignition.

"Okay," I said, "here we are."

She sat staring out the side window while I rooted around behind the seat for my purse.

"I'll come around to that side and let you out—" I started to say. But I stopped.

Mother was pointing her index finger toward the building.

"What?" I said.

She turned to me, and it was all I could do not to gasp. Her flat expression had pulled together into one of pure bewilderment. For the flash of a second, her eyes were once again their intense blue, and they were demanding answers.

"This is the Hopewell Care Center," I said. I could hear my voice growing louder, my pace slowing, as if I were talking to someone who didn't speak English. "Look, Mother, you're going to be staying here now. It's a great place, and they're really going to—"

To what? Keep you from jumping out the window? From taking a dive into the nearest fishbowl?

She was still watching me, her square jaw set expectantly. A familiar sense of tension seeped into me, and I scrambled for better vocabulary, more intelligent phrases.

"It's about your quality of life," I said. "Basically, you don't have any at home. This is going to be your home now. Trust me. I've analyzed this by every method known to man and then some."

I felt as if I were talking to the old Liz McGavock, the one who *watched* my words as well as heard them, and then pounced on them like a lioness.

But she turned slowly to look at the building again, and one hand jerked up and pointed vaguely in its direction.

"Yeah," I said. "That's the place."

When she turned back to me, her face was expressionless once again, her eyes almost inanimate. But from then until we stepped inside the building, she never took them off me, and even then they darted back to me occasionally, somehow questioning even in their lifelessness.

The entrance hall was more crowded as we walked in than it had been the Saturday before. There were several patients at the aquarium, and, remembering the koi pond incident, I hurried Mother past it to the office. Monique was waiting for us and led us briskly to the assisted residents' wing, where I said to Mother, "This is where you'll be—not back there."

Mother was asleep on the bed about thirty seconds after Monique showed us to her room. I was almost finished putting her things away when Burl came in with the chair. I'd forgotten he was even with us. He didn't seem to mind. He appeared to be quite comfortable as he positioned the chair facing the window and then checked the lock and screen, probably to make sure Mother couldn't pull one of her Houdini acts in the middle of the night.

"Nice place," he said to me.

"I thought so," I said. And then suddenly that sounded imperious to me, as if Burl were some underling and I was chiding him for being so impertinent as to validate my choice. I turned to him. "You think she'll be all right here, don't you? I mean, don't you think her quality of life was suffering at home?"

Burl folded his hands behind his back. His face was its usual deadpan, but his eyes seemed almost annoyed.

"What does that mean exactly—'quality of life'?" he said.

"Well. I see it as how much enjoyment she's getting out of

being alive. It can't be that pleasant, sitting in a chair staring out the window all day. To me, that's why she gets up all of a sudden and goes running around? She's probably looking for something to do. Here they have things for her to do that are appropriate to her condition."

Burl gave a soft grunt. "I hear about quality of life all the time at the hospital."

"I guess you would."

"They use it like it means how much sex and money you have."

"Excuse me?" I could feel my eyebrows twisting.

"Seems like if you can't use your money and your power or can't bed somebody down once in a while, you haven't got a life."

Aside from the fact that it was the most I'd heard Burl speak at one time, I was intrigued.

"Your mother," he went on, "she never talked about quality of life."

"You talked about this often?" I said. I hoped I didn't sound skeptical, because I didn't feel that way. It was beginning to dawn on me that people read me the way I had always read my mother, and I wasn't too crazy about the idea.

"Most every evening we took a coffee break together if she was still there and she wasn't too busy," Burl said. "She never said anything like 'they ought to just take this person off life support because he doesn't have any quality of life left.'" He shifted his eyes over to Mother, who was snoring softly on the bed. "She thinks every life is worth saving, so I guess that means she thinks suffering has quality. If it doesn't, then what's her whole life been about up to now?"

I knew I was staring at him, but I didn't attempt to stop. If I had, I would have missed his look, which covered my mother like a warm blanket as she slept. He didn't shake his head as if to say, "What a shame. What a waste." He gazed at her out of a face etched with wisdom. I realized then that he knew her the way I didn't, the way no one did—maybe not even Max. It made me feel small and cold.

She woke up shortly thereafter and went straight to the chair, sat down, and looked out the window.

"I think you're gonna like it here, Doc," Burl said. He smiled at her, and the web of lines on his face came to life. "I've got to go now, but I'll be back. You want anything?"

She looked at him and shook her head.

"If you think of anything, you just tell your daughter. I'll be seein' her. There's a couple things I still need to take care of around your house."

"Thank you," I said to him as he started in his deliberate way for the door. "That seems so inadequate. You've done so much."

"I'm not done," he said. And then he left.

With Burl gone, I was suddenly at a loss for what to do or say. Mother was contentedly studying the view outside her window. Everything had been organized, tidied, and straightened, and I was growing uncomfortable in the silence and awkwardness of the moment. When Monique walked in the door, I could have kissed her feet.

"If you want to leave now," she said to me, "I think that would be fine. You're doing all right for the moment, aren't you, Dr. McGavock?"

Mother didn't answer.

"I think you can take that as a yes," I said.

Monique stepped out into the hall. I crouched beside my mother's chair, and she moved her eyes lifelessly toward me. I didn't want to leave her here, and yet there was nothing I wanted more than to get out of this place—and take her with me, or not take her with me. The only thing I knew for sure was that I wanted everything to go back to the way it was before this... this...*thing* had wrecked our lives. Before I'd ever gotten lumps in my throat or wrestled with indecision or felt the burn of shame for my own coldness.

"I have to go," I said. "But I'll be back tomorrow. By then, you'll be running this place. Just cut them a little slack the first day, okay?"

She blinked and then turned again to look out the window. I grabbed my purse and stood up.

"See you tomorrow?" I said. "I'll try not to interrupt your bridge game."

Somehow I made it out the door and several steps down the hall. Monique was standing at the corner, and she smiled and pointed behind me.

"Someone's following you," she said.

I turned around. Mother was coming toward me at a brisk clip, looking for all the world as if she were rushing a lab report to Ted Lyons.

"What is it?" I said to her.

She stopped beside me and with a jerk pointed her finger on down the hall.

"Yeah, I'm leaving," I said. I looked helplessly at Monique. She just nodded. What that was supposed to tell me, I hadn't a clue. "Like I told you," I said to Mother, "you're staying here. It's the best thing."

She didn't appear puzzled. She merely stood there, looking down the hall, pointing at some nebulous destination with a jerky finger.

"You know what, Dr. McGavock?" Monique said finally—a good two minutes after she should have intervened, in my opinion. "I have a lot to show you. Why don't we get started right now and let Jill go take care of business?"

At least, I think that's what she said. I said good-bye to my mother one more time and then moved away at a near gallop. All I could hear were my own words, spoken as if I knew for a fact that they were true. *It's the best thing,* I had told her. *It's the best thing.*

But I no more knew that leaving her there to stand like a

mannequin with a ping-pong paddle in her hand was the best thing than I knew whether I was going to make it out the front door without throwing up into the nearest trash can.

I thought about it until I could no longer stand the sound of it in my head. *It's the best thing.* Then I got into the Miata and punched in a number on my cell phone.

"Blaze?" I said when Sam answered. "I need to see you."

We met at Denny's just down the street from Hopewell, Sam looking sleepy-eyed and boyish with his curly hair unbrushed and a red Stanford T-shirt thrown over a pair of chinos. But his mind was obviously wide awake as he ordered us coffee and then leaned intently toward me.

"It didn't go well?" he said.

I filled him in.

"Okay, Blaze," I said when I was through. "Where does God fit into that?"

He waited for the waitress to drop off our coffee. Then he sipped his thoughtfully while I dumped three packets of Sweet 'n Low into mine and stirred like I was trying to dissolve sand.

"I think we need to get clearer on what you can expect from God," Sam said. He nodded at my coffee mug. "You're going to get carpal tunnel."

I looked sheepishly at my hand and put the spoon on the table. "Okay, let's have it."

"If you're looking for a God who authors mathematical truths and the order of the elements and that's it, go read Epicurus."

"Nah. I've got the mathematical truths handled."

"If you want a God who grants the wishes of the people who worship him with great wealth and happy days, talk to the people who see God as some kind of Fairy Godfather."

I gave a half-laugh. "That doesn't sounds so bad. Sign me up for that."

"I can sign you up, but it isn't going to happen. That isn't God."

I stared miserably into my coffee. "Then you better tell me what God *is*, Blaze," I said. "At this point, I'm open to anything."

Sam pushed his own coffee aside so he could lean farther across the table. "You mind if we go back to Pascal?"

I shook my head.

"Okay, picture old Blaise sitting in his apartment brooding over the fact that his belief in God was merely intellectual. That kept him in a quandary as to how to satisfy the demands of both God and the world as a man of his station in life was expected to do." Sam grinned. "There were certain 'moral compromises' the men of his class allowed themselves to make. Anyway, suddenly he experiences God—for about two hours."

"Experiences how?"

"He had a vision."

"A vision," I said. "Okay."

"He called it 'the night of fire.' God apparently came to him in flames and told him what eternal life is: that he should know the one true God and Jesus Christ whom He sent. Pascal came out of that encounter a completely changed man—how did he put it? In 'total submission to Jesus Christ. Eternally in bliss for a day of hard training in this world.'" Sam looked at me, his eyes glowing as if he had just seen a vision himself. "My favorite part of the story is that nobody even knew about the vision until nine years later when he died. His servant was going through his clothes and he noticed what appeared to be extra padding sewn into his doublet. Turns out it was a piece of parchment and wrapped inside it was a sheet of paper where Blaise had written an account of his night of fire. He evidently carried it around with him in his jacket everywhere he went."

"So that's where you get all these little Pascal zingers you're always firing at me?" I said.

"No, those were found on who knows how many little pieces of paper all over his rooms. It looked like he was going to compile them in a book but never got around to it. Other people have done that since then—the collection is called the *Pensées*. That's French for 'thoughts.'"

"So there's a book?" I said.

"You want to read it?" Sam said. "I have about ten copies in different translations."

"I have no doubt," I said. I smiled at him, and I could feel myself sinking warmly into the seat. "So, Blaze, are you expecting me to have a vision?"

"I'm not saying you won't," Sam said. "But I never have, at least not to that extent. The point is, the God of the Christians—the God Pascal saw and hundreds of thousands, millions of people have seen—is a God who fills the whole being of the people who love Him. He makes us aware, deeply aware, that we're unworthy—"

"Yeah, yeah, we lick the earth."

"—and simultaneously, that He's merciful to us. He unites us with Himself in the depths of our souls so that we're humble and joyful and confident and love-filled because intertwined with Him, we're incapable of being anything else no matter what kind of suffering life slaps us with. *That* is the message Jesus came to deliver."

"Should I be happy because I just put my mother in a nursing home?" I spread my hand on the table. "I'm not being sarcastic. I really want to know."

"Not superficially happy—like Susie Cheerleader," Sam said. "But at peace here." He rubbed his fist against his chest.

"But I'm not at peace about it," I said. "I already hate it that she's in that place, because even though they call it assisted living, sooner or later she's going to be in that hallway, staring at the tropical fish." I cupped my hands around the coffee mug. "But what am I supposed to do? I can't keep her at home, not unless I completely dump everything I've been working for. Is that going to give me peace?"

"Look into the vision and ask God that," Sam said.

I looked at him blankly. "What vision?"

"Whatever vision of God you have."

"Do I have one?"

"For now, it's however you perceive God. Get that in your mind and then just ask: 'What's this about? What am I supposed to do?'"

"You want me to pray."

"Essentially. I want you to talk to God—whatever that means to you. That's acting as if. Act as if God's actually there. Don't wait for some magic hand to come down from above and move you around like a pawn. God doesn't play chess. God wants a relationship with you."

I fingered the rim of the coffee cup. "I don't know, Blaze. I don't know if God is ready for me."

Sam reached across the table and ran a finger along my cheek. "Jill, God's been waiting for you for a long time. I think I have some sense of what He feels."

He sat back and roamed the room with his eyes. I had to rub my hands on the front of my skirt because they were breaking out into a sweat.

"You are the most compelling woman I've ever known," he said finally.

I tried to laugh. "Compelling? Now there's one I haven't heard before."

"One what? You think that's a line?"

His eyes begged me to say no. There was a sincerity there I couldn't hurl another shard of sarcasm at. I shook my head.

"No, I believe you think that," I said.

"I don't just believe it—I know it." He grinned at me. "I don't understand it, but I know it."

Our smiles came together, clinking like glasses in a toast, and with it, the clear lines in my head wilted and bent and wrapped themselves around each other. All my neatly ordered compartments blurred into mushy masses. Walls caved in like melting snowbanks. There was nothing to separate me from the warm ache of looking at Sam Bakalis.

I let myself look.

EIGHTEEN

After we left Denny's that Saturday, I was no longer trying to nurture any denial about my feelings for Sam. I couldn't, because they were turning me into someone I didn't recognize.

But except for a brief chat with him on my cell phone when I was on my way to Hopewell Sunday afternoon, there was a sudden and complete silence on Sam's end. I didn't think about it much on Monday when I called him and he didn't answer at home or at his office. I did begin to wonder that afternoon when I called again and hadn't heard from him by two o'clock, when I knew he would be out of class.

I was leaving a message with the philosophy department secretary as Tabitha arrived at Mother's for her tutoring session. I'd forgotten to tell her we could resume meeting at the office now, and it had been working out so well at the house anyway.

"You okay?" Tabitha said.

"Yeah, yeah, I'm fine," I said.

"I wasn't, like, eavesdropping or anything, but I kinda heard you say Dr. Bakalis's name. I didn't know you knew Dr. B. Don't you just love him?"

I was glad I had my back to her as I hung up her coat. "You obviously know him."

"He's the advisor for our campus Christian group," she said. "Do you think he's cute?"

"Cute?" I was nearly choking. "I suppose you could call him attractive."

Tabitha giggled. "I think he's *adorable*. He's the kind of man I want to marry."

I turned to look at her and hoped my mouth wasn't falling open too far.

"So have you proposed?" I said.

Tabitha shrieked. "No! He's a little old for me." Her face was now red enough that I could no longer see her freckles. "But I hope when I'm ready to get married, I'll meet a guy my age like him. He actually told us in one of our small-group discussions that he will never marry a woman who isn't a Christian because he wants a marriage built on a solid foundation of God. Well, I can't put it exactly like he did, but it was something like that."

I was nodding, but I was clearly hearing Hercules saying, *Sammy wants a church lady.* It settled in my brain the way pancakes lay heavy in your stomach.

While she was getting herself organized at the coffee table in the living room where I currently had everything I owned strewn around, I said, "I assume you're going home for the holidays. Right?"

"Yeah, I leave in seven more days! I don't have it down to hours yet—I'll probably start that tomorrow."

"If you can calculate that, you can do calculus," I said. "Personally, I think you just have a mental block. You don't realize you're probably one of the brightest people in that class."

"Nuh-uh," she said, wide-eyed. "I just feel so dumb in there. All those boys who rattle off stuff just like that."

"They need to get lives," I said.

Tabitha giggled. I wanted to look in a mirror to make sure I hadn't switched identities. Had I just said that—that people needed to have something in their lives besides their academic pursuits? It was slightly scary.

We finally got settled, Tabitha with her usual bag of Doritos. We were only about halfway through the second problem when she looked around and said, "It doesn't feel the same without your mom here with us."

"Yeah," I said. "You don't have anybody competing for your chips."

"I liked to share with her," Tabitha said. "Made me feel like there was *something* I could do for her. Is she happy where she is now?"

"Who knows?" I said.

Tabitha nodded. Then her eyes went to the piano.

"That's so gorgeous," she said. "I bet it has an incredible sound."

"Oh, I forgot you told me you played," I said. "Try it out."

Her eyes bulged. "Are you sure? I mean, it's a baby grand."

"Yeah," I said, "but it's got eighty-eight keys, just like the rest of them. Go ahead. Play something."

I sat back on the couch and watched her approach the instrument as if she'd been summoned to the royal throne. Any second I expected her to prostrate herself at its pedals. She reverently lifted the cover from the keyboard and sat on the bench. When she started to play, I watched her, spellbound.

All at once, the living room was alive with scarlet sounds, and Tabitha herself was no longer the gawky freshman. Everything about her became charged with the vibrant electricity of a young woman embraced by the music. She eased a brilliance from the piano that I certainly had never achieved and had seen few other people do.

I hardly realized it when she stopped, until she shrugged and rocked her head side-to-side and giggled for no apparent reason. I watched the lanky, insecure kid return.

"All right, so tell me something," I said. "Why in the *heck* are you wasting your time on math? Tabitha, that was amazing. Do you have any idea what kind of talent you have?"

"It's all God," she said.

"But does God want you to waste it while you try to turn yourself into some math geek?"

She cocked her head at me. "You're not a math geek."

"Yes, I am. I was born to be a math geek. You were not."

She looked a little alarmed. "Do you mean you think I won't make it as a math major?"

"You'll get by. But you don't have a passion for it—not the kind of passion you have for playing Rachmaninoff."

"But that's just because I've taken lessons for so long. Calculus is all new to me."

I grunted. "No, I took lessons for ten years. My mother had to threaten me with house arrest to get me to practice. Today I could probably play you a nice version of 'Chopsticks.' I didn't love it the way you obviously do. I love math. You need to pursue what you have a passion for."

Tabitha left the piano bench and sat on the other end of the couch from me. She twisted her hair with her finger. "I told you before: My parents don't think music is what God wants me to do with my life."

"What is up with letting your parents decide the course of life for you?" I said. "I didn't let my mother dictate that to me—and believe me, she could dictate in her day. She'd give Mussolini a run for his money. She thought I was going to toddle along right behind her and go into medicine, but I didn't want to spend the rest of my life being compared to her, so I chose math."

Tabitha was nodding, leaning forward, studying my face with genuine interest. I'd never noticed that she listened like that—with more poise than when she talked herself.

"No offense or anything," she said, "but in a way you sort of, like, did let your mother determine what you were going to do with your life. I mean, you know, by rebelling against it."

I considered that. "In a twisted kind of way, I guess you're right."

"Not that that's bad," she said quickly. "You're the best math teacher I ever had. I think even though you did go into math because you were rebelling against your mom, it's still where God wants you to be."

"That's just a lucky coincidence, then," I said, "because I definitely didn't discuss it with God."

Tabitha stopped twirling her hair, and her eyes got wide. She was obviously having a "wow" moment.

"I just realized," she said, voice breathlessly husky. "I didn't really discuss it with God either. I mean, I talked to my parents about it and I kept praying, 'God, please let me follow their guidance,' but I never actually asked Him myself." She cocked her head at me. "How old were you when you stopped asking your mom about everything and started deciding for yourself?"

"I don't think I ever did stop," I said. "She just stopped answering."

"When was that?" Tabitha said.

I sighed. "About two months ago."

Tabitha giggled uncertainly, but I wasn't trying to be funny. I'd had my own sudden realization: two months ago my mother had ceased to be someone I fought hard against emulating and as a result had became identical to. When she had ceased to respond and give me a net I could bounce back from like an acrobat, my entire identity had been called into question. No wonder my life had been one big question ever since.

"So how do you determine the right path to take?" Tabitha said. "How would I know where God is leading me?"

I squirmed inwardly. With all of my own struggles and questions, where did I get off giving this child—this trusting, talented, good-hearted young woman—advice about anything?

But she was waiting for a response.

"This is what a friend of mine told me," I said finally. "Imagine in your mind what God is—how you perceive Him—and then talk to that. Ask the questions you've been asking me."

How exactly she was supposed to *hear* the answers that were allegedly going to come, I couldn't tell her. She seemed to know that, or at least, she didn't ask me. She simply beamed and then lunged across the space between us and hugged me.

"All right, look," I said, "why don't we rearrange your tutoring schedule so you can come here, instead of my office at Sloan, later in the afternoons. That way when we're through, you can play the piano."

"You're going to keep living here, then?" she said.

"Yeah. I don't know why—I'm just not ready to leave yet."

"This is great!" Tabitha practically squealed. "I love this!" And then she clapped—she actually clapped.

As I reached for Tabitha's calculus book, I thought, *I can't remember the last time I was so spontaneously happy that I burst into applause.* In fact, maybe I never had been.

The staff at Hopewell told me that I didn't *have* to visit Mother every day, and that my frequent visits might actually be keeping her from adjusting as quickly as she might. I followed that advice, but unfortunately, that gave me a little too much time to think— about how far behind I was in my work, about how empty the house seemed now even though Max still joined me for dinner most evenings, about how uneasy I'd become because Sam still hadn't called.

I didn't try calling him again. He obviously wasn't eager to talk to me or he'd have responded to the half-dozen messages I'd left on his home answering machine. By Friday afternoon, I was beating myself up for leaving even *one*. I must be coming across as pretty desperate and pathetic.

As hard as I tried—and I definitely tried, burying myself in K-theory computations—I couldn't help looking for a reason for Sam's abrupt silence.

That evening, I couldn't stand cross-examining myself any longer. I toyed with the idea of going over to Antonio's and seeing who was winning at darts, but what if I ran into Sam there—otherwise occupied? I grabbed my purse and took off for Hopewell. It was late, but even if Mother was in bed, I was sure they'd let me see her. Why I wanted to, I couldn't have said.

Only the hallway lights were on when I arrived, and I padded softly toward Mother's room, listening to the mutterings and the snoring and the deep, restless breathing that wafted out from behind the doors. I hesitated outside Mother's room, listening as I had so many times for the sounds of her sleep. All I heard was a frightened cry.

I shoved the door open and flipped on the light. The sides of her bed had been pulled up, and her hands were tied to them.

Several obscenities spewed out of my mouth as I literally threw my purse into a corner and began furiously untying the restraints.

"What the heck is this about?" I said. "Who did this?"

My mother was trembling, and her eyes clung to me, terrified. The minute I released her second hand, she tried to climb over the side railings. She did, in fact, get both arms over and threw them around my neck. She hung there, whimpering softly into my ear.

I put my own arms gingerly around her. Hugging my mother wasn't a thing that came naturally to me. But this wasn't my mother. This was a frightened child who'd been tied to a bed.

"Is there a problem?" someone said from the doorway.

"You better believe there's a problem!" I said.

But as I hurled those words over my shoulder at a woman with frosted hair and clipboard in hand, I could feel Mother's arms clenching me tighter and her heart pounding against my chest.

"Let me get her settled down," I said.

"I'll help—"

"No, it looks like you've all helped enough. Go—just leave me alone with her!"

The woman marched out, the intent to bring in backup etched on her face. I held my mother until she stopped shaking and peeled her arms from around my neck.

"Are you okay?" I said. "Are you hurt?"

She said nothing, so I examined her wrists myself. The restraints had been soft and obviously not fastened tightly, because there wasn't a mark on her. That made zero difference to me. The damage I imagined had been inflicted on her psyche was enough to send me into a rage. I was still raging—and only because Mother was calming down did I not pick her up and haul her out of there entirely.

Instead I carried her to her chair and wrapped a blanket around her. She leaned back and pointed a jerky finger at the window. I raised the blinds, and she gave a contented sigh and stared out into the dark. I crouched beside her.

"I'm going down to the nurses' station," I told her, "to find out what's going on here. You'll be okay?"

She didn't look at me, but I was sure she nodded.

I took off out the door and met Nurse Frosty Hair and a battalion of others halfway down the hall. I took them all on en masse.

"Why was my mother tied up?" I demanded, eyes raking them over one by one.

"She wasn't 'tied up,'" Frosty said. "We put her in restraints."

"I don't care what you call it. Why did you do it? I didn't sign anything giving you the authority to do that. There was nothing about this in the paperwork."

"You didn't read the fine print," one woman muttered, but Frosty silenced her with a hand.

"We don't usually have to restrain patients in the assisted-living area," she said, gently, as if she were talking to a child. "But it's the only way we can keep her in bed. She seems to be asleep and then the next thing you know, she's wandering the halls."

A short guy with a ponytail and a wrestler's build stepped up beside her, apparently to take care of her light work.

"Other patients were complaining," he said. "She was going into their rooms and standing over them while they were in bed.

Couple of people said they woke up and found her poking at their stomachs." He shook his head, ponytail wobbling. "We can't have that."

"And I can't have you tying her down like she's Charles Manson! She was terrified when I found her."

"You don't think the other patients were terrified when they opened their eyes and found her hovering over them?" Ponytail said.

"Why didn't you just lock her door? Or, better yet, why didn't you call me?"

"We don't call family members for every little thing."

"This is not 'every little thing'!" I said. "We *will* find another solution to this, or I'll take her out of here."

"Okay, okay—" Frosty said, her hand on Ponytail's arm, which was pumping up like a bicycle tire. "We'll try locking her door and see if that works."

"No more tying her down," I said. "Absolutely none. If there's any problem, you call me—any time, day or night. My cell phone number is on file."

I waited until every head finally nodded, however grudgingly, and they had all backed off toward the nurses' station. I saw more than heard the mutterings under the breath, the comments to each other. I couldn't have cared less if they'd been a flock of indignant pigeons. I went back to Mother's room. She was still in her chair.

"All right, this is the deal," I said, crouching once more beside her. "You can get out of bed, sit in your chair, look out the window—but you have to stay in this room at night. They're going to lock it, so don't even try the knob. I promise you this: They will never tie you to the bed again, all right? Are we clear?"

She just looked at me, and then suddenly bolted for the bed and crawled under the covers. I sank down into the chair beside it.

"You want me to talk until you fall asleep?" I said.

She closed her eyes, and I put my head on my arms on the

side of the bed. My heart had stopped racing like a freight train, but my mind was still going, thoughts careening off their tracks and colliding with every turn. I wanted Sam there.

"You're not going to believe this, Mother," I said, "but I met this guy. In fact, I met him at your anniversary dinner. He's a Ph.D. in philosophy—teaches at Stanford. We were seeing each other—well, sort of—and then, of course, he disappeared. You always said that about men, though, didn't you? You always told me to concentrate on my career—which I did until we started talking about some pretty intense things. Now brace yourself, Mother. We've been talking about God."

NINETEEN

By the time I got back to the house that night, it was after midnight. I should have been exhausted, but even after a hot bath, a glass of warm milk, and a bout with a couple of articles in *K-Theory*, my eyes refused to close. My body refused to even sit down. All I could do was pad around the house, pointlessly opening drawers, peering into closets, picking up items and putting them back down. Each shove of a drawer and slam of a door was louder and harsher then the one before it, until I shut the piano keyboard cover so hard the Steuben vase on top dropped over and rolled onto the floor, shattering into five-hundred-dollar shards of glass on the hardwood.

"Get a grip!" I said—to myself. "Just get ahold of yourself! My God!"

The word echoed in the room like a distorted version of Tabitha's Rachmaninoff. When it came back to me, it landed with a thud, somewhere in my chest.

"Okay, sorry," I said. "I'm sorry that I—what do you call it?— used Your name in vain. But I'm losing it here."

I definitely was. I was talking out loud to some invisible force I'd always denied was even there.

And yet it was somehow calming. No maniacal head-voice was screaming at me, telling me to get up and run around like a lunatic. Talking to no one had to be something of an improvement over that.

I pulled my legs up onto the bench and hugged my knees against the silence.

"Okay," I said, "so what do You look like? Let me get some kind of shape in my mind. Work with me here."

I closed my eyes. No, too dark in there—too many shadows. I stared up at the ceiling. The shape of God. I'd never even considered it.

So consider it now—before you lose your mind.

"All right, I'll tell You what I think You are," I said. "I think You're either some kind of cruel, heartless despot with a sadistic mind—or You just know a whole lot more than the rest of us do."

I narrowed my eyes at the ceiling. "You sit up there or out there or wherever it is You are, and You watch what's going on here. If You're so all-powerful, why can't You just cure my mother's disease? Why don't You swoop down and wipe out all this *stuff* that's been dumped on me that I can't handle? It's pretty obvious I can't handle it—I just took on eight people at once tonight. I don't know what to do, which is no wonder because I don't know what to *think* to begin with. Not with all this psychic pillage and plunder going on, which I can't deal with because I've never had to before. And now when I need to be clearheaded and rational, I'm turning into Tabitha Lane in a train wreck! I don't want to imagine a God who lets that happen! I want to imagine a God who cares about what's going on, who will come in here and untangle this miserable mess—because *I can't*. That's the kind of God I want You to be!"

I brought my fist down on top of the piano. Fragments of glass danced across it. I pulled my hand up to my mouth and pressed, but I couldn't hold back the weeping.

"Please be that kind of God," I said, "because I don't have it in me. I just don't."

Sometime later I stopped crying and picked my way amid the crystal slivers to the couch, where I think I talked myself to sleep.

It was after three in the morning when I woke up with the remnants of a dream already slipping away. All I could remember was the sight of my mother on all fours, knelt over Freda III, lifting her eyelids. I could almost hear Mother's pre-Pick's voice saying, *Pupils equal and reactive.*

I sat straight up on the couch. *Other patients were complaining,* Ponytail had said. *She was going into their rooms and standing over them while they were in bed. Couple of people said they woke up and found her poking at their stomachs.*

"That's it," I breathed. "That has to be it."

I was at Hopewell by seven, barely out of my pajamas, hair in a haphazard knot on top of my head. I wanted to see the night crew before they went off duty.

Ponytail didn't attempt to conceal his grimace when I walked up to the counter at the nurses' station.

"Yes, we kept her door locked all night," he said. "We unlocked it about fifteen minutes ago in case she wanted breakfast. Do you have a problem with that?"

"No," I said. "I appreciate your doing that and—"

I had to stop and choose my words carefully. This wasn't something I had done often.

"I need to apologize for last night," I said. "I was upset and I may have overreacted."

Ponytail smiled, probably in spite of himself. A heretofore hidden dimple appeared in his left cheek. "It happens," he said. "We possibly weren't as understanding as we should have been either."

I asked if it would be all right if I chatted with some of the patients Mother had made house calls to. While Ponytail was making a list, I peeked into her room.

She was already dressed, and Burl was with her.

"What are you doing here at this hour?" I said.

"I generally come by early in the mornings, right after I get off work. She likes to hear what's going on at the lab."

"Every morning?" I said.

"Pretty much. It's on my way home."

I thought he would probably have done it even if it meant a twenty-mile detour.

I spent a couple of hours interviewing four of the people on the list. Once they realized I was going to stay until I got the information I wanted, each one of them devised a way to drag out the story, branching off into all manner of unrelated topics, including their entire family history for several generations back. Finally, though, they got around to talking about Mother's night visits.

The first old guy showed me the arm Mother tried to examine. I tried not to react too strongly to the oozy-looking sores he uncovered when he pulled up his sleeve.

The next lady said Mother had yanked her covers back while she was sleeping, and she woke up to find herself being poked and pressed. When I questioned her about abdominal problems, she said that currently she was experiencing stomach pains the doctors couldn't seem to explain.

The other two residents related similar stories: One awoke to find she was having her pulse taken, the other to discover Mother's hands pressing his neck. He went on to describe his ongoing bouts with sore throats.

By noon, I was convinced of one thing—my mother hadn't just been wandering aimlessly through the halls to perform random acts of weirdness on her fellow assisted-livers. She was giving them free medical exams, based on the evidence she was picking up from her own observations.

It was a conclusion that was at the same time reassuring and chilling.

Mother slept most of the afternoon, despite the attendants' urgings to come join the rest of the gang for yoga, square dancing, and the afternoon movie. I hung around and waited for her to wake up while I figured out what I was going to say. When I found myself roaming around her room like a frenzied gerbil, I sat down in her chair at the window and muttered under my breath.

"Okay, God, so if this is You—and I'm just saying *if*—are You going to tell me what to do with all this? I'm grasping at straws here, and I hate that."

It suddenly occurred to me that it probably wasn't a good idea to be irreverent with God, just on the off chance that such a being did exist.

"Sorry," I whispered.

Talk about acting as if.

When Mother finally woke up, she bolted out of bed and came to stand next to me. She looked agitated until I got out of her chair and let her sit in it.

"I think I'm getting what you like about that thing," I said. "It kind of molds to you, doesn't it?"

She blinked placidly, and then faded off into sleep again. I crouched beside her. It was becoming my automatic position with her.

Had I conjured up the whole thing—about her examining patients as naturally as the rest of us breathed or swallowed? Was I actually starting to believe that she still had something of herself left, or did I just want so much for it to be true that I was looking for reasons to think that it was? Maybe that was what people did when they said they believed in God.

A deep ache took shape in my chest. That was a question for Sam.

I left at suppertime and went home to attempt to get some work done. What was left of my rational side told me I needed to return to the real world before it got away from me completely. However, the minute I propped up on the couch with a pencil in my hand, I nodded off. I was pulled from sleep by a faraway rapping that seemed to get closer as I peeled my eyes open. Somebody was knocking on the front door.

"Hold on," I said thickly. I staggered to the foyer and fumbled for the doorknob. When I finally got the door yanked open, Sam was standing there. Hands in pockets. Face frozen in an uncertain smile.

"Hey, you," he said.

Later, I was able to convince myself that if I'd been wide awake, I would have slammed the door in his face and let that be the end of it. Only because I was just semiconscious did I first gape like a runny-nosed toddler and then let him in.

In that same self-deceptive conversation, however, I did give Sam credit for not trying to take advantage of my near-catatonic state. There was no reach to hold me, no attempt to kiss me. He just stood there in the foyer with his hands in his pockets and said, "I wasn't sure you'd let me in. I wouldn't really blame you if you didn't."

"Why wouldn't I?" I said. Some reactions just kick in automatically, no matter how porridge-headed you are.

He rubbed the back of his neck. "Because I haven't called you in a week for no apparent reason."

"Has it been that long?" I said.

His eyes flinched. It ached in me, and I turned and went into the living room. He followed.

"I know I don't have any right to ask this," Sam said, "but could we not play games here?"

I had my back to him as I sank one knee onto the couch. I could feel him behind me, not crowding me, but with no intention of backing off either.

"Okay," I said. "You didn't call me for a week and I was at a loss for a reason. I mean, the last I heard, I was compelling."

That remark stung even me. I turned around in time to catch him wincing.

"I'm sorry," I said. "You caught me at a bad time. No, that's a lie. Seems like it's *always* a bad time with me these days."

He shook his head.

"Yeah," I said, "I'm ticked off that you dropped out of sight—

you insensitive, arrogant pig—and you'd better have a good reason or you are out of here, because I didn't let you in just to have
you do your little tap dance on my—"

I needed to say *feelings*, but I couldn't. Evidently I didn't have
to, because Sam was grinning at me. He was trying not to—but
he was flunking.

"What?" I said. "What is so funny?"

"Nothing's funny. I just missed you."

"Yeah, right," I said in my best sarcastic tone. I glanced at my
watch, fighting back a smile. "You have exactly ten minutes to tell
me a story that doesn't force me to boot you out of here."

He nodded at the couch.

"No, I'm going to make you tell it standing up, face to the
wall…of course, sit down—you're driving me nuts standing there."

I dumped my papers onto the floor with a sweep of my arm
and tucked myself into a corner of the couch. Sam plopped down
at the opposite end.

"I had to go out of town," he said.

"Something sudden, I take it."

"No, I knew about it several weeks ahead of time."

The ache in my chest nudged me to tighten up. "Look, there's
no reason why you should have told me you were going off someplace. It's not like we have some commitment."

"*I* have a commitment."

"Not to me."

"To myself—to be available to you while you're sorting things
through. I shouldn't have just dropped out of sight without some
kind of explanation, and I'm sorry."

I felt a rising disappointment. I tried to rake it out with a
hand through the hair.

"I managed to keep sorting," I said.

"I'm sure you did."

He rubbed the back of his neck. We were definitely a pair to
draw to.

"All right," I said, "go ahead."

"I went to Illinois."

"In December. Good call," I said. Then I put up my hand. "Sorry. Go on."

"You've heard of Wheaton College—maybe not, it's a Christian school. There's a department chairmanship open there, and I applied for it. I made the short list, and they flew me out for an interview. It went well, so I stayed a few extra days to really look the place over. 'Course, I nearly froze my tail off back there."

I was staring at him. "Let me get this straight," I said. "You're on the faculty at one of the most prestigious universities in the world, but you're considering taking a job at some—" I stopped myself. "At a small college that's only going to offer you one thing you can't get here—a frozen tail."

Sam shook his head. "They have a lot more to offer than that, at least in my view. I haven't been happy here since day one. Okay, maybe day two. On day one I enjoyed the prestige thing, but that wore off once I realized Stanford isn't a good fit for me. It's an incredible university but—you'll find this out once you get your degree and start interviewing—it isn't about the university name or even the money. It's about the fit." He was leaning toward me. "I've got a soul-longing," he said. "I want to teach in a place where I have a chance to see the divine fire in my colleagues, and I'm not going to see that here—not out in the open, not where it can move me along on my own spiritual journey. Is this making sense to you?"

"Nothing you say makes sense to me, Blaze," I said dryly. "But I can see how it makes sense to you. That's what matters, right?"

"Not entirely. Listen, I have to know this: Do you think I was being dishonest with you because I didn't tell you about my job opportunity? I mean, I've been thinking about it since before we met. It's not like it came out of the blue. I had plenty of chances to tell you."

"No," I said. "Now, if at some point I had said, 'Gee, Blaze, I guess you're set here for life, huh?' and you'd just said, 'Yeah, I have no plans to move elsewhere,' then, yes, I would've said you weren't honest. Not that it's any of my business—"

"But it *is* your business. At least, I want it to be your business."

He picked up one of my hands and kneaded it between his. It was another one of those firm holds I couldn't have gotten out of if I'd tried—and I didn't try.

"Up until the day before I left, I didn't think there was any reason to tell you. We were focusing on you. But then it all happened at once—at least for me."

Did I miss it? I wanted to say. But I knew that came from old habits. Something else, something new and deep, told me to shut up and nod.

"We were sitting in Denny's," he said, "and I saw it all in one piece: you so close to touching God, and me so close to touching you, really touching you."

I did pull my hand back then. "This was some goal you had?"

"No," he said. "It was something that happened in spite of my goal—which was to keep myself from falling in love with you."

"Oh," I said—eloquently.

Sam put his hand on the back of my neck and pulled me up to his face. "I love you, Jill," he said.

I didn't have to answer him. I told him in the kiss.

He pulled away just far enough to look at me. "Okay, let me just say this," he said. "If they offered me the job at Wheaton and I accepted, would you think about going with me?" He put a finger to my lips, which had already started moving. "It wouldn't be until June, and by then you'll be finished with your degree. I'm just planting a seed. There are a lot of ifs involved anyway, but can you even think about it?"

It was as if my mouth were frozen. I did manage to get out: "Is this a marriage proposal?"

"I just know I liked everything about Wheaton except that you weren't there."

"So—you're asking me to—do what?"

"I'm just telling you how I feel and asking you to think about it. That's all."

I gave him a numb nod, and he grinned—like a kid grins when his mom has said "maybe."

"Okay," he said. "Let's just put that on the back burner for now. I want to hear about you."

"Not so fast, Blaze," I said. "I still don't get why you didn't tell me about this when we talked before you left. Or why you didn't call me from there. Why all the secrecy?"

The grin faded. He looked more somber than I had ever seen him.

"Because I was scared to death of what you'd say. I'm still scared." He touched my cheek. "I want you in my life."

The questions lined up in my head, jostling for position. *I thought you wanted a church lady, Blaze. What happened to that? You want me to go find a teaching position in Podunk, Illinois, so I can be close to you even though you can't even define our relationship? You think you're the only one who has ifs?*

But I suddenly hated all of those questions, and I hated the fact that they had even entered my head. This man who was earnestly searching my face with his eyes—this man didn't deserve to have any of those questions hurled at him.

"What are you thinking?" Sam said. "Or should I ask?"

"I'm thinking…I want to tell you what's happened with my mother."

"Tell me," he said. He looked longingly in the direction of the kitchen. "You got any Max meals we could thaw out while we're talking? I haven't eaten all day."

While I warmed up the last of the cappellacci with meat sauce in the microwave, I filled Sam in. The more I talked, the more of it came to me.

After putting the plate down in front of him, I sank into the chair opposite him, another entire piece forming in my head.

"What?" he said.

"Do you think she's still trying to practice medicine?"

"It sounds like it."

"But do you think that's just an automatic reflex on her part? If I had Pick's, I might write equations on the walls. If you had it, you might still…"

He laughed. "Yeah, just exactly what is it that I do, anyway?"

"The point is, when people have dementia, do they keep doing what they did for a while, just out of habit?"

"Did you read anything about that in the literature?"

I shook my head. "Besides that, Mother hasn't actually seen patients for twenty-some years, except for looking at my sore throats and saying, 'You'll live. Go to school.'"

"So you're saying this wouldn't be a habit."

"Not unless her brain's going back to when she was in med school or something."

Sam watched me as he chewed. Then he said, "I hear another possibility in there somewhere. It could just be habit. Or—?"

"Or she's consciously clinging to her mind."

"Or?"

"Or her soul," I said. I put a hand up. "Don't start doing your little end zone dance, Blaze. I'm just considering it as a possibility. *If* she has a soul that's going to transcend everything—death, dementia, disease, whatever—then that's where her drive to heal and preserve life could possibly be. Just possibly." I shook my head. "But then I think about her trying to flush her nylons down the toilet and I'm not so sure."

"Yeah, well, I'm voting that not only is she clinging to her soul, but she's trying to tell *you* she still has a soul." Sam put down his fork and leaned toward me. "Let me just put this out there: Maybe your mother is taking Pascal up on his wager."

"If you had known my mother when she was in her right mind, you wouldn't even suggest that."

The grin went earlobe to earlobe. "I know you in your right

mind, and you took him up on it. I don't see a big difference here."

"I can't believe I listen to some of the stuff you hand me, Blaze," I said, grinning back at him.

TWENTY

The next week was the start of winter break, and I had never been so glad to see it come. Without classes to teach and office hours to squeeze in and Jacoboni to listen to, I could concentrate on my own work…and on Mother… and on Sam.

Seeing that my life was still overloaded even without classes in session was an eye-opener, and I found myself discussing that with the ceiling on a regular basis. Sam called it praying, a point I continued to argue.

"It might be saving my sanity," I told him, "but that's all I'm willing to concede right now."

"That's okay," he said. "We'll wait."

"You and who else?" I said.

He just gave me his grin and melted me down another ounce.

I did nothing for Christmas except buy a gallon jug of extra-virgin olive oil for Max, a goldfish in a bowl for Mother, and a sweatshirt with the word *Blaze* on it for Sam. He gave me a leather-bound copy of the *Pensées* by Pascal and taught me to pronounce it to rhyme with "Chauncy."

Hopewell had a bash Christmas Day, complete with several sets of carolers from various churches, a visit from Santa Claus—who turned out to be Ponytail in a very bad fake beard—and a dinner that I had to admit even Max would have eaten. Mother poured gravy over her entire plate and then ate nothing, and she didn't seem to know what to do with the wrapped gift from

Hopewell, which was put in her lap. But she did watch the goldfish I brought her with more attention than I'd seen her give anything else in a while.

"I know it's not your koi pond," I said to her, "but it's as close as I could get. Just promise me you won't pull it out and try to dissect it, okay?"

I went to see her every day, and from all accounts there were no more nighttime house calls to other patients. Frosty—whose name was actually Emily Murphy—said every time they checked on Mother, she was either sleeping, sitting in her chair staring out the window, or watching her goldfish. She advised me not to leave the fish food in her room, lest the poor little thing should bloat up and explode.

Sam and I continued our lively debates, and many of them sprang from what I was reading in *Pensées*.

"Pascal was a freak," I told Sam on one occasion. "That whole 'night of fire' thing—do you think that really happened to him?"

"Nobody can know that for sure."

"I didn't ask if anybody knows. I'm asking if *you* think it did."

Sam nodded. "Yeah, I think it did."

"But it's never happened to you."

"Not that exact experience, no. It's different for everybody. C. S. Lewis said that the day he climbed into the sidecar on his brother's motorcycle, he was still an atheist. When he climbed out at the end of the ride, he was a believer."

"Must have been some ride."

"It's definitely a ride, no matter how it happens." He looked at me, eyes twinkling. "Don't you feel like you're on a ride?"

"Yeah, on a roller coaster, which can stop anytime now, thank you."

"Nah, you don't want it to stop."

"The heck I don't!"

"No, you'd miss the best part."

"And this is about to come."

"It comes to everybody who seeks God, and you're seeking. It comes in different ways, like I said, but a seeker always eventually feels the joy—and the tears—and it becomes concrete, specific." He was molding his fingers around an invisible shape. "You will have an experience where what you've been skirting around and questioning and doubting will become *definite*. It'll be a different *experience* of Christ—the living God—but it'll be the same Christ."

Another night I told him, with disgust, that I had come to the "licking the earth" section in *Pensées*.

"According to Blaze Senior—" I said.

"I'm Blaze Junior now?" he said.

"Yes."

"Just checking. Go on."

"According to him, we're supposed to despise ourselves. No, thank you."

"You didn't read the whole thing. Let me see your copy."

I looked at him across the table at the Rose and Crown. "I don't carry it around with me."

"Okay, lemme see if I can remember—"

It was times like that, when his Chicago blue-collar upbringing slipped into his speech, that I loved him the most. He was so very real.

"I think it goes, 'We are to despise *ourselves* because we have chosen not to fulfill our capacity for good, but we are not to despise our *souls* which *have* that capacity.'"

"You're saying if we listened to our souls instead of ourselves, we'd be better people," I said.

"Right. Better people who are better able to make good choices."

"But that's only if there's a difference between our souls and ourselves."

"Good."

"Thank you. So which is which?"

"Let's use your mother as an example. We can all see that her 'self' is virtually gone—the self you knew because that was the self she chose to show."

"I'm with you so far," I said.

"But the jury is still out, at least in your mind, on whether she's left with a soul that can still feel and intuit and know things like love and respect."

"So if there is a soul that goes beyond death and dementia, blah, blah, blah, that's what it is."

"Right."

"So it would behoove me to treat her with love and respect, as part of my taking the wager."

He grinned, but the grin faded as he watched my face.

"What's wrong?" he said.

I pushed my club soda away from me. "I don't think I know *how* to treat her with love and respect. I never did before."

"Come on, of course you did. I saw you that night I was over at the house. You treated her with the utmost respect."

"No, that was fear," I said. "The only two emotions I have ever felt toward my mother are fear and anger. I never showed her disrespect because I was scared to death of her. And then I'd go away completely livid with myself for *being* afraid of her."

"That's what your *self* felt," Sam said. "Now you can look at what your *soul* felt. Deep down in there, what did you *want* to feel for your mother?"

I pulled the club soda back to me and stirred it with the straw. "I get the picture. We don't have to pursue this."

"You're scared."

"No, I'm not."

"Then there's some other reason you're slopping your drink all over the table." He took the straw out of my hand. "It's your soul that's scared. Look at it. It's terrified that you're going to lose your mother completely because you love her."

"That's where you're wrong," I said. "I've heard people say, 'I

love my parents because they're my parents, but I don't like them.'
I don't buy that. If I didn't like my mother—which I didn't—how
could I possibly love her? She molded me and shaped me into
what she wanted me to be. Then when I showed any deviation
from her design, she criticized me into wanting to be anything
but what she wanted me to be. And as a result, I'm just like her.
Hey, so I guess old Blaze was right—I do despise myself."

"And your mother's self."

"Yeah."

"But not your soul—and not hers." Sam put his hand on the
back of my neck and pulled me closer to him. "So deal with her
soul to soul," he said. "Treat her the way you always wanted to
when you were a kid."

"Sit in her lap?"

"She wouldn't let you do that when you were little?"

"No," I said. "Not that I can remember."

He let go of me and watched me closely. "What else?"

"I don't know."

"Yes, you do."

"You irritating *man!*"

"Yeah," he said. "That's me all over. Come on, spill your
guts."

That was just the point. It *was* like spilling my guts—bringing
up the stuff that had been festering and fermenting in me since I
was six years old. Bringing it out would be like throwing up, and
I hated to throw up. I would rather suffer the stomachache of the
century for hours than upchuck once and get it over with. My
mother had told me every time I was nauseous that if I would just
let it go, I would feel better.

"I wanted her to let me brush her hair," I said. "She has great
hair and all I wanted to do was brush it while we were practicing
my French verb conjugations."

"French verb conjugations?" Sam said. "How old were you?"

"I was about seven when I stopped asking her."

"And she never let you."

"No. Nor did she want me 'hanging all over her' in public, licking her ice cream cone—excuse me, frozen yogurt—or giggling when I crawled in bed with her. It wasn't long before she didn't want me crawling in bed with her at all."

I stopped and looked at Sam.

"I'm sorry," he said.

"I don't want a pity party, Blaze. Nor do I want any, 'Then no wonder you're a cold fish—'"

"Stop it," he said.

I did, because his voice was sharp.

"You are anything but a cold fish," he said. "I couldn't love a woman who didn't have a soul that burned into mine."

"Why, Blaze," I said, "how poetic of you."

It came out without the sarcasm, and I was glad.

Tabitha—and the rest of the students—returned to campus a few days after New Year's. She popped into my office the first day of classes to bemoan the fact that she wasn't taking a course from me that quarter.

"That's because I'm not teaching one this quarter," I said.

"And because I'm not taking any math this quarter."

"Bad choice," I said. "You should be taking courses in your major every quarter."

"Math's not my major anymore."

Every freckle was shining.

"What about your parents?" I said.

"They're letting me be undeclared until next fall so I can, you know, explore other possibilities."

If I had had freckles, mine would have been glowing, too.

"I'm impressed," I said. "How did you swing that?"

"After that talk you and I had, over at your mom's house that one day, I prayed about it a lot and then when I got home I just sat down with them and I go, 'I'm not happy in math and I don't think that's where God wants me.' They were, like, still kind of 'We don't think so,' but then when I told them about what you said—"

"Time out," I said. "You were quoting me? To your Christian parents?"

"Yeah. Anyway, when I was telling them about you and your mom and how you were still helping me even though you already had so much to deal with, and that you weren't just helping me with math, but with, like, life decisions, that's what got them. They said you were sent by God."

I steeled myself for the laughter that was sure to come roaring out of my throat and the sarcastic remark that would follow, but all I said was, "Pretty hard to believe."

"Believe it," she said. "So I don't have to take any more math, and I'm already happier. The only thing is, I won't see you. I mean, there's no reason for you to tutor me, so…"

She looked so glum, I did laugh. "You totally crack me up, Tabitha," I said. "First you moan and groan like somebody's torturing you because you *need* tutoring. Now you're pouting because you don't."

"I'll miss you," she said.

"I'll be right here. You can stop in."

"Oh, like I'm gonna stop in when you barely had time to see me before when you had to."

"Actually," I said, "I never *had to*. I could have pawned you off on a second- or third-year grad student."

She did that back-and-forth thing with her head that she always did when she was halfway embarrassed.

"I tell you what," I said. "I do want you to come over to the house, maybe one night this week. There's somebody I think you should meet. Come for dinner."

"Really?" she said.

"Yeah, come tomorrow night. Do you like Italian food?"

"So I'm having this little dinner party," I told my mother that evening as I sat in her room, brushing her hair while she stared out the window. "Interesting combination of people. You always liked to do that at your dinner parties—put unlikely people next to each other and watch the sparks fly. Anyway, I'm having Max, of course. Like *I'm* going to cook? And Sam—he's the guy I told you about. And Tabitha Lane. You used to eat her chips, remember? I want Max to hear her play the piano. You'd love it. Remember that Rachmaninoff piece I was trying to learn my senior year—that C-minor thing that sounded like aluminum cans going around in the dryer when I played it? She plays it and it's exquisite."

I stopped and crouched beside my mother to see her face. For a flash of a moment, something bright flickered through her eyes, and something unexpected flickered through my mind.

"Is God in there, Mother?" I said.

She didn't answer that. But she didn't say no.

I didn't tell Tabitha who Max was, nor did I tell Max about her talent. I just let him think he was cooking dinner as usual, only there would be two extra people. Of course, "dinner as usual" for Max meant tortellini filled with Swiss chard for the first course, roasted lamb with juniper berries for the second, and glazed semolina pudding for dessert.

From the look on Tabitha's face when she sat down at the table, I was pretty sure they didn't eat like that in Idaho. She did it justice, however, in spite of the fact that she was sitting across from Sam, who made her blush about every two minutes just by grinning at her. I had resisted the temptation to tell him she had a crush on him. It had, in fact, been a semi-shock to me when I realized that I didn't want to betray her trust.

We took our coffee—espresso so rich both Tabitha and I loaded it up with cream—into the living room. I lifted Tabitha's cup from her hand and said, "Would you play something for us?"

Her eyes went immediately to Sam. "Does anybody really want to hear me play?"

"Absolutely!" Sam said to her. "Don't I go nuts every time you play the Pharaoh Boogie or whatever that thing is?"

She darted to the piano as if she were going to plunk out said "Boogie," but I said quickly, "Play that Rachmaninoff piece you played for me a while back."

"Oh," she said. This time she looked doubtfully at Max. "I don't know if you'll like it. It's kind of, like, you know, heavy and dramatic."

Max was sitting up slowly in his chair.

"Go ahead," I said. "Max is into heavy and dramatic."

Tabitha played the piece for us, and just as before, the moment her fingers touched the keys she was poised, in control, self-confident. I glanced at Max a few times and saw that he had the same expression as he used to when he and my mother would spend an evening listening to Puccini's *Turandot* and moaning at intervals in some kind of ethereal angst. But most of the time my eyes were still on Tabitha. Even more than before, there was passion in the chords that crashed under her fingertips, as if she herself were being transformed by playing them.

We're seeing her soul, I thought.

It was a thought against type, and I looked inward to scoff at it. But all I saw in myself was a deep appreciation for something beautiful that I didn't want to chase away with my sarcasm. I closed my eyes and listened to her play.

No one said anything when she was finished—not until Max got to his feet as if he were at the Met and shouted, "Bravo!" as he clapped. That nearly did poor Tabitha in. She turned red down to the quicks of her fingernails. Max polished her off by saying, "Why aren't you in the music school, my dear? With a gift like that, how dare you hide it? This must be honed!"

He went on *ad nauseam* while Sam and I exchanged proud looks. For a moment there, I felt positively parental.

The relative peace in my personal life—relative only to the few preceding months—was not duplicated in my academic world. It was ironic that it seemed more separate from the rest of my life now than it had ever been when I was trying to keep it apart. The sense of separation had nothing to do with any time-management skill or mental compartmentalizing on my part. It was simply that the world of math seemed to have no connection to anything else.

Jacoboni returned from winter break with renewed confidence in his own charm. That always happened when he spent any significant time with his "Muthah" down in Tennessee. The first day I saw him, he pulled me into a bear hug, and I had to wrestle to break free. He wasn't cowed, however, and proceeded to tell me how much work he'd gotten done at home in spite of the many young women who just couldn't seem to leave him alone.

"I needed to get back here so I'd stop partying so much," he said.

"Are you still in your grandfather's will?" I said.

"Of course."

"Then you didn't party *that* much."

I sat down to check my e-mail and was all the way to "You have mail" before I realized he was still staring at me.

"What?" I said.

"Something's different," he said. "Did you do something to your hair? No, that's not it. Different makeup? No, you don't even wear makeup."

"Doing a full inventory, Jacoboni?" I said.

He put one hand in his pocket and gestured with the other one, trying to illustrate some concept he couldn't quite grasp. "I don't know. I think it's your voice."

"You did party too much. Go get some coffee."

"No, that's definitely it, darlin'. Your voice is different. I think it's softer."

"I'll tell you what's softer," I said. "Your brain. Go get some coffee, and get me some, too, would you?"

He left still convincing himself that I'd had a laryngeal transplant over winter break.

Later that day, I had my first meeting with Nigel in several weeks. I'd made some progress over break, but nothing like the quantum leap I'd assured him was going to happen. When I sat down across from him, he looked at me over the top of the progress report and frowned.

"You still have a long way to go," he said.

"I know. But now that I have my mother settled into a…well, now that my personal life isn't quite so chaotic, I can focus more. Not having any other responsibilities here this quarter, I should be able to make better progress."

Nigel took off his glasses. "I know about your mother, Jill. I'm not one for listening to talk about people's personal affairs, but I couldn't help but hear. I'm sorry."

I nodded. I didn't feel angry that a boundary had been violated. It was just that Nigel's talking about it seemed surreal.

"You're a bright young woman," Nigel said suddenly. "When it comes to math, you border on brilliant. You have a future in mathematics. But no one, not even the rare genius among us, can fix herself on her work when a part of her world has been torn apart."

The look in his eyes was almost stern. If I had known what fatherly was, I might have described it that way.

"I wish you had trusted me enough to tell me, Jill," he said. "I could have helped. I still can."

I didn't know what to say. That kind of tenderness ached in me, just the way it did with Sam, and I didn't know what to do with it. I found myself looking at the ceiling.

"Thank you," I finally said to Nigel. "But I'm not ready to abandon this now—or even put it aside. I have to finish this, and I have to finish it on time."

Slowly and deliberately, Nigel crossed one leg over the other. I waited.

"May I ask you a personal question?" he said.

I was surprised, but I nodded.

"Did—does—I don't know quite the way to say it…. Did your mother want very much for you to get your doctorate?"

"It wasn't a matter of *want*," I said. "She *expected* it. If you're asking me whether I'm doing this out of guilt or something—"

Nigel was shaking his head. "No, no, I'm not asking that. I wouldn't presume to pry."

He ought to talk to Sam, I thought. I remembered then that Sam had said he and Nigel were friends—that they prayed together over breakfast or something.

"But if I may," Nigel said, "I would just like to share with you the parental point of view."

I was even more surprised. "Sure."

"I have two sons—grown, of course," he said. "They've both done well, and I'm very proud of them. But should the time ever come when I'm unable to take care of myself, it won't be their accomplishments I'll want. I'll want their love and their support. If that meant making sacrifices for me, I would hope they would make their choices based on love, not on what I expected of them, one way or the other."

But your children love you! I wanted to tell him. *I don't love my mother. It's taking everything I have to act like I do! Good grief, Nigel, I lick the earth, for Pete's sake!*

He put his glasses back on. "I have discovered by way of a very circuitous route never to give advice, only to share what works best in my own life."

"Thank you," I said.

I started to get up, but I couldn't, not yet.

"Dr. Frost," I said. "I understand you may be a praying man."

It was Nigel's turn to look surprised. His glasses, in fact, slid straight down his nose, and he had to catch them before they tumbled to the desktop.

"I am," he said. "Though that's not the kind of thing that usually comes down the grapevine."

"We have a mutual friend," I said.

The corners of his lips twitched. "Would that be God?"

"That I don't know yet," I said. "But until the theory is disproven, would you pray for me? I mean, not here—but, I mean, when you do—pray—whenever that is—"

I was on the verge of sounding like Porky Pig. Before my stuttering led to a "That's all, folks!" I stood up. As I did, Nigel smiled.

"Your request comes a little late, Jill," he said. "I've been praying for you for two years."

Prayers notwithstanding, I was stressed that night when I saw Sam. I told him the whole dissertation thing was no longer a goal at the end of a long, straight road, that it was a veritable mammatocumulus hanging over my head.

"A *what?*" Sam said.

"It's a severe thunderstorm cloud," I said. "My mother made me learn the proper names for everything. I couldn't even say I had the flu. It had to be *influenza.*"

"Okay, that's it," Sam said. "You are suffering from a lifetime fun deficit. I am taking you to the city this Saturday, and we are going to put on the dog."

"The dog?"

"Just wear your walkin' shoes. We got places to go and things to do."

"You left out 'people to see.'"

"No people to see. Just me."

Saturday was perfect, because Hopewell was taking the assisted-living residents on a field trip to some function on campus. Sam and I drove to San Francisco that Saturday in Sam's little Jeep-wannabe vehicle with an old Phil Collins CD blasting away on the stereo.

"Your taste is all in your mouth, Blaze," I shouted over the din. "Don't you have any jazz?"

"No way. I listen to no music that sounds like it's being made up as it goes along."

We did, however, make up the *rest* of the day as we went along. We hung off the side of a cable car going up Powell Street—something Mother had never let me do, having seen too many mangled bodies in her med school emergency room days. We walked Fisherman's Wharf, ducked into several of the art galleries that had sprung up here and there between the T-shirt and souvenir shops, and ate crab drowning in cocktail sauce out of paper cups.

"This makes me want more," Sam said. "I know a great place where we can get Alaska king crab. It shouldn't be too crowded this time of day. We can probably get a table by the window."

I was already stuffed from our visit to Ghirardelli Square with its chocolate at every turn, plus the several hunks of Boudin's sourdough bread I'd consumed while standing in line for the cable cars. But I had a club soda while I watched Sam dig into a platter of crab legs like it was some kind of peak experience and finally accepted a couple of butter-dipped fillets from his fingers. With it—with the essence of the whole day—came my first taste of real contentment.

Perhaps it was good that Sam chose that moment to announce, "I've been offered the job at Wheaton."

I stopped, midway through licking my fingers.

"Are you going to accept it?" I said.

"It depends," he said. "I have some time to think about it and pray about it."

"What does it depend on?" I said.

He didn't have a chance to answer. My cell phone rang. I glared at it.

"I have to answer it," I said. "I told the staff at Hopewell to call me if there was a problem."

"Answer it," Sam said. "I'm not going anywhere."

"This is Jill McGavock," I said into the phone.

The voice on the other end said with barely disguised panic, "Jill, this is Monique. It's your mother—she's missing."

TWENTY-ONE

I was halfway out of the car before Sam even pulled it to a stop in front of the campus security building, where Monique had told us to meet her. Mother had wandered away from the group during the field trip, and Monique had assured me she was probably still on campus.

But I could see Monique through the front window, talking on her cell phone, and the look on her face didn't foreshadow good news. Even as I marched myself toward the door, the cold fear cut me off at the knees. There was nothing left in me to shout at her when she set down her phone and came to me.

"Still no sign of her," she said. "But Jill, she was separated from the group for only ten minutes at the most before they discovered she was missing. She couldn't have gone far."

"How long ago was that, though?" Sam said behind me.

Monique pressed her lips together and then said, "A good hour."

Sam put both hands on my shoulders as if he thought I was going to lunge at her, but I didn't move. I put my hands in my hair and tried to think.

"We should call Max," I said.

Sam took the phone from me.

"He'll probably know some places she might have gone," I said to Monique.

Her face went soft. "Jill, I don't think she went anywhere consciously. I think she just drifted off."

"That's okay, " I said. "I just have to look for myself."

I went for the door with Sam on my heels.

"Jill, we have plenty of people on this," Monique called after me.

"Now you have more," I said.

When we were outside, Sam covered the cell phone with his hand. "Max wants to know what we want him to do," he said. "He's pretty upset."

I took the phone and tried to calm down. If Max was already having a breakdown, my joining him in one was only going to make matters worse—and they were bad enough as it was.

"Max," I said, "do you have any idea where Mother would go if she were free to wander around campus? Do you think she'd go to the Rodin garden? You hung out with her here more than I did."

"The music school," he said. His voice sounded old and frightened.

"Really?" I said.

"I can meet you there in five minutes," he said and hung up.

I know the look I gave Sam was bordering on panic. "I think he's losing it. He says she might have gone to the music school. Why would she do that?"

Sam took my arm and headed east. I scoured every inch with my eyes along the way. No sign of my mother.

Max was already standing in front of Braun Music Center when we got there. His entire face was trembling. I took hold of him by both bearlike shoulders.

"We are going to find her," I said. "We just have to think this through. Why do you think she might be here?"

He shook his head. "She's not. I just looked."

I glanced up at the three-story building. "You went through the whole place already?"

"I looked in the rehearsal room where the chamber orchestra practices. That's the only place she would go. Jill, have we lost her?"

"Why the heck would she—?" I stopped and forced myself to take a deep breath. "Okay, let's stay focused. You only looked in that one room?"

Max gave an agonized nod.

"Maybe she had the idea of going there but couldn't find her way. That could be right, huh?" I turned to look at Sam. He was already headed for the front door.

"Let's spread out," he said over his shoulder. "Ask if anybody's seen her."

Looking not much better than Mother herself probably did at that point, Max nodded again and moved toward the door.

"We'll *find* her," I reassured him again. "Don't give up on me now."

He shook his head and lumbered off to the left. I tore up the stairs to search the third floor.

Since it was Saturday, the narrow hall was empty and quiet except for a few random pianos and the tangle of notes that seeped out of the sparsely occupied practice rooms.

I poked my head and my questions into the occupied ones, but nobody had seen Mother. Nor was she in any of the lounges along the way.

I was standing in one of those lounges, looking around frantically, when I heard Sam calling me from below. I leaned over the stairway railing.

"Come on down," Sam said. "Max has a lead."

I flew down the stairs, and Sam met me. "Somebody down in the music library told Max she saw a woman that fit your mom's description wandering through here about forty-five minutes ago. Lady said she asked if she could help her, but the woman just turned around and walked out."

"Did she say where she went?" I said.

"She left the building," Sam said. "The woman thought it was a little strange so she watched her, and she did go out the front door."

I was already half running down the hall with Sam right beside me.

"At least we know she was here," he said. "So you were right. She's going to places that are familiar to her."

"I still don't know why she'd come here. Okay, forget that. Where else?"

Max was at the front door, his face ashen. "She was here, Jill," he said. "She was looking for the chamber orchestra, I know it. She used to come in when we were rehearsing and I would let her conduct sometimes. She had a passion for the music. You should have seen her face—"

I put a hand on Max's arm. "So where else would she go that was familiar to her? You obviously have all the secrets."

Max looked at me helplessly. It was Sam who said, "I don't think it's necessarily a secret. What about the lab?"

"All the way over at the medical center?" Max said. "Could she get that far?"

"She got *this* far," Sam said. "We can at least go rule it out."

I dug in my bag and handed Sam the phone. "Call the lab and ask them to watch for her. Tell them not to let her leave if they see her—but not to call security and not to try to restrain her. If they just keep talking to her, she'll probably stay. The number's already logged into the phone."

"Got it," Sam said. "Max, let's take your car."

After Sam spoke to the people at the lab, none of us said a word on the way to the hospital. Max was too busy driving like he was going for the Winston Cup. Sam and I had our faces practically pressed to the windows, watching for Mother. The crowd was thinner than it would have been on a weekday. It would have been easy to spot her even in the fading light, but she wasn't there.

Please, please, please, I thought. *Just let her be at the lab. Let her be all right. Please.*

It was dusk by then and outside lights were winking on even

as Max pulled in through the circular drive and let Sam and me out.

"I'll be there as soon as I park," Max said. "Just tell her I love her—just tell her—"

I was still nodding as I closed the car door, but I couldn't stop to reassure him yet again. I couldn't even reassure myself. There was no way she was here. It *was* a long way from Braun, and she was confused…and frightened.

Or was that me I was thinking about? As we hung a left inside the front door, the floor in front of me started to roll. Sam locked his arm around my shoulders and stopped me.

"You okay?" he said.

"No!" I said.

"I mean physically—you're white as a ghost."

"It doesn't matter! We have to get down there."

"Hey." Sam pulled my face up to his with both hands. "I told you, when I called nobody had seen her yet, which probably means somehow we beat her here. I'm going to alert the people at the information desk and then I'm going to wait out front and see if I can spot her. You go ahead to the lab and wait for her there. It'll give you a chance to get yourself together before you see her."

"And I *am* going to see her," I said.

"Of course you are. We're on the right track." He looked at me earnestly. "You're the one who knows her."

"Obviously not! Max knows things about her I *never* would have guessed."

"Max knew her *then*. But you're the one who knows her *now*. He knew her self. You know her soul."

He kissed me on the forehead and left for the information desk. I went on toward the lab, the words *please, please, please* pounding in my head.

Although the lab had a full staff on Saturdays, the halls were almost empty, except for a woman in a green housekeeping uniform who was cleaning the windows on the doors. The sight of her made me stop in my mental tracks. Why hadn't I called Burl?

I opened my bag, but I realized Sam still had the phone. I considered heading back to get it from him, but I wanted to check again with the lab staff. Besides, Burl should be around here someplace working. This was about the time he came on duty—if he worked Saturdays.

I readjusted the bag on my shoulder and headed once more for the hemo lab, but my walk was slower now and heavier. What Sam had said weighed on me. *He knew her self. You know her soul.*

It wasn't the words that slowed me nearly to a crawl. It was the fact that I believed them.

I loved my mother. If anything else happened to hurt her, I would never be the same. I would never be anything at all.

I threw my head back and looked at the ceiling. "Please, please, please," I pleaded. "Just—please."

"Jill?"

My head jerked. It was Ted Lyons.

"Ted!" I said. "Have you seen my—"

"She's here."

"Where?"

He put his finger to his lips. "She's right around the corner. I think you're going to want to see this before she sees you."

He beckoned me to the corner and peered around the wall, hand still up to keep me quiet. Then he took me by the arm and leaned me forward so that I could see what was happening, just six feet away.

My mother was standing outside the closed door to what was once her office. She was wearing a white lab coat that was at least ten sizes too big for her, and she was holding a clipboard against her chest. Standing in front of her was Burl.

"I should have known," I said.

Ted put his hand up again. "Listen," he whispered.

Burl was talking in his usual sandpaper monotone. "You're just as good as you ever were, Doc," he said. "I told you that a dozen times. You're just good in a different way now, that's all."

"It's a shame."

A shiver went through me. Ted put his hand on my shoulder. My mother had said that. She had said "It's a shame" in a voice as deep and clear as I remembered it.

"No, it isn't any shame," Burl said. "What do you got to be ashamed of? You gave these people twenty-five years. What more do they want? It's time for you to rest now—enjoy life."

"I have work to do," she said. "I have work."

"Maybe so, but not here. See?" He pointed to the nameplate on the door. "Somebody else is doin' the work. It's gettin' done. I'm keepin' an eye on it."

Mother looked vaguely at the nameplate and then down at the clipboard.

"Here," she said, and she handed it to Burl. He stuck it casually under his arm.

"They'll appreciate gettin' this back," he said.

"Tell them. Blasts in transformation," she said. "Myelodysplasia."

"See?" he said. "You still got a lot of that in there. But it's time to move on. Time to find another reason for gettin' up in the morning."

The look that crossed her face squeezed at my chest. "Dr. Elizabeth McGavock," she said.

"That's right, Doc," Burl said. "That's who you are and who you'll always be. But that ain't all. *Isn't* all, excuse me."

He nodded his head at her. She nodded hers back, as if it were some ritual they had performed a hundred times.

"That isn't all you are," he said. "Now you're gonna go home and find out what else."

"Home," she said.

I stepped forward. "Right, Mother," I said. "I'm here to take you home."

I went to her, blinking back the tears so hard that I could have given Deb Kent's eyelids a run for their money. Slowly she turned her face from Burl to me. Her eyes flickered something, then faded. But before they did, I saw what it was. It was the light of recognition. It was a fleeting brush with love.

We took Mother back to Hopewell, and I announced that I was going to stay with her. Ponytail went off to find an extra bed they could roll into the room for me.

Mother fell asleep almost before I could get some dinner into her. When I was sure she was definitely out, I stuck my head out the door and looked for Sam. Max had taken him back to campus to get his car, and he said he wanted to come back and talk before he went home.

He was sitting in the recreation area, bouncing a ping-pong ball on a paddle.

"Hey, Blaze," I said.

He did one last behind-the-back hit and tossed the ball and paddle onto the table. His arms came around me and pulled me to the couch beside him.

"Did you get her settled in?" he said.

"For the time being. But I'm staying here tonight. She's liable to be really restless."

"And what about after tonight?" He grinned. "You going to move in here?"

I shook my head. "No. I think I'm going to move her back to the house."

He stared at me.

I would have stared at me, too. I didn't know I'd made that decision until it came out of my mouth—not clearly anyway. But I'd known from the minute I saw her with Burl that I couldn't leave her.

"It won't be tomorrow, obviously. I'll have to make arrangements."

"You're going to be her sole caregiver?" Sam said.

"No. I'll get a home health aid, somebody experienced with dementia patients this time. That could take a while. I haven't worked out all the details. I'm really just thinking out loud."

"Then think about this," Sam said. "Think about bringing her to Illinois with you."

It was my turn to stare.

"I asked you to come with me," he said.

"You asked me to think about it—if they offered you the job and if you accepted it."

"It's where I need to be…if you're there with me."

I turned my head to get my bearings, but they were nowhere to be found. I gave him a half laugh. "Do you want to throw a few *more* things into this pot before I start stirring?" I said.

"I think you ought to have all the options in front of you. Otherwise I wouldn't have said anything tonight, especially after the day you've had. But it sounds like you're making some big decisions pretty fast. I just want to throw my two cents in the pot—or my two carrots—or whatever the right thing is to toss into this metaphor."

He grinned, but I didn't. I pulled back from him so I could look him full in the face.

"I need straight answers here," I said. "What exactly are you saying?"

"Exactly? I'm not sure."

"Then let me give you multiple choice, okay, just so I'm clear?"

"Sure," he said.

"A: You want me to, I guess, marry you? Move to Illinois and bring my mother with me and we'll take care of her in our home. Or B: You want me to marry you and move to Illinois and find a nursing home for my mother there. Or C: You want me to come to Illinois, find a house for Mother and me, get a job, and continue to date you…" I let that one trail off. "Choice C is not an option."

"Why not?"

"I love you," I said. "You know that. But for me to uproot myself and, more importantly, *my mother* when she obviously needs things she's familiar with and go to Illinois with you with no definite future plans—" I shook my head. "I can't do that, Sam."

He rubbed the back of his neck. "And I can't ask you to marry me."

"Because you'd feel like you were marrying me *and* my mother."

"No, that's not it."

He took my face in his hands. I didn't pull away, but I could feel myself stiffening.

"There is no doubt that I love you," he said. "I want you to come to Illinois with me so we can see where this relationship goes. I don't mean move in with me. We'd get you your own place and of course I'd help you out financially, especially since you would be bringing your mother."

I did pull away then. "Until when, Sam? Until she dies or I have to put her back in a home?"

"No. I told you your mother has nothing to do with it."

"Then what?"

He leaned over his knees, arms propped across his thighs. I tilted my head back to look at the ceiling—and it hit me as if the tiles were coming down from it and slapping me in the face.

"I'm not a church lady," I said.

He didn't answer.

"Your father told me that," I said. "'Sammy wants a church lady,' he said. Of course, who listens to a man who's three sheets to the wind—or to the eighteen-year-old freshman who said 'Dr. B' could never marry a woman who wasn't a Christian? Now if *you* had said it to me yourself at some point, Blaze, I might have believed it and saved myself a lot of—"

I was going to say *heartache*. I didn't. But I was sure Sam could see it on my face. I was certainly feeling it, in the very pit of my soul.

"That's it, isn't it?" I said softly.

"We just need a little more time," he said. "Because, yes, I do need to know that the woman I marry is walking the same path I am, and that path has to be Christ."

"Then why did you even bring up the Illinois thing in the first place?"

"Because you're so close."

"But not close enough."

"You're making it sound like I have all these criteria you have to meet before I can marry you, and it's not like that," Sam said. "I do love you, everything about you."

"But I'm not a Christian. That's it. Period. End of discussion." I put my hand on his arm. "There's no other way to make it sound different, Sam, because that's what it is."

"But you're so close," he said again.

"Maybe I am," I said. "But now I'm finding out it's not a choice I'm making—it's an ultimatum you're giving me."

"It is *not* an ultimatum!"

For once, his voice was unsteady and quavering. But I had never been more sure of what I needed to say.

"Then if it's a choice," I said, "let me make it. In my own time. Let me get there the way I'm supposed to get there. You said it yourself—we need time."

He sank back against the couch cushions. "So what does that mean?"

"It means you go to Illinois if you need to, and I'll stay here and take care of my mother until I'm sure it's right to put her back in a home. In the meantime, I can keep seeking and we can—"

"Keep our relationship going long distance," Sam said.

"People do it."

He was quiet—for an endless moment.

"I can't see it working with us," he said finally.

"Why not? I have no intention of going out and looking for another guy. I wasn't looking for one when I found you. Don't you think you can be faithful if I'm not right under your nose?"

"No, it's none of that," Sam said. I could see the frustration in his hands. "Your seeking God has been so much a part of our relationship. I want to be with you when you finally embrace Christ."

I looked at him, long and hard. His chin was jutted out, his eyes fixed on me. He wanted to win.

And as far as I was concerned, this was no longer a debate.

I put my hand up to his face, and he put his up to hold it.

"Is that really it?" I said. "Or is it that you don't think I'll continue to seek if you aren't here to guide me along?"

"I didn't say that."

"I'm not saying you did. I'm asking you if that's in there somewhere."

He took his hand away and used it to rub the back of his neck.

"It is, isn't it?" I said. "Sam, don't lie to me. I have to know this."

He looked down at his lap. "Yeah. Yeah, I guess it is."

"Then I think that's our answer." I closed my eyes. "Choice D: You go to Illinois and find a woman you don't have to wait for."

"And what about you?" he said.

I had to fight back tears to answer him. "I'll stay here...and find God."

TWENTY-TWO

I was awake most of the night, listening to Mother's soft, even breathing and whispering to the ceiling. I fell asleep not sure there would ever be answers. I woke up the next morning knowing there would be.

They came over the course of days—weeks.

I scheduled an appointment with Dr. McDonald for both Mother and me, so that he could observe her and give me his best guess on just how fast her disease was moving. He told us her behavior indicated that the frontal lobe was deteriorating more rapidly than with the majority of cases, but that she seemed less agitated and confused than almost any Pick's patient he'd seen.

"How long will I be able to care for her at home with help?" I said. "Before she needs total professional care. I just need an estimate."

He studied me for a while, until I thought his eyes began to swim.

"Eighteen months at the most," he said finally.

"That's all I need to know," I said. I put my hand out. "Thanks so much for your time. I know these are hard questions to answer, but I needed to have an idea."

"You call me anytime," he said. He looked at Mother. "You're a fortunate lady, Dr. McGavock."

It was a statement that would have sent me through the ceiling six months before. Now it merely sent me *to* the ceiling. Looking there, I whispered, "Thanks."

Monique, of course, tried to talk me out of taking my mother home, but once she realized I'd made up my mind and that I had everything arranged, she was on hand to see Mother off. Emily Murphy—Frosty—was there, too, sleepy-eyed but anxious to give Mother and me her best wishes.

"I admire your courage," she said to me. "We all do."

To Burl, who was of course there to haul Mother's belongings back home, she said, "Thanks for all you've done around here. Can we call you if anything else needs fixing?"

"You have my number," Burl said.

"Did I miss something, Mother?" I said to her as we drove off. "What is it with Burl? Does he even have a home, or does he just go from house to house doing repairs and then sleep in his truck?"

"South San Fran," she said.

"What? He does *not* drive all the way down here every day from South City. Does he?"

I asked him that myself when he'd unloaded all Mother's stuff and was having a cup of coffee in the kitchen. It was a little tough to have a conversation, with Max singing selections from *Turandot* at the top of his lungs while he made conchiglie with cream sauce, but I managed to get it out of Burl that he was born and raised in South San Francisco, though he now lived in Redwood City. As the oldest in the family, he grew up taking care of his brothers and sisters, particularly one brother who was slightly mentally retarded.

"I talked to him like I'd talk to anyone else," Burl told me, "and any kid made fun of him knew he had me to reckon with."

"What happened to him?" I said.

"He died in '79—had leukemia on top of everything else. Doc McGavock took a special interest in his case. That's how me and her—excuse me, her and me—" he gave me a solemn nod— "we got to know each other."

He nodded at me again as if that explained everything sufficiently and went on sipping his coffee.

It was that way most evenings from then on—Max cooking and Burl puttering and sitting by the hour with Mother, talking or not. The nurse often stayed for supper, even though she was off at three. Dr. McDonald himself had recommended her—brought her out of early retirement, he said, because he wanted Dr. McGavock to have the best.

The nurse wore a cross and said a silent blessing before she ate and had a light-hearted aura about her that obviously didn't come from crystals or the Tao. From the first hour, which she spent merely observing Mother and asking me questions, I had no desire to call her Freda. We called her Laura because, well, that was actually her name.

On Sunday nights, Tabitha joined us, too, basically to practice with Max, who was coaching her for her music school audition. If it was nice weather, she and I would end the session sharing the inevitable Doritos on the front porch, often with Mother on the other side of her, dipping her hand in and out of the bag.

I worked on my dissertation during the day while Laura was there, checking in over at Sloan once a day to pick up mail, and twice weekly I met with Nigel. Because I wasn't teaching, I didn't have office hours to keep, so I moved most of my stuff out of my office, under Jacoboni's scrutiny.

"You're a better person than I am," he said to me the day I went in to get my final load.

"That's common knowledge, Jacoboni," I said. "You're getting your doctorate, man. Show some original thought."

"I love my grandfather, but there is no way I would leave this program with only months to go just to take care of him."

"In the first place," I said, "you love your grandfather's money. In the second place, I'm not leaving the program. I've gotten an extension on my dissertation, and I'll probably graduate in August, maybe December—it depends."

"But you're losing your funding, aren't you?"

"In May, yes, but I don't need it. I've given up my apartment at Escondido. I have a place to live and money to live on until I finish here and get a job. But I'm not looking that far into the future. It's day to day in my situation."

"Wait a minute. Hold on. Back the truck up and pull it over to the curb!" His face was actually flushed. "Did I just hear you say you were living one day at a time?"

"Something like that."

"All right, let me see some ID."

"What?"

"You can't possibly be Jill McGavock. The Jill McGavock I know and love does *not* live for the moment."

I couldn't help smiling at him. "You may love me—in your own perverted little way—but you definitely do *not* know me."

I hiked the box up on my hip and headed for the door.

"Well, here, at least let me get that for you," he said.

He put out his arms to take the box. I pushed it toward him, but for a moment I didn't let go, so that we were both standing there, hands touching at the bottom of the box, faces within inches of each other.

"You really can be kind of charming, Alan," I said. "I hope I haven't been too much of a witch to share an office with."

If he was surprised, he covered it well. What he didn't cover well was the sudden urge to drop the box and enfold me in some tight, too-long hug. But he knew better than to try.

I squeezed his hand and said, "Thanks for putting up with me. It couldn't have been easy."

"What wasn't easy was me keeping my hands off you, darlin'," he said.

I left that hanging in the air and departed with my box. *You've got him,* I said to the ceiling. *That case is way out of my league.*

There were, of course, rough patches in all areas. One area that was nothing *but* rough was Sam. *Ironic,* I thought. The rest of my life had begun to fall into place because of divine answers, yet the one person who was most responsible for getting me to even ask the questions was out of my life.

The night we found Mother at the lab, he left the nursing home looking confused and frustrated. The next time I saw him was the day before spring break started. He came by the house while Burl and I were pulling weeds in the tulip bed, which meant I was in sloppy gym shorts and had my hair piled on top of my head, rooster fashion. I was the picture of well-groomed confidence all over.

He, on the other hand, stood with his hands in his pockets, as at ease as he'd been the first time I met him. Admittedly, it had been at least five weeks since our last conversation, but I thought he could have had the decency to look a little forlorn. I could feel my forgotten walls rebuilding themselves, bricks stacking up on fast-forward, but I punched the stop button on that. I had already lost Sam. I didn't need to lose me again, too.

"What's up?" I said.

"You got a minute?" he said. He glanced at Burl.

"Sure, but it's a little crowded inside. Let's go in the back. It's nice by the koi pond."

"Koi pond?" he said. "I thought you had that drained."

"Burl filled it back up. There are enough of us here to make sure Mother doesn't go for a swim."

In the backyard I offered him a chaise longue and sank into one myself. I watched him as he folded his long, lean frame into a lawn chair, and I felt an old but familiar ache. The lanky body, the olive skin, the dark curly hair—they could still get to me. With any luck, he wouldn't grin. One eye twinkle and *I'd* have thrown myself into the koi pond.

"So," I said, "what can I do for you?"

He waited, as if he expected me to say more. When I didn't, he tilted his head at me.

"You look great," he said.

"I'm sure I do," I said. "Garden dirt's a good look for me, don't you think?"

"Everything's a good look for you," he said. "You're still beautiful."

"Sam, it's only been about a month since I saw you. Did you expect me to go down the tubes?" I put my hand up. "I didn't mean that the way it sounded. Thank you. I appreciate the compliment. But look, before either of us can get our other foot into our respective mouths, why don't you tell me why you came? I'm not going to bite your head off."

"I can see that," he said. "You're really doing well, aren't you?"

"Sam," I said.

He scratched at his scalp. "I came to apologize."

"There's no need. We got things out in the open. It's okay."

"It's not. I have to tell you this. You were right."

I caught my breath, as if that were going to stop me from hoping. I nodded carefully.

"I should have told you about my vow to myself that I would never marry a woman who wasn't a Christian. I let myself spend time with you because I really did want to help you. I deluded myself—told myself I wasn't falling in love with you. And then when I knew that I did love you, I thought any minute you'd tell me you believed. Anyway, I was in denial that there was any reason to tell you. I'm sorry."

The look on his face was genuine. I hoped the one on mine was not. I didn't want him to see the disappointment that was churning in my chest.

Not disappointment that he hadn't come back to say he'd changed his mind about us. Disappointment that he didn't ask if I'd changed my mind about God. He didn't even ask.

I didn't tell him that I had replaced the ceiling with a real image of God, and I was talking to Him on a regular basis. That I had finished the *Pensées* and was now studying the Bible. That my weekly meetings with Nigel picked up the Christ-centered discussions where Sam and I had left off. That Tabitha and I prayed together—well, that she rambled on to the Lord as only Tabitha could do while I listened in sacred fascination. That I was looking for a church. That I talked to Mother about all of it.

I could have told him all of that and he might have turned around and taken me in his arms instead of climbing back into his SUV and leaving for Illinois to look for a house over spring break. But I didn't tell him any of it, because he didn't ask. Because he assumed that without him, it wouldn't happen.

And I had made my own vow to God: I would never marry a man who didn't know my soul.

Things settled into a somewhat off-center but workable routine, and by the beginning of May I actually began to have time on my hands. The weather was California spring-beautiful—soft and clear—and my body began to long for the Loop.

I hadn't been up there since the last time Sam and I had run it. I was holding together nicely without denying myself the occasional cry or pillow thrown across the room, but I was also avoiding "our" places—like the Rose and Crown and Antonio's. I hadn't seen Sam since that day before spring break, and I didn't want to increase the chances. I wasn't sure if I could handle the extra pain in my chest. It was there. No matter how disappointed I was in him, no matter how much better I knew I now was as a person, the ache of being without him was always there. I knew the pain was more genuine that the cold, unfeeling state I'd lived in before, so I could live with it. But if I saw him and he grinned or pulled me to him with one hand on the back of my neck, could I live with that?

When finals were over, however, I decided it was worth a chance. Before she left to go home for the summer, Tabitha told me Sam was planning to leave the minute his grades were turned in. So one evening before sunset I put on my running shoes, left Mother on the front porch with Max and Burl, and went to the Loop.

Deputy Dog was still at her guard post. If she recognized me, she didn't let on. I wondered vaguely if maybe *she'd* asked him out once I'd stopped showing up with Sam. There was a time when that would have been an amusing thought.

The first hill was a killer after several months of neglect, and I had to slow to a walk when I got to the top. I was leaning into a stitch in my side when I saw the little dirt path, leading off the main running road like a tantalizing string beyond the forbidden fence.

I stood up straight and looked at it. It had really been the beginning of something for me, going down that path with Sam to the Jill Tree. It would hurt to go back there—but it would be sadder not to. I had, after all, come so far since then. I wanted to feel the difference of sitting in that tree now.

I didn't even look back to find out if Deputy Dog could see me. I just hoisted myself over the fence and jogged lightly down the path.

My tree was even more gnarled and misshapen than I'd remembered it, and I felt almost sorry for it as I climbed aboard its long, horizontal trunk.

"How've you been?" I said, patting the bark. "How loony is that? I'm talking to a tree."

It's no loonier than you taking your mother out of a perfectly good facility and playing Nurse Nancy with her at home, I told myself.

No crazier than you assembling that motley crew you've got running your house.

No weirder than you talking to God.

I looked up at the sky. The sun was heading down behind the hills, leaving them warm and golden. It wasn't weird, I decided. I was doing it, and it was working. Maybe it wasn't changing the things I really wanted God to change—but it was changing me.

I shifted my weight on the tree trunk and tried to get comfortable, but I was restless. It was as if I didn't fit here anymore.

I slid to the ground and, dusting off the seat of my shorts, headed back to the main path. There was no one on it, and as I went into a gentle jog up the hill, I remembered how much I'd loved the silence at one time. No one in my face. Nobody to prove anything to. And then there had been the space of time when I couldn't stand the aloneness—and I'd call Sam and that would always make it right.

I pressed my hand to my chest. *Okay, God,* I thought. *I think I've learned all I'm supposed to learn from this particular pain. Could we move on, please?*

I heard a noise on the path ahead of me and my insides jumped.

It was just a large jay, swooping down to inspect the shells of someone's dropped sunflower seeds, but I knew why it had startled me. This was the spot where I'd seen Sam emerge from prohibited territory, long before I really knew him. I stopped and looked beyond the fence. There was a path there—like the one to my tree—that led over the top of a rise in the same way. Beyond that, I could see branches just over the rise, wavy branches that seemed to be beckoning to me like teasing fingers.

I leaped over the fence and jogged up the path to the top. Before me was a tree straight out of a Dr. Seuss book. Its base was broad and stood staunchly in the ground, and the primary branches that stemmed from it had grown out and up in a firm and sensible way, like the prongs on a candelabra. But from there, its offshoots sprang up in wavy twigs, ever more whimsical-looking as they stretched and wiggled toward the sky. Toward God.

It was so Sam, I laughed out loud.

"All you need is a big goofy grin," I said to it.

And then, of course, I had to climb it. It wasn't a thing I'd done much in my life. Climbing trees had been right up there next to hanging out the side of a cable car in my mother's recollection of ER days. But I did manage to get myself up far enough to see all of the Loop in silhouette against the blazing sunset.

"A night of fire," I said to it. "Blaze Senior would be in his element."

I swung my legs and looked up into the wavy branches that danced happily above me. Maybe I was in my element too. It was surely the most peaceful I had felt since…since ever. In spite of the pain of losing Sam, in spite of the heartbreak that might be ahead with my mother, in spite of the mist of uncertainty that now hung over my plans for the future, I was quiet within. And I knew why.

Well, Pascal, I thought. *I don't need to wait for the coin to fall. I've made the toss, I've acted as if, and I know how it has landed.*

I knew because I'd loved and I still loved and I was always going to love—God, myself, the unlikely assortment of people in my life. And for a person so cold, so rigid, so rational, so terrified, that could only have come from the source of all love. It could only have come from God.

The sun was making its final descent, leaving a burning rim above the Loop's silhouettes. "This must be *my* night of fire," I whispered to the blaze.

Like Pascal's, my moment was immediate, interior, intense. But in that moment, I felt a stunning sadness. I did know love, in all its exaltation and pain, but it hadn't been love that had been too stubborn to tell Sam that I was coming to know the Christ he so wanted me to. It had only been the remainder of my old self-hate.

It was almost completely dark, but I couldn't leave until I'd let that go. I could never allow that to stand between myself and love again.

I leaned against a solid branch and closed my eyes. Even as I did, I could hear footsteps on the main path—probably Deputy Dog coming after me, citation book in hand. I pressed harder against the tree and waited for them to pass. They didn't. The footsteps went dull against the dirt path as they came toward me. And then I heard the voice.

"Hey, you."

My eyes came open. "Sam?"

I looked down. I could barely make out a figure in the dark, but I would have known the tall, lanky frame anywhere.

"Are you okay?" he said.

"Yeah. Are you?"

"Yeah. I went by the house. Max told me you were up here somewhere."

"I thought you were gone. I thought you went to Illinois."

It was absurd, of course—the two of us making small talk while I sat in a tree gaping down at him and he stood on the ground gaping up at me. And somehow acting as if we *hadn't* once had a love that had ached inside me.

I should go down, I thought.

"I'm coming up," he said.

He had obviously done it a number of times before, because he was beside me before I even realized my hands were shaking, much less had a chance to stop them. As he pulled himself up onto the branch, I could see that his face was taut and that his eyes were intense behind his glasses. He dispensed with the pleasantries.

"Jill, why didn't you tell me you believe now? I just need to know why. If it's because you found out you didn't love me and it was easier to just let me go, I can deal with that. But I need to know."

I was shaking my head. "No, that's not it."

"Then why?"

I didn't even hesitate. "Because you didn't ask me. Because you seemed to assume I couldn't do it without you. Because I'm stubborn, proud, selfish. And because I lick the earth."

He opened his mouth.

"I'm not finished," I said.

He closed it.

"But according to Pascal—you know Pascal?"

He nodded.

"According to Pascal, I may be absolute scum myself, but my

soul has the capacity for good, because my soul is of God. You know God?"

He nodded again.

"So do I." I let the debate voice drain away. "I should have told you what was happening with me. After all you did for me, you deserved at least that."

He was watching me, and his eyes were shining even in the dark.

"Okay," I said, "I'm finished now."

"You're sure."

"Yes. Except why come looking for me now? How did you find out?"

He leaned toward me. "My men's group gave me a going-away dinner tonight. There I am sitting next to Nigel Frost, and I can't help myself. I ask him if Jill McGavock has finished her dissertation. He looks at me like I have two heads, maybe three, and says, 'Do you know Jill?' I tell him I do, and he says, 'I'm surprised Jill didn't come to you with the questions she's been bringing to me. You two would have made a good team. She's like you—a very intelligent believer.'" Sam looked at me soberly. "I shouldn't have had to have Nigel Frost tell me. I should have asked you. No—I should have known by looking at you that day." I could see him swallowing. "I'm sorry, Jill."

I nodded.

"That's it?" he said. "You're not going to tell me how arrogant I was?"

"I'll tell you I think you lick the earth too," I said.

A grin was twitching at his lips. He knew before I said it, before I nodded, before I moved toward him, waiting for him to reach behind me and pull me to him—he knew I still loved him.

"I am so sorry, Jill," he said. "I want another chance. Please."

"I can't leave here and go to Illinois," I said. "Not right now."

"I know."

"I can't tell you how long it will be before I can."

"I know that, too."

"But I do love you, Sam. I really do."

Then he did pull me to him, his hand on the back of my neck, and he kissed me until I could barely breathe.

"Is this Pascal's payoff?" I whispered.

"Nah," Sam said. "This is God's."

The publisher and author would love to hear your comments about this book. *Please contact us at:*
www.multnomah.net/pascalswager

Acknowledgments

I wish to express my sincere appreciation to the following people, who helped to make this book a reality:

- Dr. Bill Newsome and Rev. Zondra Newsome, for far too many gifts to enumerate.

- Bill Jensen, for introducing me to Pascal.

- Kristen Boyd, Jessica Purcell, and Dana Roland, for their insights into the Stanford experience.

- Keith Wall, for sensitive, intelligent editing.

- Greg Johnson, for being my agent and friend.

- Rev. Anne Wolf, for spiritual guidance and theological expertise.

- Dr. Michael Torre, professor of philosophy, University of San Francisco, for unveiling the mysteries of philosophy, and Marijean Rue for putting them into terms even I could understand.

- Dr. Steven Foung, director of Clinical Laboratory Services, Stanford Hospital, for giving his valuable time.

- Betty Morse, for sharing her painful firsthand knowledge of Pick's Disease.

- Kelly Gordon and Tracy Lamb, my personal assistants, for maintaining order along the way.

- Jim Rue, my husband and friend, for twenty-eight years of life-passion.

God bless all of you.

Other Books by Nancy Rue...

ADULT FICTION
Retreat to Love

YOUNG ADULT FICTION
Row This Boat Ashore
The Janis Project
Stop in the Name of Love
Home by Another Way
The Lucas Secret and Other Stories by Nancy Rue
Boys and Other Things That Fry Your Brains
Bringing up Parents and Other Jobs for Teenage Girls

RAISE THE FLAG SERIES:
Don't Count on Homecoming Queen
"B" Is for Bad at Getting into Harvard
I Only Binge on Holy Hungers
Do I Have to Paint You a Picture?
Friends Don't Let Friends Date Jason
How Perfect Is Perfect Enough?

YOUNG ADULT NONFICTION
Handling the Heartbreak of Miscarriage
Learning Guides for The Christian Series

CHILDREN'S FICTION (AGES 8–12)
CHRISTIAN HERITAGE SERIES:
"The Salem Years"

The Rescue	*The Samaritan*
The Stowaway	*The Secret*
The Guardian	
The Accused	

"The Williamsburg Years"
The Trick
The Stunt
The Discovery
The Rebel
The Thief
The Burden

"The Chicago Years"
The Misfit
The Ally
The Threat
The Trap
The Hostage
The Escape

"The Charleston Years"
The Prisoner
The Invasion
The Battle
The Chase
The Caper
The Miracle

"The Santa Fe Years"
The Capture
The Pursuit

THE LILY AND FRIENDS SERIES:
Here's Lily!
Lily Dobbins, M.D.

CHILDREN'S NONFICTION (ages 8–12)
It's a God-Thing: The Beauty Book
It's a God-Thing: The Body Book

EVERYTHING IS ON THE LINE...

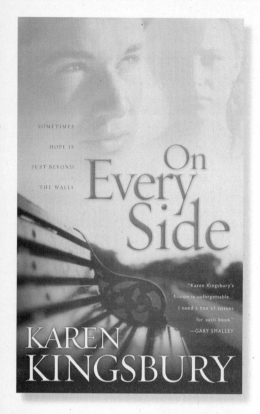

SOMETIMES

HOPE IS

JUST BEYOND

THE WALLS

On Every Side

"Karen Kingsbury's fiction is unforgettable... I need a box of tissues for each book."
—GARY SMALLEY

KAREN KINGSBURY

"Karen Kingsbury's
fiction is unforgettable...
I need a box of tissues
for each book."
—GARY SMALLEY

For Faith Evans, an up-and-coming newscaster. A woman of honor and integrity, who finds herself making a stand against the one man she never imagined would be her enemy...

For Jordan Riley, a powerful attorney dedicated to fighting for human rights—and against God. A man still reckoning with the boyhood loss of the three women who once meant everything to him...

For Bethany, Pennsylvania, a small town no one ever dreamed would become the center of national attention. But it has. All because of a beloved, hundred-year-old statue of Jesus Christ that stands in Bethany's park. A statue that some say is a clear violation of separation of church and state. A statue that has to come down. A statue that suddenly becomes the focus of a bitter conflict—one rife with political intrigue, social injustice, and personal conflicts. Before it's over, everything that Jordan, Faith, and the town of Bethany stand for will be challenged.

Will love be enough when the battle rages on every side?

ISBN 1-57673-868-X

TEARS ARE FALLING LIKE SPRING RAIN…

"*Spring Rain* contains all the mystery, suspense, and romance a reader could want."

—ANGELA ELWELL HUNT, bestselling author of *The Note*

"A realistically portrayed story of love and forgiveness, filled with emotion and grace…. A compelling read."

—*ROMANTIC TIMES* Magazine

Seaside, New Jersey. Small town, U.S.A., where everyone knows everyone else's business…or thinks they do. Even so, there's nowhere else Leigh Spenser would rather live, no place she'd rather raise her young son, Billy. It's taken a lot of hard work, but Leigh has finally put memories and rumors to rest and found peace in Seaside. Then Clay Wharton comes home. It only makes sense. Clay's estranged twin, Ted—Leigh's closest friend—is dying of AIDS. Even life-long resentments and bitter battles over life choices wouldn't keep Clay from his family now. Leigh will just have to avoid him—to make sure Clay never discovers the secret she's protected for so long. If only circumstances would stop throwing Leigh and the man she once loved together, forcing them to face powerful emotions neither wants to acknowledge. But it's not until Billy's life is in danger that Leigh and Clay discover the answers they've been looking for all their lives. Answers they can only find together. A powerful, moving drama of family conflict, social issues, redemption, and God's unparalleled forgiveness.

ISBN 1-57673-638-5

HE SURVIVED THE NAZI TERROR…NOW CAN HE FACE HIS OWN SON?

G.K. BELLIVEAU

go down to silence

> "A deeply felt…affirmative odyssey."
>
> —BOOKLIST, January 2001

Jacob Horowitz is a man with an untold story—the tale of his former life of terror and persecution at the hands of the Nazis. It's a story that may never be known…because Jacob is dying.

But when the Jewish business tycoon receives an invitation to visit Pierre, a friend and former member of the Belgian underground, Jacob decides he must return once again to the land of his nightmares—and take Isaac, his estranged son, with him.

In this powerful, vivid, and fast-paced narrative set alternately in the trauma of his youth and his complex present, an aging and embittered Jacob must choose whether or not he will reconcile with his son, his past, his God, and himself.

ISBN 1-57673-736-5

WHEN YOUR MIND IS THE BATTLEGROUND

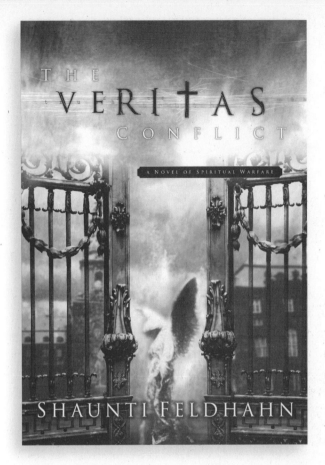

A heavenly battle is raging for the hearts and minds of a young co-ed, a college, and a nation. In this work of fiction, Harvard University is a centuries-old battleground in the struggle between good and evil, and one student has no idea she's about to be thrust onto the front lines.

Claire Rivers arrives at Harvard an enthusiastic freshman but is ill prepared for the challenges she encounters to her Christian faith. Students and professors who proclaim "tolerance" and revel in alternative lifestyles greet her beliefs with disdain—even hostility. But Claire soon faces an even greater challenge…

Working with a godly professor and protected by unseen members of the heavenly host, she uncovers disturbing information of a shocking plot against *veritas*—God's truth—at the university and beyond. Will Claire risk all by helping to expose and transform the darkness—or give in to it?

ISBN 1-57673-708-X

A MYSTERIOUS DISAPPEARANCE…A FAMILY IN TUMULT…VOLATILE SURROUNDINGS… CAN ONE WOMAN CONNECT THE PIECES IN TIME?

When nine-year-old Ally Buckley turns up missing, fear spreads throughout the New England fishing village of Bowden's Landing, where Sadie and her family live and worship. But when Sadie discovers one of Ally's drawings among her husband's possessions, she suspects danger may be closer to home than she had ever known.

ISBN 1-57673-659-8